Finding Margo

Center Point
Large Print

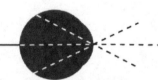

**This Large Print Book carries the
Seal of Approval of N.A.V.H.**

Finding Margo

The *Finding Home* Series
BOOK 1

Jen Turano

CENTER POINT LARGE PRINT
THORNDIKE, MAINE

This Center Point Large Print edition
is published in the year 2017 by arrangement with
Gilead Publishing LLC.

The text of this Large Print edition is unabridged.
In other aspects, this book may vary
from the original edition.
Printed in the United States of America
on permanent paper.
Set in 16-point Times New Roman type.

ISBN: 978-1-68324-271-0

Library of Congress Cataloging-in-Publication Data

Names: Turano, Jen, author.
Title: Finding Margo / Jen Turano.
Description: Center Point Large Print edition. | Thorndike, Maine :
Center Point Large Print, 2017. | Series: Finding home series ; book 1
Identifiers: LCCN 2016048754 | ISBN 9781683242710
    (hardcover : alk. paper)
Subjects: LCSH: Large type books.
Classification: LCC PS3620.U7455 F56 2017 | DDC 813/.6—dc23
LC record available at https://lccn.loc.gov/2016048754

For Dave, Kristin, Meghan, and Kaitlyn.
Love you!
Jen

Finding Margo

chapter one

In the heat of summer, under the dark sky of a moonless night, three Amish children disappeared from their beds, never to be seen or heard from again. Until . . .

Present Day

With the roar of the crowd still reverberating in her ears, Margo Hartman stepped past one of her many bodyguards and into the relative quiet of the dressing room she'd been assigned for the evening. Waiting right inside the door as another guard checked the room for any hint of a threat, she returned the nod he finally sent her and watched as he strode out of the room, closing the door firmly behind him.

Unfortunately, the door did not remain closed for long, bursting open a mere moment later to reveal one of Margo's personal assistants, Fauna Silverman. "Fabulous performance, Ms. Hartman. Simply fabulous." She dashed across the room, sizzling with the energy of a woman who'd clearly had far too many energy drinks that night. "You were on fire during the last set and totally rocked the final song. How were the boots?"

Allowing herself the luxury of hobbling across

9

the dressing room in those thigh-high boots instead of pretending she was completely at ease wearing six-inch heels, Margo sat down on the vanity stool and grimaced. "Painful, although I lost feeling in my toes about twenty minutes ago, so that's a plus I guess."

"Looking fierce does have its drawbacks." With that, Fauna moved to Margo's side, handed her a bottle of sparkling water, took a second to blot the perspiration off Margo's face with a fluffy towel, and then tossed the towel aside. She then began the difficult job of prying Margo's long legs from boots that didn't seem to want to release them.

By the time Margo was bootless, Fauna was breathing heavily, sweat was trickling down her face, her green and purple bangs were plastered against her forehead, and Margo was no longer sitting on the vanity stool. Instead, she was sitting on the floor, having landed there right after Fauna gave the last boot an enthusiastic tug.

"Sorry about that, Ms. Hartman." Fauna picked the boots up off the floor and folded the leather over her arm as she straightened. "Let me tuck these away and then I'll help you up."

"There's no need to apologize, Fauna, and there's no need to help me up just yet. I'm perfectly fine where I am at the moment." Margo stretched out her legs, wiggling her toes and wincing when the feeling began coming back to them. "Since this was the last night of my national tour, instead of packing those boots away, feel free to keep them for yourself. I certainly have no desire to wear them again."

A crease settled between Fauna's eyes. "Sebastian won't like it that you're abandoning what he refers to as the soon-to-be-in-demand fashion item of the year. According to your temperamental stylist, he had to beg the designers at some fancy design studio in Paris to create the boots in the first place. I heard they cost you more than I paid for my first car, which *was* a beater car, but . . . still."

Having made her first million by the time she was sixteen, and having made many more millions in the years since, the cost of the boots wasn't a concern. Her talented and incredibly opinionated stylist, on the other hand . . .

"Maybe I should hold on to the boots until Sebastian forgets about them," Margo began. "Or better yet, why don't you order your own pair from that design house and have them send me the bill."

Fauna's eyes sparkled. "It really is a shame the tabloids don't report how nice you are, Ms. Hartman. They always seem to prefer writing those highly exaggerated tales about you."

"That's because exaggerated tales sell, whereas niceness . . . well, I'm afraid that doesn't attract much interest."

Walking over to a portable wardrobe used to store costumes changes, Fauna slipped the boots inside their box before she smiled at Margo. "I imagine you're looking forward to enjoying some time away from all the press and paparazzi who've been following you on this tour."

Margo leaned forward, pushed aside the strand of blonde hair that fell in her face, and rubbed a foot that had begun tingling. "I'm pretty sure the paparazzi's not going to give up trailing after me, considering they make a lot of money from photos of me. Although I must admit I am looking forward to not having my every minute scheduled. I love touring, but after months of it, I'm relishing the idea of sleeping in a bed that doesn't have wheels under it or is in a hotel. I'm also looking forward to sitting on my deck at home, looking out over the ocean, and doing absolutely nothing for hours on end."

Before Fauna had a chance to respond to that, a brisk knock sounded on the dressing room door. A second later, the door opened, and Margo's agent, Daphne Johnson, strode in. She was dressed in a black suit that screamed success, with four-inch heels lending her the height she believed was imperative for a powerful agent to possess. Moving across the room, she stopped directly in front of Margo, a frown puckering a forehead Margo knew had recently been injected with the latest anti-wrinkle serum.

"What are you doing on the floor?" were the first words out of Daphne's mouth.

"What are you doing here?" Margo countered.

Daphne pursed her lips. "You neglected to send me an itinerary of your schedule for the next few weeks. Because of that, I had no choice but to track you down tonight in order to go over some of the appearances your mother approved for you while you were on the road."

Struggling up from the floor while tugging down the short skirt she was wearing, which had hitched up to mid-thigh, Margo crossed her arms over her chest. "I don't remember being consulted about my mother approving any future appearances for me while I was on tour."

Daphne dropped her briefcase on a small table. "She wanted to make certain to capitalize on the publicity your tour attracted. That right there is why I've arranged for you to sit down and speak with *Vogue, Cosmopolitan, Glamour*, and do a round of the morning shows, after which you'll do the late-night circuit."

A prickle of temper began traveling up her spine.

While it was true that her mother had always been involved in her career, having been responsible for taking Margo to her first professional audition when she was fourteen years old—an audition that had landed her a coveted role on a popular cable show—Margo was no longer a child. She was twenty-three, although some-times she felt forty, and was perfectly capable of deciding what public appearances to make. She was certainly capable of deciding if she even wanted to make those appearances in the first place.

Working steadily after she left the cable show, singing instead of acting, Margo had managed to obtain the title of Pop Princess. Retaining that title, however, had turned into an obsession with her mother, Caroline Hartman. She was constantly pushing Margo to release new material and go out on tour as often as possible. And while Margo truly loved her career and loved the tens of thousands of fans who supported her, she was . . . tired.

The national tour she'd finished only that evening had been exhausting, what with all the rehearsals, traveling, and then performances. Being asked to keep up the whole Margo Hartman persona—exhausting in and of itself because of both the physical image her fans expected from her at all times and the chirpy personality she'd cultivated over the years—was enough to have her gritting her perfectly aligned teeth.

She would have thought her own mother, the one person in the world who should have been looking after her daughter's best interests, would realize she was just about ready to have a nervous—

". . . *and then,* after you're done with all those interviews, your mother and I would like you to consider an offer I've recently been approached about—an international tour. One that will see you traveling from England all the way to China, and then ending with a few shows in Australia."

A strange buzzing noise began in Margo's ear right after Daphne's words settled in her mind.

"Did you just say I've been offered an opportunity to do an international tour?" she asked slowly.

Daphne smiled and nodded, setting her poker-straight, asymmetrical-styled black hair swinging back and forth. "You have, which is a huge achievement on your part, as well as an enormous honor. International tours aren't offered to every singer out there these days."

Curling her still tingling toes into the plush carpet that blanketed the floor of her dressing room, Margo narrowed her eyes. "Should I assume you think I should accept this offer?"

"It would be career suicide to do anything *except* accept the offer. And while I remember you mentioning something about taking some time off, now is not the time to do that. You're a hot commodity, Margo, and we have to strike while the iron is hot. That means you'll have a few weeks to do all the interviews I've lined up, then a few months to tweak your show. That will allow your publicist to promote it properly. And then you'll be flying across the world and cementing your position as the number one female singer of the decade."

With her stomach turning queasy and the buzzing in her ears intensifying, Margo drew in a deep breath. Catching Daphne's eye, she smiled the smile she'd practiced for hours in the mirror—a smile that would have made any beauty pageant contestant proud. "If you'll excuse me, Daphne, I just remembered . . . I . . . uh . . . told some friends of mine I'd meet them for dinner. I really don't want to disappoint them by being late."

Daphne frowned. "I didn't see anything on your personal schedule about meeting friends for dinner tonight."

"While we could get into how inappropriate it is for you to somehow have access to my personal schedule, we really don't have the time, which means I think you and I are done for the evening."

When Daphne didn't bother to take that less-than-subtle hint and leave, Margo squared her shoulders and headed for the door.

"Where are you going? You haven't changed out of your last stage costume, and we need to go over the details for the interviews I've lined up for you."

Not wanting to say something she'd certainly come to regret, Margo took the shoes Fauna was holding out to her—a funky pair of hot pink canvas slip-ons—bent over and stuck them on her

16

feet, and then left the dressing room without another word.

Three bodyguards immediately surrounded her when she hit the hallway, and with two of them flanking her and one leading the way, they whisked her straight out of the building and into her waiting limousine.

Settling into the cushy seat, Margo rubbed at the throbbing that had begun at her temples. She could only hope the quiet of the limousine would fend off the migraine that had shown signs of rearing its ugly head the moment Daphne marched her way into the dressing room.

As her driver turned onto a road that led away from the fans still swarming the streets outside the concert venue, a sense of weariness she'd never felt before in her life settled over her.

Closing her eyes, the unexpected thought flashed to mind that life would be much easier if she could simply pack a bag and turn her back on all the demands everyone seemed to want to—

Her eyes shot open, her lips began to curve, and as the limousine continued purring down the road, a plan she couldn't believe she was even contemplating began to take on a life of its own.

chapter two

One week later

As the miles passed by and states became blurs of cornfields and endless ribbons of highway, Margo couldn't help but wonder why she'd waited so long to rebel against the insanity she was expected to maintain on an almost daily basis.

Turning up the volume to a song she'd discovered on the playlist Fauna had given her before she'd snuck out of California—not that she'd allowed her assistant to know she was leaving town—Margo raised her voice and belted out the lyrics to the chorus. Her belting came to a rapid end, though, when her iPod slipped off the seat of her slightly vintage Mini Cooper and silence settled over the car.

Finding that to be a sad state of affairs, Margo flipped on her directional signal, pulled the Mini Cooper over to the side of the road, and brought it to a stop. Reaching across the small console, she patted around the floor of the passenger side, locating her iPod a second later. Tunes blasted to life again when she reattached the cord to the funny-looking device that allowed her to use her iPod through the Mini Cooper's cassette player.

For the briefest of seconds, she considered

sending Fauna a text to tell her how much she was enjoying the playlist, until she remembered that she and her mother shared a cell phone plan. That plan, unfortunately, was set up so that her mother could track Margo's every move, a condition Caroline had insisted on, stating it would calm her anxiety over her daughter traveling to so many different places.

Not wanting to chance giving her mother a straight-up map to her, Margo pushed the urge to text Fauna aside, sat back in the driver's seat, and allowed the warmth of the sunny June day to drift over her from the open sunroof.

Switching her attention from the sky to the fields and forest that spread out before her, Margo turned down the volume and simply enjoyed the sounds of the country—a melody of chirps, buzzes, and the wind blowing through the trees.

Shaking her head when she realized she was beginning to think more like a country singer than a pop star, she knew it was time to get back on the road. The last thing she needed was to dawdle in the middle of nowhere, itching to write down lyrics that centered around pickup trucks, brawny men wearing flannel shirts, and women walking around in flirty cotton dresses. *That* would definitely give the tabloids some great fodder for their stories, all of which would revolve around the idea that Margo Hartman had certainly lost her mind.

Tucking a strand of the hair she'd dyed a mousy brown back underneath her baseball hat, she selected a song with a dance-club vibe from the playlist. Nodding her head to the beat and banishing all thoughts of banjoes to the back of her mind, she checked the rearview mirror, amused to discover not a single car on the road with her at the moment.

The lack of anyone else in sight gave her a sense of freedom she'd not felt in years. There were no insane members of the paparazzi trailing behind her, no agents annoying her with a filled-to-the-brim schedule she hadn't been consulted about, and no mother—whom Margo was certain she loved but didn't always like—voicing her strong opinions every other minute.

Easing the Mini Cooper into gear and onto the road, she let out a bloodcurdling scream a mere second later when she caught sight of something flying straight toward her windshield.

A nasty sounding *splat* immediately came from that windshield, just before whatever it was that hit her car rolled upward, dropped straight through the sunroof, bounced off her head, and landed between her chest and the steering wheel.

Screaming at the top of her lungs when wings suddenly obscured her view, Margo jerked the steering wheel to the right, got the car off to the side of the road again, then shoved what turned out to be a duck into the passenger seat. With hands trembling like mad, Margo switched off the ignition and reached for the door handle. She paused, though, when the duck let out a sad sort of quack right before it keeled over on the seat and became completely motionless.

For a full minute, Margo simply sat there, staring at the duck, uncertain what she should do. Animals, no matter what type, had always disliked her, which was exactly why she'd never had so much as a fish for a pet and had no desire to get a pet anytime in the near or distant future.

Having a duck drop on her head was something straight out of one of her nightmares. But now, with the poor creature not moving so much as a single feather, Margo was pretty sure she wasn't in any danger of being mauled—although she certainly intended to proceed with extreme caution.

The first order of business, unfortunately, should be to see if the duck was dead. Reaching out a single finger, she gave it a little poke, snatching her hand back when the duck stirred, let out a weird-sounding snort, and then lapsed into silence again.

Blowing out a breath as she debated her options, and knowing one of those options should revolve around finding the duck some help, Margo got out of the car. Looking up and down the road, her sense of delight over being completely alone vanished when she didn't spot so much as a single car zooming her way.

Tipping back her baseball cap, she swiped a hand over a forehead that was getting somewhat sweaty. Readjusting the brim, she squinted down the road, relief edging through her when she spotted something moving toward her. That relief turned to confusion when that something drew closer and turned out to be a horse and buggy driven by a woman who seemed to have some type of bonnet covering her head.

The only explanation that came to mind was that she'd landed smack-dab in the midst of a film set. Before she could think that through, though, the horse and buggy turned down what seemed to be a dirt road since dust was now billowing around. It then disappeared from sight before Margo could flag it down.

Trudging back to the car, she slid behind the wheel. Seeing that the duck was still lying motionless on the passenger seat, she carefully stretched her arm over it, opened the glove compartment, and pulled out the map she'd purchased at a gas station.

Snapping it open, then giving it a good rustle because that's what it felt like you should do after you opened a map, she propped it against the steering wheel and traced her finger across the lines in the state of Ohio. She stopped on the town of Millersburg, which she thought was somewhere nearby. Glancing to the tourist attractions listed on the side of the map, Margo felt the oddest chill run over her when she spotted all the Amish things to do in Millersburg.

There were Amish farms to visit and Amish foods to try. There was Amish furniture to buy and tours promising insight into the life of the Amish. A working Amish farm operated as a bed and breakfast—although a disclaimer stated the owners were no longer Amish, something that must have been important to disclose, though why that would be Margo really didn't know.

She rubbed her arms to banish the chill she was still feeling, brushing her uneasiness aside as she chalked it up to the travel fatigue she was evidently experiencing.

Folding the map up, although it turned into a struggle to get it to refold neatly, she stuck it in the space beside the console. Looking back to the duck, she smiled when she heard the faintest sound of a snore coming from it. Taking that as a positive sign, she started up the Mini Cooper again and headed down the road.

Keeping an eye out for more buggies, because she really didn't want to run into one of those since running into the duck had been enough of a shock for one day, she drove a little over two miles before she spotted a sign directing the way to Millersburg.

Reaching the town of Millersburg ten minutes later, she dropped her speed to the posted limit and smiled as she took in the sight of one of the quaintest little towns she'd ever seen.

Bright pots of colorful flowers were set out everywhere, and shop fronts were immaculate, with many of them offering well-maintained painted benches that beckoned a person to sit for a while.

Bringing the car to a mere crawl, Margo spotted a group of boys walking out of an ice-cream shop, pulled over to the sidewalk, and rolled down her window. A few minutes later, armed with somewhat contradictory directions to the local animal clinic given to her by incredibly cute and enthusiastic boys with dripping cones, she pulled back onto the street and hoped she was going in the right direction.

She'd made it all of a single block before another unexpected chill slid over her, leaving her short of breath as sweat beaded her forehead and then began rolling down her cheeks.

Trying to suck a deep breath of air into lungs that had become constricted, she looked around, searching for the source of what had caused an honest-to-goodness panic attack.

A blink of an eye later, a reason popped to mind.

Something was oddly familiar about the town, even though she knew she'd never been there before. Somehow, and she didn't understand how, she *knew* this place, knew it as one vaguely remembered a distant memory.

A quack from her passenger had her pushing all thoughts of déjà vu and creepy feelings aside as air flowed back into her lungs. Glancing to the duck, she smiled when she found it sitting up on the seat, stretching its neck before it looked her way.

"Thank goodness you're not dead," she said, earning a quack of what seemed to be agreement in return. "But even though you're looking much better, I've just been told where to find an animal clinic, so you and I are off to have a little visit with a vet. And then, hopefully, that vet will know what to do with you."

Taking a right turn on the street the majority of the boys had said the animal clinic was on, Margo found it without any problem and eased the Mini Cooper into a parking space.

Turning to the duck, she considered it for a long moment. "Before I pick you up, I'm going to be upfront and tell you I don't know much about animals. I apologize in advance if I pick you up wrong, or if you don't like to be picked up at all, I'm sorry about that as well. But I can't leave you in the car because I've seen stories about animals dying in hot cars. Since I've almost killed you once today, I think I've reached my limit."

Getting out of the car, she walked to the other side, opened the passenger door, and took hold of the duck with both hands. Swallowing a shriek when it ruffled its feathers a bit, she straightened, kicked the door closed, and headed for the animal clinic, holding the duck out as far away from her body as possible.

After climbing up the three steps that led to a covered porch filled with pots of brightly colored flowers, Margo stopped in front of the closed entrance door. Before she could figure out how she was going to open it, though, it was opened for her.

Keeping the duck held out in front of her, a tricky thing since it had started to wiggle, Margo hurried into the waiting room, then turned to thank the person who'd been kind enough to get the door for her.

Every word of thanks got stuck in her throat when her gaze settled on the most compelling man she'd ever seen.

He was tall, well over six feet, and had a rugged face—although that ruggedness was softened by two dimples, one residing on either side of his mouth. He had an inviting smile, which he was sending her way, but he also had a distinct sense of unleashed power about him, one that suggested he was not a man to take lightly.

Dark hair, not quite black but darker than brown, grazed the collar of his buttoned-down blue shirt, and when he lifted his arm to brush aside a shaggy strand of that hair, muscles strained underneath the fabric.

He was clearly a man who didn't bother with the

grooming products most of the men she knew used daily, an idea that was strangely appealing. Before she could stop herself, her feet began moving in his direction, until the duck gave a loud quack and brought her immediately back to the situation at hand. That situation, odd as is seemed, consisted of her holding a duck, gawking at a complete stranger, and evidently losing her ability to speak.

"Are you okay?"

Shaking herself—apparently not a wise decision when holding a duck because it immediately began ruffling its feathers again—Margo managed to get out an "I'm fine" before the duck started pecking at her fingers, as if it had quite enough of being held and wanted her to release it.

Since the pecks were becoming painful, Margo wasn't reluctant in the least to let the animal go. Unfortunately, a second after she let it go, instead of flying to safety, the duck plummeted to the ground, becoming completely motionless.

Bending over, she was just about to scoop it up when it shot to its orange feet, lowered its head, and charged her, quacking as she'd never heard a duck quack before.

Abandoning any and all plans she might have had to impress the compelling man who'd opened the door for her, Margo let out a scream that would have done any side character in a horror movie proud. Jumping on the nearest chair as the duck waddled after her, she could only stare at it in stunned amazement as its quacks intensified and it began to waddle faster than she knew ducks were capable of waddling.

Having no idea what to do next, or even where to go, Margo settled for making a few shooing motions with her hand. That shooing, however, did absolutely nothing to stop the duck from its advance.

"Hey now, little one, there's no need to make such a fuss."

Freezing mid-shoo, Margo's mouth dropped open as the *compelling man,* or whatever his name really was, scooped up the duck and cradled it against a chest Margo couldn't help but notice was . . . impressive.

That cradling—or perhaps it was the comfort of being held in the arms of a man who was certainly capable of protecting it—had the duck quieting almost immediately, right before it nuzzled the man with its orange beak.

"You must be the vet," was all she could think to say when he looked up from the duck and back to her.

Flashing a grin her way—one that had her knees going weak, which she'd certainly read about in romance novels but had never experienced before—he shook his head. "The vet would be my brother-in-law, Dr. Ian St. James. I'm just one of the sheriff deputies in town, Deputy Brock

Moore." He nodded to the duck. "I think you might have been holding this little girl too tightly, which is why she probably went after you."

"That's a girl duck?"

Brock frowned. "You don't know your duck is a girl?"

"Oh, that's not my duck. My car ran into her, or rather my windshield did, and then she rolled up the windshield and fell through my sunroof."

"Really?"

Margo lifted her chin. "I don't think a person can make up a story like that."

"You might have a point." He tilted his head, considered her for what felt like forever, and then frowned. "Have we met before? You look awfully familiar."

Unwilling to explain why she looked familiar to him since she was finding it refreshing to *not* be Margo Hartman at the moment, she settled for a shrug. "A lot of people say I have a face that resembles someone they know. It must be because I'm rather ordinary."

"I wouldn't say you're ordinary," he countered before he turned and nodded to a woman who'd just stepped out of a back room. "Doesn't this woman look familiar to you, Mrs. Hershberger?"

Turning to the woman Brock had just addressed, Margo found herself looking at what could only be a member of the Amish community the town of Millersburg was known for. She was dressed in a plain blue dress, covered with a white apron, while a white cap covered her hair that had been pulled into a bun. Wire-framed glasses with thick lenses distorted eyes that might have been green, eyes currently narrowed on Margo.

"She looks like Sarah Yoder," Mrs. Hershberger finally said. "Except that Sarah has lighter hair."

Before Margo could say anything to that, she found herself being considered once again by the blue-eyed, obviously far too curious Deputy Brock Moore. Fighting the urge to squirm—or drop her chin, which would hopefully prevent him from realizing she looked *exactly* like Margo Hartman—she was spared further scrutiny when he sent her another smile and nodded.

"You do look like Sarah Yoder, and I bet you're here in town visiting them, aren't you?"

"I'm afraid not. I don't know anyone named Yoder, and I don't live anywhere near Ohio."

"Ah, a tourist, are you?"

"I suppose you could say that."

"Well, make sure to check out a few of the shops in town, and you'll have to try a meal at the Millersburg Diner." Brock's smile widened. "They serve a mean slice of pie there, as well as homemade ice cream to go with that pie."

Even though Margo limited her calorie intake because her fans and the press noticed any pounds she might put on, and could be vicious in their remarks about those pounds, she found the idea of pie and ice cream incredibly appealing. Perhaps even more appealing than she was finding Brock Moore.

Shoving aside that ridiculous thought since it was completely random, and was almost along the same lines of her wanting to pen a country song, Margo inclined her head. "Pie does sound appetizing, Deputy Moore. But I suppose I should settle the problem of the duck before I consider doing anything else."

"Did someone say they have a problem with a duck?"

Looking past Brock and Mrs. Hershberger, Margo found a man in a polo shirt and slightly worn jeans stepping through the back door. He immediately walked around the front counter and joined them.

"What happened?" he asked, taking the duck from Brock.

"I hit her with my car," Margo said, wincing when the man, obviously the vet, sent her a look that almost seemed to suggest she'd done so deliberately. "I didn't run it over. It flew into my windshield and then dropped through my sun-roof."

With his brows drawing together, the man shot a look to Brock, who laughed as he shook his head.

"I don't think she's been drinking, Ian. I mean, I could administer a breathalyzer test, but I think it would be a waste of time. Her reflexes were impressive when the duck went after her, and I don't remember ever seeing a person jump up on a chair so fast."

Margo drew herself up to what she knew was an impressive five feet eight inches. "I'm not drunk."

"Then I most certainly do apologize," Ian said. "It's just not every day that one hears a duck has dropped through a sunroof, although that will be a story I'll be telling for years." He smiled. "I'm Dr. Ian St. James, by the way, and with that said, I'd better take a look at this little girl."

Turning, Ian walked back to the front counter and set the duck on top of it. He ran a hand over her head, smoothed her feathers, then squeezed her middle, earning a quack of protest in response. Glancing to Margo, he smiled. "She doesn't appear to be suffering any noticeable injury. However, do you remember how fast you were driving?"

"I'd just gotten back on the road, so I might have been going five miles per hour, maybe ten?"

"At those speeds she might have avoided any lasting injuries, but I'm going to take a few x-rays just to be sure there's no internal injury." Picking up the duck, he headed around the counter, opening a door that Margo assumed led to the x-ray room.

A mere second after the door opened, the sound of yipping filled the air. A second after that, something began scrabbling across the linoleum floor, almost as if it was in such a hurry to reach the main part of the waiting room that it couldn't get its feet to find any traction.

A mass of brown fur that looked exactly like a mop without a handle on it scampered around the corner of the counter, wagging a tiny little tail as adorable yips spilled from its mouth. Those yips came to an immediate end, though, when the pooch suddenly caught sight of Margo, turning it into a snarling, teeth-baring beast.

Before she had the sense to jump back on the chair again, the dog, no bigger than a loaf of bread, lurched forward and sank its razor-sharp teeth straight into the hem of her Dolce & Gabbana jeans.

chapter three

It took an enormous effort for Brock to swallow the laugh threatening to burst out of his throat.

After prying the four-month-old Yorkie mix off the leg of the woman he knew only as *the tourist* since she'd yet to tell them her name, Brock felt the puppy turn into a mass of wiggles and tail-wagging as it nuzzled its snout between the buttons on his shirt. The coldness of its nose left Brock smiling.

"I cannot apologize enough," Ian said to the woman who was sitting on one of the plastic chairs that lined the waiting room. She was getting her ankle wiped down by Mrs. Hershberger, one of those women who always seemed to have the right piece of equipment or supplies available, this time a wet cloth and a bottle of rubbing alcohol. "Pudding is usually a very pleasant puppy, but I'll definitely be enrolling her in obedience classes so something disturbing like this never happens again."

"I'm afraid it's not the puppy," the woman began. "It's me. I have this strange effect on animals, especially dogs, and this wasn't the first time I've found a dog attached to my leg."

Ian turned his head to evidently hide a smile. After he apparently believed he had his amusement under control, he turned around. "Even so, Pudding can't be allowed to think chomping on someone's pant leg is acceptable. And speaking of pant legs"—Ian nodded to the rip in the woman's jeans—"I *will* compensate you for the cost of your jeans."

The woman smiled and waved that offer straight aside. "There's no need for that, Dr. St. James, especially if you're about to tell me that since you feel so bad about the . . . uh . . . puppy trying to deprive me of my leg, you'll take care of the duck for me. I'm hoping, since you're the local veterinarian, you'll know where it came from and who might be missing it."

"How about you tell me a little more about where you hit it, and we'll go from there, Miss . . . ?"

For the span of several seconds, the woman didn't say anything, but then she smiled a smile that seemed a little too bright, and nodded, just once. "I'm Marge. Marge . . . um . . . Simpson."

Brock wasn't certain, but he thought her smile faded ever so slightly before she hitched it back into place and took a rather absorbed interest in the ceiling.

"Like the cartoon character?" Ian asked slowly.

Pulling her attention away from the ceiling, Marge scratched her nose, muttered something that sounded like "I'm an idiot" under her breath, then nodded again. "It's unfortunate, but yes, I do share my name with a cartoon character that has . . . um . . . blue hair." She blew out an overly dramatic breath and Brock wouldn't have been surprised to see her raise a hand and dash it across her forehead. "It's been one of my greatest trials in life, one I don't care to talk about. So let me tell you what I remember about running into the duck."

Less than three minutes later, Marge, although Brock was almost certain that wasn't her name, finished her story and looked expectantly at Ian. "So there you have it. From what little I could tell you, any ideas about who that duck might belong to?"

"I'm not sure," Ian began, looking to Mrs. Hershberger who'd finished up with Margo's leg and was standing by the front counter. "Would you have any guesses about that?"

Mrs. Hershberger tilted her head. "I think it must have come from Jonas Yoder's farm, seeing as how that's the farm nearest to where Marge thought she was when she hit it. They have a nice flock of white ducks at that farm."

"Hasn't everyone been saying I look like a Sarah Yoder?" Marge asked.

"A lot of families named Yoder live here in Millersburg." Ian said before he took a step closer to Marge and frowned. "But now that you mention it, you do look like Sarah, and Sarah is the daughter of Jonas. You can meet her for yourself if you'd like to take the duck back to them. It might be amusing to chat with a woman who looks so remarkably like you."

Marge wrinkled her nose. "Don't the Amish prefer to stay to themselves?"

"Some do," Mrs. Hershberger said. "I'm Mennonite, although that's by marriage since I was born Amish. We Mennonites mingle a little more than the Amish, but the Yoder farm is a classic example of how true Amish live. Since Dr. St. James has a full schedule today, and I don't have a car, it would save us the trouble of having to make special arrangements to see the duck returned if you'd agree to take it out there."

"I suppose I could make the trip," Marge said slowly before she turned to Brock, narrowed her eyes just a touch on the puppy that had now fallen asleep in his arms, then lifted her gaze to meet his. "You wouldn't have time to take the duck there, would you?"

Before Brock had a chance to answer, Mrs. Hershberger spoke up, taking it upon herself to speak for him.

"This is tourist season, Marge. And that means our poor deputies, along with members of our police department, are just run ragged." She smiled. "That's why I'm sure you won't mind doing us this teensy favor. I'll even write down the directions to the Yoder farm, as well as the name of an adorable bed and breakfast I'm sure you'll enjoy staying at tonight."

Marge blinked. "Oh, I'm not staying here, Mrs. Hershberger. But thank you for offering to do that for me. I'll just grab the duck and get going soon since, again, I was just passing through and really had no intention of stopping in Millersburg until I . . . well, there's no need to bring up the duck episode again, is there?"

Pressing her lips together, as if she was holding something back, Mrs. Hershberger suddenly took to smiling, a smile that almost seemed to Brock to be a bit calculating. "At least you'll have a little time to shop around our town while Dr. St. James gets the x-rays done on the duck, slightly delayed because of the unfortunate Pudding incident. I'm sure it won't take more than an hour or two to make certain the duck is fine."

Ian opened his mouth, an obvious argument on his tongue, but then closed his mouth somewhat rapidly—which Brock thought might have come about because Mrs. Hershberger seemed to be stepping on the poor man's shoe.

"An hour should be sufficient to determine if the duck is okay," Ian finally said, earning a scowl from Mrs. Hershberger that he completely ignored. "And because you now have some time to visit a few of the shops here in town, do let me reimburse you for the damage done to your jeans. That way you'll be able to buy yourself a treat, and I'll be able to stop feeling guilty that my puppy attacked you."

Marge got up from the chair and shook her head. "I normally pay a lot of money to get that whole holey jeans look, but precious little Pudding just made this particular pair of jeans far cooler than they were when I bought them. So, thank you, but no. You don't owe me anything."

Sending the puppy he was still holding a small smile, even though Marge gave Brock a wide berth as she headed for the door, she turned and nodded. "I'll be back in one hour." With that, she walked out of the clinic, leaving Brock with the most unsettling feeling that the woman calling herself Marge was hiding more secrets than her true name.

Deciding that, as one of the sheriff deputies of the town, it was his job to look into any and all suspicious activities of visitors, he handed Pudding to Mrs. Hershberger and followed her.

Pulling off the baseball cap that was beginning to give her a headache, Margo took a second to throw it into the Mini Cooper, then retrieved her Kate Spade handbag from the back seat. Slinging its strap over her shoulder, she headed down the sidewalk to where she thought she'd find Main Street again, pretending not to notice that the far too appealing, yet evidently far too curious Brock Moore was walking right behind her.

Clearly his training to become an officer of the law had allowed him to realize something wasn't quite right with her. But since she had no intention of coming clean with who she really was, and she didn't want him to join her because he definitely made her nervous—which then made her say things that were completely idiotic like "I'm Marge Simpson"—Margo picked up her pace and darted into the first shop she encountered once she reached Main Street.

To her delight, she found herself in a shop that primarily sold quilts, and even though she didn't know a single person who'd want an old-fashioned quilt for a present, she decided she was going to buy one just for kicks.

Wandering around the shop, she couldn't resist touching the soft fabrics surrounding her, each one seemingly softer than the last, and each one tempting her to buy out the store.

"They're all made by hand."

Looking up from the quilt she'd been con-sidering, Margo found a woman approaching her. She was dressed remarkably similar to how Mrs. Hershberger had been dressed, although this woman didn't have glasses and was smiling in a polite but not overly friendly way. That smile, though, faded in a flash when the woman stopped in her tracks and simply stood there, staring at Margo.

"Good heavens, has anyone ever told you, you look just like—"

"A famous woman?" Margo asked, hoping that

by implying she got that all the time, the woman would think she wasn't talking to Margo Hartman, but just someone who looked like her.

"No, not a *famous* woman. I was going to say a local one." She smiled again. "I bet you're here visiting relatives, aren't you?"

"I'm sorry, but no, I'm not here visiting relatives." She turned back to the quilt she'd been considering. "This is so beautiful. It is for sale, isn't it?"

Glancing behind her when she didn't get an answer, she found the Amish woman looking perplexed, a look she'd seen often when people were trying to place her but couldn't quite put their finger on exactly who Margo was.

"It is for sale," the woman finally said, her cheeks turning a little pink. "Every quilt in the store is for sale, although I should warn you that the quilt you're interested in is the most expensive quilt we have."

"That's fine. I'm sure the price is fair. And besides, I really love it."

Pulling the quilt off the display rack, Margo handed it to the woman. "I'm just going to look around a little longer, but I want that one for sure."

For what felt like an incredibly long moment, the woman continued staring at Margo before, thankfully, she inclined her head. "I'll wrap this up while you look."

Stepping into another aisle, Margo wandered

down it, stopping right in front of a window that just happened to have Brock Moore peering into it. Lifting a hand, she sent him a regal wave paired with the beauty queen smile she'd perfected over the years.

Brock gave her a halfhearted wave in return before he strode away, adopting an air of nonchalance as if he hadn't just been caught following her.

"And that's what happens, Mr. Deputy Guy, when you try to mess with a pop princess."

"I'm sorry, were you saying something to me?"

Turning from the window, she found the Amish woman standing directly behind her.

"I was just talking to myself, something I do regularly, although . . . you probably don't want to know that, which means . . . I think I'm ready to check out now."

As she made her way to the cash register, she found that two other Amish women had shown up, both of whom were watching her closely.

Sending them a nod, she busied herself with finding her wallet, then paused when one of the women moved to stand next to her. The weight of the woman's stare had Margo fidgeting. Turning, she arched a brow the woman's way. "May I help you with something?"

The woman shook her head. "I thought you were someone I know, but . . . I was mistaken. I'm sorry."

Wanting to distract the woman from figuring out who she really was, even though Margo was pretty sure the Amish didn't watch TV, go to concerts, or peruse the latest tabloids, she blurted out the first thing to spring to mind. "I just met Mrs. Hershberger over at the animal clinic, and she seems to think I look like someone named Sarah Yoder."

"That's exactly who you look like," the woman now ringing up the quilt for Margo said. "Honestly, you could be her sister or . . . twin." She nodded to the quilt. "Sarah Yoder made the quilt you're buying, which is such a lovely coincidence, isn't it?"

Since the fine hairs on the nape of Margo's neck took that moment to stand straight up, as did the hair on her arms, Margo was thankful she could even summon a nod in response to an observation that gave her a serious case of the heebie-jeebies. Pulling some bills from her wallet, she handed them over to the woman manning the cash register, told her to keep the change, picked up her package, and then practically ran out of the store, gulping in a breath of air once she reached the sidewalk.

Ignoring the fact that the Amish women who'd been in the quilt shop with her were now all pressed up against the window, probably wondering what was wrong with her, Margo started down the sidewalk again, deciding it was past time she found something to eat. After lunch, she was hoping the duck would be ready to go, which would let her get out of this town that was giving her the creeps.

Locating the Millersburg Diner Brock Moore mentioned with no trouble at all, she soon found herself sitting in a booth, on a vinyl bench, stuffing herself to the gills on a remarkable meal of creamed chicken, stuffed peppers, and truly the best slice of pie she'd ever eaten in her life.

That she'd just blown the strict diet she always maintained didn't seem all that important to her at the moment, and with a pat to a stomach that was feeling very well fed indeed, she glanced up from her plate. Unfortunately, glancing back at her over the high seat of the next booth was a teenage girl, and with a quick look around the rest of the room, Margo realized she was attracting the notice of every single person in the diner.

Knowing it was only a matter of time until someone recognized her, since the only thing she'd done to disguise her appearance was dye her hair, Margo reached for her purse. The last thing she needed was for someone to call the local paper, which would then lead to an entire army of paparazzi jumping on planes to see what Margo Hartman was doing in the heartland of America.

She knew the kinds of stories that could spring up about her unusual trip. Everyone would wonder in their articles why Margo Hartman had chosen to drive a Mini Cooper, and an older model

Mini Cooper at that, clear across the country without bringing a single bodyguard or personal assistant with her.

A mental breakdown would be discussed, as would a romantic breakup with some unknown man, and then she'd be followed for the rest of her trip, forced in the end to return to California, especially because . . .

She really didn't have a bodyguard with her, which, now that she thought about it, could pose a problem, especially if her identity became widely known.

After licking the last remnants of the apple pie from her fork, she set it aside, rose from the table, settled her bill at the front of the diner—which was a little different but efficient—and then walked out into the warmth of the June afternoon.

Keeping an eye out for the oh-so-attractive Brock Moore, telling herself she wasn't *really* disappointed when she didn't see him lurking around to keep tabs on her, she strolled back to the animal clinic and stopped to tuck her newly purchased quilt inside her car's minuscule trunk. Then she walked up the steps of the clinic and entered the waiting room.

"Ah, Marge Simpson, you've come back."

For a moment, Margo didn't realize Mrs. Hershberger was speaking to her. But looking around, she not only realized she was the only person in the waiting room but remembered the ridiculous name she'd given instead of her own, choosing the name Marge because it was almost Margo if you switched the *e* for the *o*.

With her lips twitching at that random idea, Margo moved across the room and stopped at the front counter Mrs. Hershberger apparently manned. "I *have* come back. And you'll be pleased to learn that I took your advice and did a little shopping, finding the most exquisite quilt I've ever seen. After that, I went to the diner, had the most incredible piece of pie I've ever tasted, and now that I've been well fed, I'm here to fetch the duck. After I drop it off at the Yoder farm, I'll get back on the road and back to my adventure."

"One never knows where one may find an unexpected adventure." Mrs. Hershberger eyed Margo for a long moment before she bent to a pad of paper and began writing. "I heard tell from my niece that you bought one of the most expensive quilts offered in that shop, and then heard from a cousin that you ordered the creamed chicken for your lunch." Mrs. Hershberger gave a bit of a chuckle. "My relatives do enjoy keeping me abreast of all the local news."

"I'm surprised that, with so many tourists here, a tourist shopping in a quilt shop would be considered *news*."

"Hmm . . ." was all Mrs. Hershberger said to that before she lifted her head. "I've written down directions to the Yoder farm, as well as taken the liberty of listing that delightful bed and breakfast where you may want to stay for the night after all. It's not a good thing for a young woman to find herself alone on a dark, desolate road, especially in these dangerous days we live in."

The thought that she *was* a woman alone caused a little tingle of apprehension to run down her spine, until she pushed that way of thinking aside. It would definitely put a damper on her adventure. Clearing her throat, Margo nodded. "I'll keep that in mind, Mrs. Hershberger, although I probably should point out that it's just afternoon now, not night. And on that note, if I could just get the duck, I'll get right on delivering it to that farm, and then I'll be on the open road with plenty of daylight to see me to my next destination."

Releasing a sigh and looking what could only be described as disappointed, Mrs. Hershberger straightened, then headed toward the door leading to the back offices. She returned a moment later with a pet carrier in her hand.

"Dr. St. James didn't find a thing wrong with this little dear, so she's free to go home. If you would be so kind as to tell them at the Yoder farm that Dr. St. James will drop by in the next day or two to check on the duck and retrieve the carrier, we'd surely appreciate it." With that, Mrs. Hershberger walked around the counter, handed Margo the carrier, and then took to shaking her head when Margo immediately held the carrier as far away from her as possible.

"She won't hurt you."

"Best not to take any chances," Margo countered. Then, after exchanging the expected good-byes and promising to follow the directions Mrs. Hershberger gave her, Margo breezed out of the clinic.

After getting the carrier settled on the front seat of her car, since a good deal of her luggage was taking up the entire back seat, she couldn't resist taking a peek around. A sliver of disappointment slid through her when she looked up and down the street but didn't catch so much as a glimpse of a certain attractive deputy.

Sliding behind the wheel of her car, she found the duck peeking out at her through the grate that kept her safely enclosed. "You may live in a weird town, but you do seem to have some fine-looking men wandering around it, although—a girl like me can't do much more than admire fine-looking men, what with all the attention the press likes to give me regarding my love life, or lack thereof."

Smiling when the duck let out a quack of obvious agreement, she propped the directions Mrs. Hershberger had written out for her on the dashboard and started her engine. Getting back on Main Street, she hung a left, drove past all the quaint little shops and the diner, and found herself strangely relieved when she left the town behind.

After checking her odometer, then the directions on the dashboard, Margo glanced back to the road, then to the duck. "We go three miles down this road, take a right, and find a dirt road that has a scarecrow on it. That's a sign we've reached the right farm . . . the Yoder farm."

Two quacks were the duck's reply to that, and laughing, Margo switched her iPod on and spent the next two miles belting out the lyrics of the latest Rihanna tune.

Cresting a rise, she found a pretty lake on the other side of it. "Ah, would you look at that. I bet you've taken a swim in there before, haven't—"

A blast of a horn had her gaze pulling from the lake back to the road, a sense of horror stealing the breath right from her when she caught sight of a large truck.

It had come out of nowhere, but there was no question it was heading directly her way.

Jerking the wheel to the right even as her foot pressed on the gas, she found herself whispering a prayer for help—right before her car went airborne and then dropped straight into the lake.

chapter four

Considering he'd always prided himself on being a rather savvy law enforcement type, and even though he'd been away from the FBI for over six months now, Brock couldn't believe he'd been caught in what he'd hoped would be an informative reconnaissance mission by a woman claiming to be Marge Simpson.

Obviously, his investigative skills had become a little rusty since he joined the county's sheriff's department on a temporary basis. Still, one would have thought he'd at least be able to avoid detection by a woman who'd somehow managed to have a duck land on her head, and then was set upon by a less-than-killer puppy named Pudding.

Cranking the air up a notch in the Jeep he preferred to drive over a departmental car—a perk he'd been given because of the unfortunate circumstances surrounding the reason he was in Millersburg working as a deputy in the first place—Brock turned from Main Street onto a rural road that led away from town.

Easing off the gas a few miles later when he saw a buggy cresting the hill in front of him, a sight he still wasn't used to seeing, he waved to Mervin Fisher, who sent him a nod in return.

Speeding up once the buggy had traveled a

sufficient distance away, Brock continued to keep an eye out for other buggies—something he never thought would become a daily part of his life when he lived in Virginia. But until he was satisfied his sister's death was, in truth, a suicide, he wasn't leaving Millersburg.

Fortunately, his position with the FBI would be waiting for him when he settled matters here. But in all honesty, though his determination was still firmly in place, his faith in his ability to learn what had actually happened to Stephanie was fading as months went by without uncovering any leads suggesting she had been murdered instead of taking her own life.

The only thing that kept him going at this point was helping Stephanie's husband, Ian, find a sense of closure, along with hoping he could provide his parents with knowledge that would ease the guilt they felt over the belief their daughter had killed herself.

All the evidence he'd uncovered so far pointed to a suicide. But because Stephanie had been a woman of incredibly strong faith, and insanely happy married to a man she claimed was the love of her life, Brock didn't buy the verdict of suicide the coroner provided a week after her death.

Suicide made absolutely no sense, at least to him and to Ian, which was why Brock had agreed to allow his brother-in-law to pull some strings he had with the local sheriff's department and get

Brock hired on in a temporary capacity. No one but Ian knew Brock was in Millersburg to conduct his own investigation. They'd just put it around town that Brock had wanted to lend Ian his support in what was certainly a concerning time of need, but that he'd also needed a way to pay his bills while he lent that support.

The problem he was facing now, though, was that he was running out of time. The deputy position Brock was filling wasn't permanent, and the man he was filling in for was due back from medical leave in a few weeks.

Cresting another small hill, Brock glanced to one of the small lakes that were a common sight throughout Ohio, then squinted when something caught and held his attention. That something, if he wasn't mistaken, seemed to be . . . a car.

Flooring the gas pedal, Brock turned the Jeep off the road and raced to the edge of the lake, shoving the gearshift into park before he was out the door.

Kicking off his shoes, he dove into the lake and began swimming, sucking in a huge mouthful of water when he swam into something oddly soft, yet solid at the same time. Coughing up the water he'd almost swallowed, he shoved the hair obscuring his view out of his eyes and started to tread water, finding remarkably bright green eyes staring back at him.

It was Marge . . . Marge Simpson, or whatever

her name really was. And directly behind her was the duck, quacking every few seconds as if she'd had just about enough drama for one day and wanted everyone to know she'd had enough.

"Deputy Moore, fancy meeting you out here. Although I do think you may be taking the whole following me business a little too seriously, what with the idea you've now followed me straight into this charming lake."

The unexpectedness of that wry comment, when he'd been expecting a cry for help instead, had Brock swallowing another large gulp of horrible-tasting lake water. Choking on it, he sank underneath the water for the span of a few seconds, and then was suddenly pulled straight back up to the surface and flipped to his back. Before he could do much more than cough out some more water, Marge, the woman who'd obviously driven her car into the lake, began towing him to shore.

When the absurdity of that settled in, he couldn't help but laugh, which turned out to be a huge mistake since the water sloshing around them went straight up his nose.

"Stop flailing around or we'll both end up drowning."

"I'm not drowning," he managed to get out in a somewhat wheezy sort of voice.

"You could have fooled me."

Thankfully, she released her hold on him, and

with the duck trailing after them, they swam to shore, climbed up the bank of the lake, and fell onto some cool grass.

After coughing up what felt exactly like an entire lung, Brock sat up and glanced to the woman beside him. Marge was lying in the grass on her back, and the duck, oddly enough, was sitting on her stomach.

"I see the duck seems to have had a change of heart about you," was all he could think to say.

"We saved each other, so that makes us friends for life." She pushed up to her elbows and sent the duck a fond smile. "I was panicking after the car hit the water and immediately started filling up. But then I realized the poor duck was stuck in the pet carrier and it was sinking below the water. I got the door to it open and the duck swam out, but then the car tipped, and I found myself under water. I thought for sure that was it. That I was going to the place in the sky. You know, heaven. But then the duck pecked me and I ended up following it through the sunroof."

"I'm sorry I didn't drive by sooner so I could have helped you get out of the car."

"I'm sorry that maniac lost control of his truck and was driving in my lane, but—" She set the duck gently into the grass and sat up, looking around. "Where is that truck?"

Looking around as well, Brock didn't see a

single sign of a truck. Frowning, he turned back to Marge. "Are you sure there was a truck?"

"Of course I'm sure. A person doesn't forget a sight like that."

"Do you think the driver of that truck saw you?"

Marge tilted her head. "I would have to say yes, because he honked at me, and that's when I turned the wheel of my car and ended up in the lake."

"You're sure it was a he?"

"Since it was a really big truck, and it was clearly a maniac driving it, I'm going to say I'm almost positive it was a guy."

"We could spend hours discussing the social correctness of a statement like that, but"—Brock rose to his feet—"do you remember where you went off the road?"

She pointed to a spot between a few trees, not far from the main road. Striding over to that location, Brock looked around until he found a set of tire tracks that simply left the road.

Walking up the road, he found another set of tracks, ones made by larger tires that had run off the main road just a foot or two.

Joining Marge again, he saw she'd flopped into the grass once more and the duck had resettled on her. "I found some tracks that suggest your story checks out. That's good news for you since I won't have to administer that breathalyzer test I was considering having you take."

"Words to make a girl's heart go pitter-patter for sure."

Smiling, Brock down next to her. "Because we've evidently moved beyond the stranger-courtesy stage, what with your heart going all . . . pitter-patter . . . how about if you tell me who you really are and what you're really doing in Millersburg?"

"I think I'd rather cling to the idea we're still in stranger-courtesy country. Taking a relationship too far too quickly can only lead to hurting hearts, not pitter-pattering ones. So you may just continue calling me Marge, and I'll continue calling you Deputy Moore."

"But you really aren't a Marge, are you?"

She gave an airy wave of her hand. "If you ask me, people put entirely too much importance on names."

He grinned, something he'd rarely done since his sister died.

There was just something about the woman who looked a little like a drowned rat, lying in the grass beside him with a duck settled on her—something that intrigued him.

He couldn't remember the last time he'd been intrigued with a woman, even though he'd had his fair share of relationships.

His grin faded straightaway as a less-than-comforting thought sprang to mind. *Intrigued* was a word guys saved for that special woman, someone they knew was *the one,* or could be *the one,* or—

"Why are you staring at me?"

Brock blinked away those particular thoughts. "Your eyes are closed. How do you know I'm staring?"

"I'm a girl."

"While I might not know your name, *Marge,* I'm fully aware of the fact you're a girl."

She laughed. "Good for you, but I was simply trying to point out that girls know things like when a guy is staring at them. My psychiatrist says it's an instinctual thing, like when animals know a tornado is coming."

"You have a psychiatrist?"

"Everyone in California has a psychiatrist."

Leaning forward, he cleared his throat. "If you're about to tell me you escaped from an institution, which is why you won't tell me your name, it would explain a lot and have me feeling so much better."

"I've never been institutionalized. But if I *was* currently suffering from some type of mental breakdown, I have to imagine the symptoms of that breakdown would have me denying such information. And I have to wonder why you'd feel better having a crazy person running around your town over a—"

"Over a what?" he prodded when she suddenly stopped talking.

Her only reply was to start humming what he thought might be a Beyoncé tune.

"At least tell me you're not a criminal."

Her humming stopped as her lips curved at the very corners. "If I was, I'd hardly own up to that to a deputy, would I?"

Refusing a smile of his own, Brock nodded instead. "An excellent point, *Marge*. And because it's clear you're not going to tell me anything more about you, I'm going to suggest we abandon our lovely spot by the water. We'll head back to town—together if you had any doubt—and contact your insurance company. Then we'll start the process of figuring out what to do about the fact that your car in now residing on the bottom of the lake since I can no longer see it."

Opening her eyes, she squinted back at him. "I don't really want to go back to town because—now, don't take this the wrong way—it's creepy. Besides, I need to get the duck back to its farm. The poor thing has had a rough day and deserves to be reunited with its duck family."

"We can stop at the Yoder farm first. That won't be a problem since it's not far from here. But after that, you will need to contact your insurance agent. Your car, I'm sorry to say, is probably a total loss, so you'll need a claim processed as soon as possible."

A pucker gathered in the middle of her forehead. "What will a claim do for me?"

"It'll start the wheels turning to get you a check for the value of your car. You do have car insurance, don't you?"

She pushed herself to a sitting position, rearranged the duck on her lap, and suddenly brightened. "I saw an insurance card in my glove compartment before I left California." She smiled and shook her head. "I had no idea insurance companies would pay for an entire car, though—particularly if someone lost their car in a lake, something I can't imagining happening very often, or . . . at all."

Brock considered her for a long moment before he nodded. "Okay, now I'm getting a clearer picture of what's going on. Tell me if I'm right. You're from a really wealthy family, your parents recently decided to cut you off so you'll appreciate the value of a dollar, and that didn't sit well with you. So you ran away."

"Not even close."

"Then who *are* you?"

"I'm just an ordinary woman, taking a little road trip across the country."

"Ordinary women don't bother to disguise their appearances, nor do they make up unusual names for themselves."

"Marge is a very ordinary name."

"If you're over sixty, which, clearly, you're not."

"Maybe, like I said back at the clinic, my

59

parents wanted to name me after their favorite cartoon character."

"I didn't realize the Simpsons had been around so long."

She narrowed her eyes. "What do you mean by that?"

Blinking, Brock smiled a charming smile. "I think this is one of those times where it would be in my best interest to stop talking."

"I'm not old."

"Of course you're not, but you're also not a Marge."

"For a moment, he thought she was going to continue arguing with him, but then she shrugged. "Okay, fine. You're right. I lied about my name."

"But you're not going to tell me what your real name is, are you?"

She frowned. "How did you know I was trying to disguise myself?"

"You skin and hair have lightened up considerably since you got out of the lake."

"I *knew* I should have bought the permanent hair dye, but there wasn't really any time to have my spray tan touched up before I got on the road."

"Usually only really *wealthy* people get spray tans."

"No, they don't. I read an article in *GQ* a few months back about exotic dancers who spray tan all the time. It increases their tips if they can show really sharp tan lines."

"You read that or you actually *are* an exotic dancer?"

She tilted her head. "You know, that would have been a great cover, me being an exotic dancer. And I could have told you I'm on the lam, running from my Neanderthal of a manager. But . . . no, I'm not."

And then, before he could ask another single question, she suddenly set the duck aside, jumped to her feet, dashed straight for the lake, and dove in.

With a flutter of wings, the duck took off after her, leaving Brock sitting by the side of the lake, feeling as though he'd missed some pertinent part of the conversation.

By the time he finally had the presence of mind to go after her, she was already swimming back to shore, dragging something behind her as the duck swam next to her, keeping pace with her every stroke.

Wading into the water as she drew closer, Brock held out his hand. Then he pulled her through the muck that edged the space between the lake and the shore before he hauled her straight up against him.

For a moment, he simply held her, surprised by how right she felt in his arms, until she stumbled a step away from him, tipped back her head, and grinned as she caught his eye.

"Saw my purse." She held up a fuchsia bag

that had some strands of algae attached to it.

"You could have told me. I would have gone in after it."

"And yet another instance when you've set my poor little heart all a-flutter." She trudged up the bank and plopped down on the grass.

Pulling the purse into her lap, she blew out a breath. "This will prove once and for all if the sales associate who sold me this bag was telling the truth when he said it's completely waterproof. He certainly was right about it being able to float."

"I didn't know being waterproof was a key selling point for a lady's handbag." He joined her on the grass.

"It's not. I am, however, notorious for leaving my bags too close to the surf, which, unfortunately, ruined quite a few of my possessions over time. When one of my assistants, er . . . friends learned about these waterproof purses, I thought I'd give one a go."

"You spend a lot of time at the beach?"

"A fair amount of time, and no, I'm not a professional surfer, if that was your next guess." She unzipped her purse, pulled out her cell phone, grinned, and then stuck her hand back into the bag. "Nothing's wet."

"Then I suppose your driver's license is in fine shape as well."

She looked up. "You're very tenacious."

"I've been told it's part of my charm."

"You should know better than to believe people who are obviously prone to exaggeration." Returning her attention to her purse, and after digging around the contents for a moment, she pulled out a wallet that exactly matched the bag. She surprised him when she handed it over.

"I wasn't expecting you to actually cooperate," he said.

"See, that's part of *my* charm. Doing the unexpected."

More amused by her every second, Brock flipped open her wallet. Her license was front and center. Reading the name printed on it, he frowned.

Margo Hartman.

Turning his attention to *Margo,* he studied her face for a few seconds, looked back at the picture on her license, and noticed she was normally a blonde. But when that didn't help him recognize her, he looked at the name again, then handed her the wallet.

"I know you seem to believe I should know exactly who you are. But in all honesty, I have to say I don't think I've ever heard of Margo Hartman. Or if I have, I've forgotten exactly who you're supposed to be or what you're supposed to have done."

chapter five

To Brock's absolute confusion, instead of seeming upset over the fact he had no idea who she was, Margo suddenly looked as if she'd just woken up on Christmas morning and found an enormous pile of presents waiting for her.

Her green eyes were sparkling, her cheeks were flushed, and even with her hair sopping wet and straggling down her face, Brock realized Margo Hartman, whoever she was, was a very attractive, very quirky woman—and he found her strangely . . . fascinating.

"My poor little heart really is going pitter-patter." She raised what he just noticed was a well-manicured hand to that heart in question. "And how fabulous that you truly don't seem to know who I am, which I don't think anyone has ever told me before . . . as in ever."

Brock quirked a brow her way. "Should I assume you're someone who must be slightly famous?"

If anything, she looked more delighted than she had a mere second ago. "I am. I am *slightly* famous." She beamed a smile his way. "This is excellent."

"It . . . is?"

"Of course."

Realizing she probably wasn't going to expand

on that particular statement since she'd started humming another tune under her breath, one of those pop tunes he heard every now and again on the radio, he cleared his throat. "I would have taken you for older than the twenty-three your license states."

Her humming came to an abrupt stop. "That, Deputy Moore, is not a way to keep a woman's heart going pitter-patter. How old are you?"

"Thirty-one."

"I suppose I can see that, although I thought you were more along the lines of thirty-five."

"I *look* like I'm thirty-five?"

"Not at all. You just have this old-soul feeling about you." She smiled. "You *look* like you're twenty-seven."

"Well, all right then. Mature yet keeping up a youthful appearance. I can live with that."

"And now you're supposed to say you didn't mean I come across as a lot older than twenty-three, probably just like twenty-five or so."

"I think I'm changing my mind about your age since I don't think twenty-five-year-olds run away from home, which is what I'm beginning to think you're doing. I haven't figured out why you seem to be disguising your identity or why a *slightly* famous person would be running away from home in the first place but"—he smiled—"it'll come to me."

Lifting her chin, she smiled in return. "Because

I'm slightly famous, I had to disguise myself a little bit for this trip. And since I told you my name, I don't really have any secrets left to hide, so . . . I left California because I have this mother who can be a little much to take sometimes. I decided I needed space from her, and from some business associates as well, if you must know. That space just happens to be growing wider the farther I travel across the country, which is . . . wonderful."

"Why would you need space from business associates?"

Margo shrugged. "They've overstepped their responsibilities one too many times. Since I would feel bad firing them, it was better for me to simply leave town for a while."

"See, now I'm questioning you're *only* twenty-three again."

"Why would you question that?"

"Because most twenty-three-year-olds are still spending their time at entry-level jobs, not talking about firing business associates. Better yet, I think they still like to wander around malls, shopping in stores with remixed tracks of music blasting and enough perfume sprayed around that it's difficult to breathe."

"I've never *wandered* around a mall in my life, preferring smaller shops. And I doubt you were wandering around malls either when you were twenty-three."

Since he'd actually been studying for the bar exam, having finished up with law school, she had a valid point. Not that he was going to bring up the fact that he was an attorney, or that being an attorney had led to his being recruited by the FBI.

He inclined his head in her direction. "I apologize. That came out wrong and sounded completely insulting to twenty-three-year-olds everywhere, didn't it?"

"It did, but since you were polite enough to apologize, I forgive you."

"Thank you."

After exchanging smiles, they settled into a comfortable silence. He'd always enjoyed people who didn't need to fill silences with conversation. But the idea that he seemed to be enjoying Margo Hartman's company far more than he could remember enjoying any woman's company in a long time was surprising.

He didn't have the time, or the luxury at the moment, to become distracted from the job he'd come to Millersburg to complete. And until he resolved the mystery he knew surrounded his sister's death, he needed to remember that. Still, a little flirtation never hurt anyone.

Getting to his feet—since even a little flirting needed to be put aside when things like contacting insurance companies and figuring out if cars could be pulled from the depths of this particular lake were necessary—he held out a hand to Margo. Instead of taking it, though, she handed him the duck, which had returned to her side. Then she collected her purse and got up from the grass.

Shading her eyes with one hand, she blew out a breath. "I think my car is well and truly sunk now. It's too bad I stuck the quilt I just bought in the trunk because it was so pretty. It would have been a little tricky to save, though, what with the whole sinking thing going on."

"But you saved the duck," he reminded her, giving the duck a scratch, which had it letting out a quack.

"There is that." Her eyes suddenly widened as she turned to him. "All my clothes were in the car, and my make-up, lotions, iPod, and shoes."

"Hopefully someone in town will know who to call to see if we can pull your car from the lake. That will let you retrieve your luggage, but everything might be ruined."

She shook her head. "My luggage is supposed to be waterproof as well, exactly like my purse."

"Good to know, although your insurance company would probably reimburse you for the cost of the items lost. You can ask them about that when we give them a call. But since I know you're worried about the duck, we'll take it to the Yoder farm first."

"How will I contact my insurance company

when my insurance card is in the glove compartment of my car?"

"Can't you call someone who'd know that information?"

Margo bit her lip. "My . . . friend Fauna would know, but I don't want to turn my phone on to get her contact information since that could lead my mom directly to me."

"Your mom would go to those lengths to find you, *and* she has the resources to go to those lengths?"

"You should never underestimate the resources a determined mother can find when she puts her mind to it."

"So noted," Brock said. "And because you don't want to turn on your phone, I think I have the contacts to find this Fauna's phone number. Then you can use my phone, or a phone at the sheriff's department, and we'll go from there. I should warn you that you'll have to fill out a lot of forms about the car. And while you do that, I'm going to ask around, see if anyone knows anything about that truck that ran you off the road. Do you remember anything about it?"

"It was big, maybe dark in color, and . . . that's about all I remember," she said as they walked toward his Jeep.

"And obviously driven by a complete idiot, since that person didn't stay to help you, or even call the accident in."

Margo brushed that aside. "It doesn't really surprise me the driver didn't stick around. I bet he was texting when he drifted into my lane, giving him only a split second to honk his horn, which at least had us avoiding a collision before it sent me into the lake."

Pulling open the passenger side door of his Jeep, he caught her eye. "I know what I'm about to ask you is going to make you think I'm incredibly paranoid. But keep in mind that I witness strange things in my line of work, so . . . Because you've admitted to being slightly famous, you don't happen to have anyone running around out there who might want to see you harmed, do you?"

"Like stalkers?"

He nodded.

Margo tilted her head. "I don't think so because no one knew I was planning on leaving California. It was one of those impulsive decisions. Besides, the people who might be inclined to follow me, fans if you will, are an odd assortment of people. Most of them have limitations because of a lack of money or . . . mental stability."

"I'm going to have to Google you," he muttered.

Her face fell. "That would ruin the fun."

Shaking his head, even as he fought the urge to laugh, Brock waited until Margo climbed into her seat, handed her the duck, and then moved to the driver's side of the Jeep. Sliding behind the wheel, he switched on the ignition, and a moment later got them back on the road and heading for the Yoder farm.

"I hope we're not ruining your seats since we're both still really wet and dirty," Margo said, drawing his attention.

"Don't worry about that. My brother-in-law borrows my Jeep all the time to transport his animals, so, believe me, it's had worse than wet and muddy jeans sitting on these seats."

"Does your sister live here in town?"

"Stephanie died a few months back."

Taking him by surprise when she reached out and touched his arm, Margo gave it a small pat. "I'm so sorry for your loss. Was she sick?"

"No, she wasn't sick."

Margo looked at him for a moment, and then, as if she realized he didn't want to dwell on the death of his sister, she nodded and turned to look out the window, humming another song under her breath. If he wasn't mistaken, this one seemed to be a tune he'd learned in Sunday school when he was a child.

"Is that 'This Little of Light of Mine' you're humming?" he asked after they'd driven for about a mile.

"Hmm?" was all she replied, earning a glance from him in return.

For some reason, she was sitting as still as a

71

statue, her posture almost rigid as she continued staring out the window with eyes that weren't blinking, her face pale underneath the remnants of her spray tan.

"Is something the matter?"

Blinking exactly one time, she turned toward him. "Have you ever had the feeling that you've been somewhere before, but knew you hadn't?"

"You think you've been here before?"

She nodded. "I keep getting this weird vibe, like a déjà vu kind of thing. I mean, I know I've never been here since Ohio is not exactly a vacation destination my parents would have ever chosen to bring me to. They're more the French Riviera or Venice type. But this place seems familiar to me."

"Maybe you've read a book on the Amish, or seen one of those PBS specials on them."

Shaking her head, Margo looked out the window again. "I don't think so, although we did cover the Amish in school one time, back when I was in high school. We didn't spend a lot of time on the subject, though. Just enough to learn the Amish don't use electricity or phones, or at least don't have phones in their houses. And they don't drive cars, but I do think they now have indoor plumbing, although I'm not absolutely sure about that." She turned back to him. "Do you know much more than that?"

"I'm afraid I don't. I'd never been around the

Amish much until I moved here a few months back. But the farm we're going to now is Amish, so that might give you at least a glimpse into their lives."

Flipping on his turn signal, Brock drove the Jeep down a dirt road, and then pulled to a stop in front of the Yoder farmhouse. Turning in his seat, he leaned toward Margo, not liking the fact she was now looking a little green.

"You should have told me you were getting carsick."

"I don't get carsick," she muttered.

After thinking about that for a few seconds, Brock opened his door and got out of the Jeep, but then leaned back in. "I think it might be for the best for you to stay here. I'll take the duck back."

With a stubborn lift of her chin, Margo rolled her eyes. "Because I hit the duck, and then she and I saved each other from drowning, we're now bonded. I can't very well just hand her off to you and not say a proper good-bye. That would be rude."

Brock smiled and inclined his head. "Since I know better than to argue with that kind of logic, fine. You can return the duck." Shutting his door, he walked around the Jeep, opened Margo's door, and took the duck from her as she jumped to the ground.

Handing the duck back to her when she held out

her hands, he turned and found a woman already walking their way, waving to them as she stepped farther from the house. "That's Sarah Yoder. The woman I said you remind me of—"

A gunshot came from out of nowhere and had him spinning around, catching sight of the duck plummeting to the ground as Margo simply stood there, a telling red stain spreading across her shirt.

Lifting her head, she met his gaze with eyes that were wide with shock, right before those eyes rolled back into her head and she plummeted toward the ground, exactly like the duck.

chapter six

Forcing her eyes open, a tricky job because they felt as if they'd been glued shut, Margo winced as a bright light blinded her. Its intensity caused her to squeeze her eyes shut again.

A trace of panic stole over her. She had no idea where she was, but because of the bright light, she thought there was the distinct possibility she might very well be . . . dead.

Curiosity had her eyes opening just a slit, but instead of finding Saint Peter or anything resembling the pearly gates, she saw more white. Then a shadow flickered through the white, right before a figure loomed up directly in front of her.

She blinked, blinked again, and then smiled.

She'd always known angels would be lovely, and this one was no exception, what with his beautiful blue eyes and sculpted face. That face was a little fuzzy, though, and she was having the hardest time focusing on it.

"Margo? Can you hear me?"

All thoughts of angels disappeared in a flash because angels certainly wouldn't have such raspy voices. She'd always thought if she was actually given an opportunity to hear an angel, that angel would sound exactly like the chimes one heard when the bells rang at church.

Her lips curved into a grin at that odd thought, but it faded almost immediately when an annoying beep suddenly drew her attention. It sounded exactly like something one would hear in a hospital.

She didn't like hospitals, what with the sick people who stayed there, and all the . . . blood.

She definitely didn't like blood. Didn't like the look of it, the smell of it, or even the thought of it, which was why she decided right that very second to stop thinking about blood before she did what she usually did when faced with the nasty stuff—faint. Or puke. It just depended on the circumstance.

Blinking a few more times to clear her vision—while banishing blood to the farthest recesses of her thoughts, where she knew perfectly well it would still linger, waiting for a chance to wander front and center again and freak her out—she allowed her gaze to travel around the room.

Looking up, she discovered that the white light, much to her relief, was coming from some fluorescent bulbs, which suddenly went dark. Shifting her gaze, she settled it on the large man again, the one she'd mistaken for an angel, and realized a second later that he was the man she'd met when she stopped in a small town. He was Brock something or other, although why she'd stopped in that town was a little foggy. But Brock . . . now *he* was becoming clearer by the second, especially since he wasn't a man a girl wanted to forget—as in ever.

"So you *are* awake." He moved closer and bent over to catch her eye.

Trying to send him the smile she was famous for because, after all, she'd been told it was one of her best assets—although by whom she couldn't remember at the moment—she frowned when her lips didn't seem to want to lift. "What . . . happened?"

"You're in the hospital. You've been shot."

She blinked. "Shot?"

"I'm afraid so."

She blinked again, then her eyes widened. "Was there . . . blood?"

As Brock opened his mouth and started what she thought might have been an explanation for her being shot—or maybe about blood—the room started turning fuzzy again. His voice began sounding like it was coming from a long, long tunnel. Before she knew it, his voice faded right away and everything went dark as complete silence settled over her.

The distinct sound of snoring pulled Margo from a sleep that had to be the best sleep she'd had in years. Lifting a hand, she rubbed it over her eyes, pausing mid-rub when another snore drew her attention. Turning her head on an incredibly stiff pillow, one that certainly didn't come close to being as soft as the ones she kept on her bed in California, she frowned when she saw Brock Moore sleeping in a chair next to the bed she was in.

Second by second, memories came back to her.

She'd been at a farm, trying to return a . . . duck.

Her lips twitched at that unusual state of affairs, but the twitching stopped in an instant when she remembered something had happened at that farm—something that might have been mildly, or more than mildly painful and . . . unexpected.

"Nice to see you're back in the land of the living."

Shifting her gaze, she found that while she'd been thinking about a duck and wondering about troubling situations she couldn't really remember, Brock had woken up and was stretching. The stretching had far-too-impressive muscles rippling underneath the T-shirt he was wearing, one that bore the logo of some old rock band.

"How long have I been out of it?"

"About a day and a half."

She sucked in a sharp breath as her gaze darted around the room.

"I'm in a hospital," she said, more as a statement of fact than a question.

Brock leaned forward, looking a little wary. "You *are* in a hospital."

"I don't care for hospitals."

"So I've been told."

She blinked. "Who told you that?"

"How are you feeling?" Brock asked, completely ignoring her question.

Taking a moment to consider her answer, she frowned. "Strangely enough, I feel great, but . . ." She shot a look to the IV hanging beside her bed, the mere sight of it turning the great feeling she'd just claimed to be enjoying into something not so great. Drawing in a deep breath as she fought to remember what brought about her being admitted to a hospital, her mouth dropped open and stayed open for a few seconds. She finally closed it, but only because her mouth was incredibly dry and keeping it open hadn't helped that situation.

Releasing the breath she'd forgotten she'd taken, she forced herself to meet Brock's still-wary gaze. "Tell me the truth. I think I remember you telling me I'd been shot. How bad is it? Do I have time to set my affairs in order?"

At first she thought Brock had turned his head to save her from seeing the tears in his eyes. But then she realized that although his shoulders were definitely shaking, the sounds rumbling out of his large body were not sobs. They were more along the lines of stifled howls of laughter.

"Are you *laughing* at me?"

Turning back to her, he raised a hand and dashed them over eyes that were certainly watering, but not because he was crying. Taking a far longer time than Margo thought was necessary to compose himself, he settled back into the chair, gave a last snort of amusement, and then shook his head at her.

"Oh, that was great. I can't remember the last time I laughed like that."

"I'm so happy my being shot amuses you. I wonder if you'd be as happy with me if I were to chuckle over the idea a doctor had to dig a bullet out of you."

Instead of sobering Brock up, that had him burying his face in his hands as he dissolved into gut-wrenching laughs, which then turned into hiccups. He got up from the chair, moved to a pitcher sitting on the portable tray table, poured himself a cup of water, and swallowed the entire contents in one large gulp.

To give the man credit, though, he did pour more water into a clean plastic cup and bring it to her.

Taking a sip, she enjoyed the feel of the cold water sliding down a throat that was certainly parched. Then she took another sip as Brock reclaimed his seat.

"Should I assume I'm not at death's door?" she finally asked when she'd finished about half the water.

"You have a *flesh* wound, Margo. The bullet barely nicked you on your upper left arm."

"But . . . I distinctly remember blood, and . . . the duck. What happened to the duck?"

Sobering, he leaned forward. "The duck took the brunt of the bullet."

"She . . . died?"

"That didn't come out right at all, did it? No, the duck's fine, or as fine as can be, considering her wing got nicked."

Margo raised a hand to her heart. "She'll never be able to fly again?"

"I didn't say *that*." Brock pressed his lips together, almost as if he didn't want to smile again, then nodded. "We think she might have reacted sooner to the gun being discharged than we did. And when she started flapping her wings, she must have freaked you out. You probably stepped back, saving you from a bullet to the chest. The bullet did clip the duck's wing, but didn't leave her with a debilitating injury."

"I was only nicked by the bullet?"

"Well, yes, but we didn't know that when Sarah Yoder and I were rushing you to the hospital, because you were unconscious. And then, after one of the doctors examined you, he said you needed a few stitches. He had no idea, though, why you weren't coming around."

"I have stitches?"

"You do, like . . . uh . . . three of them. But don't look under your hospital gown, because from what I've been told, not only do you not like hospitals, you don't like wounds, and you really can't tolerate the sight of blood."

81

Margo narrowed her eyes. "Who told you that?"

"Are you going to be completely annoyed with me if I tell you your mom did?"

"You called my *mom?*"

Brock looked anything but contrite. "I didn't have a choice in the matter. We had no idea what was wrong with you, which meant numerous tests were being ordered, very expensive tests. Since I couldn't find a health insurance card in that lovely waterproof bag of yours, I had to reach out to someone, so I found your mom's number in your list of contacts on your cell phone and called her."

"You turned on my cell phone?"

"How else was I supposed to run down someone who'd be able to tell us about your medical history?"

"You could have used the same way you told me we could run down Fauna."

"Well, sure, but that would have taken a lot more time, and your phone was right in your purse."

"But now my mom knows where I am."

"I'm afraid that's true, but she did provide us with the information we needed, saving you a lot of pokes and prods in the process."

"What did she tell you?" Margo forced herself to ask.

"That you have an unusual aversion to the sight of blood, one that causes you to pass out or even vomit on occasion. That aversion was apparently a huge disappointment to your father since he, or so I've been told, wanted you to pursue a career in medicine." He smiled. "Your mother also told us you've been known to descend into unconsciousness for hours, one time for even an entire day, after encountering blood. So part of the mystery of your symptoms was solved through that one phone call."

"You said I've been out of it for a day and a half, so clearly I'm injured to a greater extent than your amusement about my condition suggests."

"No, you're not. You've simply been suffering from a nasty case of exhaustion, brought about, according to what we've been able to learn about you, by a national tour." He cocked a brow her way. "I'm absolutely waiting with bated breath to discover why a *slightly* famous person would go on such a tour."

The ringing of a cell phone, hers since she didn't know many people who had the theme song to *I Dream of Jeannie* as a ringtone, saved her from responding to that unfortunate bit of truth.

"Ah, and speaking of your delightful mom, I imagine that's her calling . . . again." Brock picked up Margo's cell phone from the tray table and held it out to her. "I've discovered that if you don't answer when she calls, she'll just keep calling back, which now has that ringtone of yours stuck permanently in my head."

Margo promptly closed her eyes. "I'm still far too groggy to deal with my mom."

Brock blew out a resigned-sounding breath. "Fine. I'll answer it and tell her you're sleeping, but . . . you owe me for this."

Opening just one eye, Margo watched as Brock swiped the front of her phone with his finger before he put it to his ear.

"Mrs. Hartman, you don't know how I was longing to hear your voice again, and . . . you haven't disappointed me. What may I do for you now?" He got to his feet and walked over to the window, pushing up one of the blind slats with a finger. "It's Deputy Moore, Mrs. Hartman—the same man you've been speaking to for the past day and a half."

Margo's lips curved immediately into a smile. Her mother was not what anyone could call an easy woman, and since Brock had admitted he'd spoken with Caroline Hartman numerous times, he had to know how difficult she was. Yet he hadn't hesitated to take the call, sparing Margo an uncomfortable conversation with her, at least for now.

"Yes . . . I told you, I'll have her call you the minute she's capable of holding a conversation with you, and—" He flipped the blind back into place right before he stopped talking and held the phone away from his ear, the demanding tone of her mother's voice bursting out of it. Sending

Margo a wink, Brock returned the phone to his ear and shook his head.

"I already told you someone will meet you at the airport. No, I'm sorry to say it won't be me. It'll be my brother-in-law and . . . no, he's not a law enforcement officer . . . yes, he's a very competent driver . . . no, I don't think he's ever gotten a ticket . . . I'll certainly tell Margo you've been calling, but there's no point handing her the phone since she—"

Brock's brows drew together. "Hello? Hello?" Shaking his head again, Brock walked across the room and set the phone down on the tray. "She hung up on me."

"Don't take it personally. She does that to everyone." Struggling to find a more comfortable position, Margo stiffened when Brock moved directly beside her. He leaned toward her, put his arms around her, and, treating her as gently as he'd treated Pudding, the vicious mop of a dog that had clearly wanted to chew off her leg, he got her settled more comfortably. Tucking the hospital blanket snugly around her legs, he sat back down in his chair, and then went about the unnerving business of watching her.

Little flutters began traveling through her stomach, a strange situation since she'd never felt any type of flutters before around a guy, not even with any of the actors and boy-band singers she'd gone out with over the years.

Granted, some of those dates had been more for publicity purposes than romance, but they'd been attractive men, highly successful, and had understood the world she lived in since they lived in that world as well.

The flutters quickly disappeared as reality took that moment to rear its ugly head.

She was Margo Hartman, a woman who was too famous for her own good, and she had no business thinking about how appealing Brock Moore was. It simply wouldn't be fair to pull him into a world a small-town deputy had likely never imagined.

There was absolutely no point in even enjoying the sense of attraction she felt for him because it was a known truth that relationships between people like him and people like her never worked. Her world was too different, too hectic, and too intense to expect a normal guy to accept it. The few famous friends of hers who'd tried to have a normal relationship with a normal person had all failed spectacularly. They'd been left with nothing but nasty tabloid stories that showed up every now and again, great fillers for whenever the entertainment industry was having a slow day.

A flash of heat traveled up her neck when an unpleasant thought struck. She was thinking in a somewhat narcissistic fashion, and it wasn't likely that Brock, an intriguing and gorgeous man, would ever be short on female company.

He hadn't even shown her the slightest bit of masculine interest, not even after he'd obviously learned exactly who she was. That was . . . odd in a completely delightful way, one that had the flutters returning and her toes curling underneath the blanket Brock had tucked around her.

"While I know you're probably still tired, although for what you've been through, you look great," Brock said, breaking the silence and banishing her flutters, at least for the moment, "I'm afraid we're going to have to turn to matters of business. You see, the FBI has become involved in your case, and . . . they've asked me to go over a few questions with you."

"Why would the FBI be interested in what was clearly an accident? And is it a normal event for them to share information with a deputy from the sheriff's department?"

"It's a professional courtesy," he said a little vaguely as he flipped open a laptop he'd apparently brought out while she'd been dwelling on flutters and other ridiculous things. "And as for the shooting being an accident, that's highly unlikely."

Margo brushed that aside. "It's not. I read in the papers all the time—because, you know, when you're on tour, you read a lot of papers—that people are constantly getting shot by accident. I bet I was shot by a hunter who mistook me for . . . I don't know, a deer or something, and then, when he realized he'd shot a person, along with a duck, he was too scared to come forward."

"It's not deer season."

"Do you really think hunters observe all the rules all the time?"

"It wasn't a hunter."

"You have no way of knowing that for certain."

Brock cocked a brow her way. "Have you always been this stubborn?"

Margo cocked a brow right back. "What's *your* explanation, then?"

Turning to his laptop, Brock typed out a few words, waited a few seconds, then turned the laptop around so she could see it. Five photographs of men stared back at her—men she, unfortunately, had seen before.

"These"—Brock gestured to the screen exactly as if he was on a game show, pointing out the attributes of some fabulous prize—"are some of your stalkers. Your most dangerous ones." He turned the screen around again. "And because you are considered, much to my embarrassment since I didn't recognize you, somewhat of a *national treasure,* the FBI has become involved. There would be a huge outcry from your fans, of which there are apparently many, if some crackpot managed to do away with you."

"One would hope a person didn't have to be famous to get this kind of attention from the FBI."

"One *would* hope, but we're talking about you

and the most dangerous of the stalkers who are known to be stalking you."

"I highly doubt any of my stalkers know I'm in Ohio. As I clearly remember mentioning to you before, they have severe limitations in their abilities to get close to me. Because of that, I think it's more likely the intended target was you, the local law enforcement officer. I'm sure at least a few criminals out there don't want you catching them, so, since no one seems to want to take the hunting scenario I presented seriously, it stands to reason that the person who shot me today was really just a bad shot and was aiming for you."

"You know, that *is* an interesting theory. But since I haven't been in this position long, nor am I intending to stay here forever because I'm more along the lines of a temporary deputy, I doubt anyone dislikes me so much that they'd try to murder me. You, on the other hand, seem to bring out the crazy in people, so we'll start with the craziest of the bunch." He turned the laptop around again and nodded at the pictures. "Which one would you believe is the craziest of this bunch of stalkers?"

"I've never heard of a temporary deputy," Margo said, finding she had questions of her own that needed to be answered.

"Since I'd never heard of a slightly famous person who turned out to be a little more famous than slightly, we can count ourselves even." He looked up and smiled. "I'll have you know I felt like a complete idiot when I got you to this hospital and everybody started acting really strange when I told them your name, then took to mocking me when they realized I had no idea who you were."

"And then they told you?"

"Nah, I Googled you, a direct result of the ribbing I took when I might have said, to combat the original mocking, that I *did* know you were slightly famous."

She grinned. "Sorry, that was my bad."

"It was your bad. And you're lucky. After not disclosing to me, a representative of the law, exactly who you are, I still took it upon myself to confiscate phones from people who thought it was their right to snap pictures of you while you were unconscious."

The flutters immediately returned. "You confiscated cell phones?"

Brock gave a bit of a shudder. "It was one of the toughest jobs I've ever had to do, but since the two bodyguards your mom hired showed up a few hours ago, and are guarding your door even as we speak, my time has now been freed up. That means we really should go through the files on your stalkers."

Not particularly caring to delve into the twisted minds of the fans who seemed to believe she was more to them than just an entertainer, Margo turned to stalling again. "I'm surprised the bodyguards beat my mom here, especially since she has access to a private jet."

"She's arriving later on today. I guess she had some pressing appointments, which have delayed her getting to you."

Margo narrowed her eyes. "What *type* of pressing appointments?"

"I'm not sure you've sufficiently recovered enough to be given that information."

Drumming her fingers on the blanket that covered her, she caught Brock's eye. "Since I apparently suffered only a flesh wound and a little case of exhaustion, I'm fine. Out with it. What type of appointments did my mother tell you she couldn't miss?"

Shifting on the chair, Brock blew out a long breath and opened his mouth, then delivered his words really fast, as if that might take the sting out of them.

"Your mom is scheduled to have a facial, followed by a massage, and then she has an appointment she said she simply cannot miss with someone she claimed is the *stylist of the decade,* some man named Sebastian."

chapter seven

The very idea that her mom had not canceled her facial, massage, and stylist appointments the moment she'd learned her one and only daughter had been shot had Margo's teeth clenching.

It wasn't that she didn't know Caroline was an incredibly self-centered woman. However, one would think that—given the disturbing nature of what had landed Margo in the hospital in the first place, that being a gun fired her way—her mom could have summoned up at least a few maternal feelings. Those feelings, then, would have had her rushing to her daughter's side, taking a seat on the uncomfortable hard plastic chair Brock was currently sitting in, and, maybe, although this would have been a stretch, holding Margo's hand or placing a cool cloth on Margo's forehead, wringing it out in a basin filled with fresh water every few minutes before she started the process again.

Realizing she'd begun traveling into the realm of complete fantasy, Margo forced a smile and turned it Brock's way, not caring to see the clear sympathy in his eyes.

"I'm not surprised about the appointments, Brock. My mom knows only too well that once the media gets wind of this little fiasco, they'll descend on Millersburg in droves. She's not a woman who ever wants to be caught looking anything but her best when the paparazzi start turning their lenses her way." Her smile faded just a touch. "She's going to have an absolute fit when she sees the condition I'm in, what with my hair being dyed and my spray tan fading. And I don't have any of my clothes since they're in the Mini Cooper and that's on the bottom of some lake."

"Not to worry about that, because your mom has apparently persuaded Sebastian to come with her, and"—Brock smiled—"he's bringing you clothes, make-up, and I'm going to guess a good bit of attitude, since your mom told me she had to pay him an exorbitant amount to convince him to make the trip."

Margo's mouth dropped open. "She's bringing Sebastian here?"

"She is, but she already told me he won't be happy in Millersburg. So to appease this man, I've been given a long list of items that need to be waiting for him in the hotel suite she had me book. One suite for Sebastian, one suite for your mom."

Margo cleared her throat. "Did you have to get soy milk, avocadoes, sushi, and sparkling mineral water?"

"I'm afraid I was unable to deliver on the sushi, but I did manage to rustle up some soy milk, avocadoes, and mineral water, although I'm not certain how sparkling that mineral water is going to be."

"Bless his heart." Margo shook her head. "Sebastian is a bit of a diva. But he *is* very much in demand these days. Not only does he style a good majority of the A-listers, but he used to work in a hair salon, which means he can do hair as well as dress a person." She shook her head again. "I hate to think how much he's charging to accompany my mom here. And I hate to think about how large the tip is going to have to be to soothe his indignation when he sees what I've done to my hair."

"I'm sure he won't be too indignant since you *have* driven your car into a lake *and* been shot in a very short period of time." Brock turned back to his laptop. "But to get to the bottom of those two incidents, we do need to go through this list of stalkers I got from the FBI. Before we do that, it might help if you give me a quick summary of your history, to help me build the picture of your life, so to speak."

"Why would you want to do that?"

"If I understand you a little better—what makes up your life, your habits, or even know more about the people you associate with—it'll help me develop a more thorough profile of whoever might want to harm you."

"So it's normal for the FBI to ask a deputy from

the sheriff's department to collect information like this? Seems a little . . . peculiar."

"I wouldn't say it's normal, but since the few FBI agents who have come to Millersburg are currently out in the field, investigating what needs to be investigated, I . . . volunteered to get this initial information from you."

Having the weirdest feeling that he was being a little sketchy, but having no idea why, Margo took a sip of water before she nodded. "Where do you want me to start?"

"Why don't you start with telling me how you got into singing?"

"Is that one of those strange techniques? Having me talk about something so far into my past that it's supposed to loosen me up and make it easier for you to pry intimate details out of me the farther we get along in this interview?"

"You obviously watched far too many of those repeat TV crime shows while you were off on tour, didn't you?"

"I might have watched a few," Margo admitted with the very corners of her lips edging up. "And because you have been watching over me for a day and a half, and because you got me to the hospital in the first place, I'll play along." She took another sip of her water, and then she launched into the story of how she'd risen to fame.

Starting with the first time she sang in the church choir at age six, a church her parents hadn't belonged to but one of her many nannies had, she found the words pouring faster and faster from her lips—especially when Brock seemed genuinely interested in the tale she had to tell.

She told him about how she loved going to that church and being a part of that church family. How one nanny, Josie Hathaway, had continued to drive Margo to that church even when she'd finished up her bachelor's degree and stopped working as a nanny to pursue a career in accounting. She even told Brock about how her mom had decided church wasn't appropriate for people of their sort when Margo was about thirteen, and then how she'd rebelled against her mom's wishes for the first time in her life.

Refusing to abandon the one place she'd felt accepted for who she was, not who her parents were or how much money they had, she'd struck a bargain with her mother. She agreed to go out on the casting calls her mom wanted her to try, but only if she was allowed to continue with her church activities.

Her mom had agreed all too quickly, and before Margo knew it, she'd landed her first big job with a cable show, which combined teenage drama with an old-fashioned musical vibe. The show propelled Margo to stardom.

Throughout Margo's teenage years, her mom tried to convince her that all that church business was silly. Margo had remained adamant about needing the church to keep her grounded with all the craziness that surrounded her, and God had certainly allowed her to achieve that. Until . . .

She'd fallen a little from her faith of late, something she hadn't realized until just that moment.

"Margo, are you okay?"

Blinking, Margo settled her gaze on Brock. "I'm sorry. I think I just stopped talking, didn't I? Right in the middle of my story."

"I'm sure you're still dealing with the effects of some of the sedatives you were given after your doctor realized you were suffering from exhaustion. You're bound to lose your train of thought for the next few days until you fully recover."

"I was boring you, wasn't I?"

Brock settled back in the chair. "Not at all. Because you're a pop singer, I would have never guessed you got your start in music at church."

"That's because the tabloids and entertainment shows aren't exactly interested in a story about Margo Hartman singing in the church choir. They're more interested in stuff like me dating Robert Pattinson or Hugh Jackman."

"You dated Hugh Jackman?"

"Of course not. He's married and he's practically old enough to be my, well, not father, but maybe older uncle. He was just eating at the same restaurant I was, and I stopped by his table to say hello, having just seen one of his films.

Someone snapped a picture, and voila! I was dating him."

"Have you ever thought about reconsidering your career choice, what with all the attention you receive—and not all of it wonderful?"

"I have, but then I realize I've got a lot of nerve whining about my life when I have so much. A few negative things don't outweigh the enjoyment I get from taking to a stage, or spending hours in a recording studio, working on a new song."

Brock glanced at his screen. "Those negative things being guys like Carl Franklin?"

Taking her last sip of water, Margo set the cup aside. "Poor Carl. Who would have thought he'd become so obsessive just because I offered him a ride home after one of my concerts?"

"You offered one of your fans a ride home?"

"He wasn't a fan. He was working the concert as security, and I overheard him telling someone his ride fell through and he didn't have a way to get home. However, before you begin that lecture I know you're dying to give me, I didn't drive him home. I had my driver drop him off while I caught a late dinner with friends. But why are you singling out Carl?"

"He seems to be the most likely of your stalkers to have followed you here." He looked back to his laptop. "From the email update I received a few minutes ago, four of your stalkers have been located in California, but Carl seems to be missing. His mother admitted to the FBI agent who pounded on her door last night that Carl's been out of the state for around a week. She claims he went off with some mysterious woman. But that seems a bit far-fetched, given the fact she didn't know anything about this woman and couldn't even tell us her name."

"Carl can be charming when he puts his mind to it. He's not creepy-looking like you'd imagine a stalker to be, so I'm not sure you should dismiss the idea that he went off with some woman."

"It seems too much of a coincidence that Carl would just happen to leave town and you would just happen to get shot in the same week."

"Maybe, but Carl doesn't drive. It's a bit of a stretch to think he'd find some mysterious woman who would travel across the country with him so he could shoot me."

Frowning, Brock typed something on the laptop and then nodded. "That's a good point, but until we know for certain he's not behind the attempt on your life, you're going to have to keep a bodyguard with you at all times. Once someone actually builds up the nerve to shoot at an intended target, they normally don't give up until they're either caught . . . or their target is dead."

The whole idea of keeping one of her body-guards with her at all times was almost less appealing than the alternative option. She knew every single one of her bodyguards was going to be watching her like a hawk after she'd managed to give all of them the slip back in California—

She drew in a sharp breath as the perfect solution sprang to mind. Turning her attention to Brock, who'd returned to keying something into his laptop, she considered him for a long moment.

Brock Moore was a man who knew a thing or two—or three, for that matter—about protecting a person. He also had a compassionate side one didn't expect from a man like him, a compassionate side that had seen him soothing both a duck and a vicious dog that went by the name of Pudding.

She would be safe with him, but she'd be able to enjoy herself while she was being kept safe, and, well, she wouldn't have to say good-bye to him just yet.

Not allowing herself to dwell on the idea that saying good-bye to him might be the most logical thing to do, because it wasn't exactly a good idea to spend a lot of time in the company of a man she was definitely attracted to, she pushed that idea aside and opened her mouth.

"I have a proposition for you."

Looking up, Brock frowned. "A . . . proposition?"

"Yes, and it's a good one, one that will double

your salary. Or even better, now that I think about it, triple it. And it'll be rewarding for you as well."

His frown deepened. "I have no idea what you're suggesting."

"You're a protector, Brock, and I need a good protector right now. I'd like you to work for me as my personal bodyguard, and to make sure you'll say yes, forget the tripling your salary thing. I'll pay you whatever you want. Money is no object as long as you agree to come work for me."

Brock narrowed his eyes on her, shut his laptop, and then, after sending her a very curt "No thank you," he got to his feet and strode from the room.

chapter eight

Leaning against the split-rail fence that enclosed a portion of the Yoder farm, Brock watched as a small team of FBI agents searched the grounds, looking for any evidence that might assist them with tracking down the person who shot Margo.

The only piece of evidence found had been an old rifle stuffed into a large haystack. Because Jonas Yoder, the patriarch of the Yoder family, had insisted he didn't "cotton to guns," and insisted none of his children did either, there was every indication the rifle was the one used to bring Margo down.

The only problem with the rifle, though, was that after closer inspection, it had been clear that someone had wiped it down, leaving not so much as a single print, nor was there even a serial number on it that could be traced. That meant it was all but useless and would hardly lead to the person responsible for shooting Margo.

The memory of Margo crumpling straight into his arms left Brock furious, that fury mixed with a great deal of regret over the fact he'd behaved like a complete idiot with her at the hospital a few hours earlier.

Granted, she'd taken him by surprise when she offered him a position as her personal bodyguard, but that was no excuse for his abrupt departure from the room.

He had the sneaking suspicion she didn't even realize she'd insulted him by tossing the tripling his salary thing in his face, or the *money is no object* nonsense, but that wasn't why he stormed from her room in such a regrettable way.

He hadn't even parted ways with her because of the veiled insult in her offer, as if being a local deputy wasn't exactly the most coveted of positions to obtain, as if it wasn't *rewarding* enough for him.

He actually enjoyed the job of deputy, not that his current position as a sheriff's deputy was what he really did for a living. But since Margo had no idea he possessed a law degree and actually worked for the FBI, there really was no reason to blame her for her misconceptions regarding his professional aspirations or lack thereof.

In all honesty, he'd walked away from her so abruptly because he'd begun to question whether or not he was capable of protecting . . . anyone.

He failed to stop someone from shooting her and the poor duck, a circumstance that was incredibly difficult to swallow since she'd been standing only a foot away from him when she was shot.

Before that, he hadn't even taken into consideration that she might be in imminent danger when he found her in the middle of the lake, swimming away from a car that had been forced off the road—although, in his defense, he'd had no idea she was a celebrity and might have a stalker trying to do her in.

He'd also not been able to dig up a single shred of evidence that his sister had been murdered instead of killing herself. The guilt he felt for being incapable of clearing the stain of suicide from a life that had been well lived and should have never been ended in such a way was tearing his soul apart.

Brock had been told more than once that he was a throwback to the days when men were men, and chivalry was not dead—an idea he'd whole-heartedly embraced until he realized it simply wasn't true because . . .

He'd been living his life as a fraud, parading around as a man who upheld the idea he was a protector of the weak and of those in need, when the reality was . . . he was nothing of the sort.

A real protector wouldn't have allowed anyone to harm his sister or failed so miserably in avenging her death, but that's exactly what he'd done. And he knew perfectly well that with the passage of time, and with no answers found, it was becoming more and more doubtful that he'd ever solve Stephanie's case.

"I'm sorry to interrupt your thoughts, Deputy Moore, but I wanted to check in with you to see if you've made any further progress on the case."

Looking up, Brock found Jonas Yoder, the patriarch of the Yoder family, walking his way, his straw hat tilted back from his forehead and his glasses slipping down on his nose.

Jonas wasn't a man who said much, or at least not to the *English*, as the Amish liked to refer to outsiders. Nevertheless, he'd been more than willing to cooperate since the shooting, allowing the authorities full access to his farm, and even having his wife set out lemonade for everyone.

"I'm afraid we haven't," Brock admitted. "And since the rifle turned out to be cleaned of any prints, it's doubtful it'll be of much use, even though it has been sent off to the lab."

"How is the young lady who got shot?"

Brock smiled. "From what the doctors told me, she's expected to make a full recovery."

Tipping his hat farther back, Jonas nodded. "I heard tell she's from California."

"She is."

"I also heard tell she looks like my daughter Sarah."

"She does. In fact, if you discount the fact that Sarah's Amish and Margo's not, I'd think they were twins."

Jonas looked at Brock for a long moment before he gave another nod and then turned around and walked away.

Wondering if he'd unintentionally insulted

Jonas by suggesting his daughter could be taken for a pop star's twin, Brock watched the man disappear before he headed for his Jeep. There was little point in staying out in the field with the other agents since he was on leave with the FBI, and besides, his time would be better spent in town.

Reaching the town limits of Millersburg twenty minutes later, Brock was forced to bring his Jeep to a mere crawl because of the unprecedented amount of traffic clogging Main Street.

News vans were lined up and down the street as reporters, mixed with what seemed to be every person within a five-mile radius, darted around, some even dashing into the middle of the street, completely oblivious to the cars trying to negotiate through the traffic.

Trying his best to not hit any jaywalkers, while resisting the urge to issue tickets to all the people breaking that particular law, Brock finally made it to the street where his brother-in-law's animal clinic was and turned down it. Inching along, he kept an eye out for a parking spot, praying he wouldn't have to drive into the next county to find one.

A moment later, he laughed out loud when he found Mrs. Hershberger standing between two parking spaces that were clearly labeled Reserved for Animal Clinic. She was shaking her finger at a man in a car with a TV station logo on it, apparently letting him know she wasn't budging so he needed to drive on.

Mrs. Hershberger's finger shaking came to an end when she spotted Brock and waved him forward, stepping aside only when he was right up next to one of the parking spaces. After easing into that slot, he got out of the Jeep and walked over to join Mrs. Hershberger, who'd begun guarding the one parking space left.

"Mrs. Hershberger, I could pull something heavy over for you that would block this space instead of you having to stand here."

Shaking her head, Mrs. Hershberger crossed her arms over her chest. "I tried that. My blockade kept being disturbed, so I'm out here until Dr. St. James returns from fetching that poor girl's relatives from the airport." She moved a step closer to the road and waved away a car that had taken to edging toward the prized parking space. "Are there any updates?"

Thinking Margo wouldn't appreciate him letting it get out that she'd only suffered a flesh wound, especially since those normally had a person in the hospital for about an hour or two, he smiled and sent Mrs. Hershberger a nod. "I'm pleased to report that Ms. Hartman is expected to make a full recovery, and she was awake and completely coherent the last time I saw her, which was just a few hours ago."

"How delightful to learn she's not gravely injured," Mrs. Hershberger began before she suddenly took to looking unusually earnest. "Do you think she'd be up for visitors later on this evening? My sister has put together a home-cooked meal for the wee lamb, and we'd surely love to know she was not being forced to settle for hospital food when there's tasty food to be had."

"I'm afraid she's not allowed any visitors, Mrs. Hershberger, what with the possibility that someone deliberately tried to kill her and all. But I'll be sure to tell her about your sister's kind offer of a meal."

"I'm sure no one would mind if my sister and I, two peace-abiding women who certainly would never even consider trying to harm anyone, simply stopped by to pay her our best wishes."

Having no idea how to respond to a Mrs. Hershberger who'd just turned remarkably pushy—something he'd never witnessed a member of the Mennonite or Amish community do—Brock called on all the training he'd obtained throughout law school and experience in his career to produce a reply that was pleasant, but didn't actually promise anything.

"While I certainly know you and your sister would never set out to harm anyone, Mrs. Hershberger, I don't think Ms. Hartman will be in Millersburg for much longer. Since she seems to have made a somewhat surprising recovery, I would imagine her mother will whisk her out of town and onto their private jet as soon as possible."

"Oh dear, that won't do at all," Mrs. Hershberger muttered before she turned on her sensible shoes and hurried down the sidewalk, apparently forgetting all about her mission to save Ian a parking spot.

Unable to help but feel as if he'd landed in his own personal episode of the *Twilight Zone*, Brock took a moment to drag a heavy bench to the front of the parking space, hoping that would ensure it would be available for Ian when he returned from the airport. A far-too-familiar ache settled in his chest when he recognized the bench as one his sister had painted a cheery red.

Stephanie had always enjoyed finding a good bargain, and when she met and then married Ian, and then the two of them moved their veterinarian practice to Millersburg, she spent endless weekends antiquing and visiting garage sales. Her mission had been to find treasures in need of sprucing up that would then give their animal clinic an atmosphere of country charm.

Ian had flat-out refused to change a thing about the clinic since Stephanie died. He'd even balked at the idea of bringing on another veterinarian, saying he wasn't ready to have anyone else work in the practice he and Stephanie dreamed of growing together.

Even though Brock saw his brother-in-law struggle with a heavy workload every day, he knew that workload was what was holding Ian together. Because of that, he simply stopped by and helped with whatever he could, allowing Ian the time he needed to heal from his devastating loss.

As a sense of regret settled over Brock again, he gave the cheery bench a pat and glanced at the sky, wondering if his sister could possibly be watching over him and Ian. When he didn't get a sign, such as a cloud in the image of his sister, he dropped his gaze and headed down the sidewalk.

As he walked, he couldn't help but question how everything had turned so grim. He'd always thought if a person led a good life, God would take care of them. But Stephanie had been the very essence of good, and yet . . . she was gone.

Pushing aside those thoughts since they always left him feeling unsettled and he didn't have time to deal with that feeling at the moment, Brock reached Main Street and turned in the direction of the hospital. The closer he got to the hospital, the more his feet seemed to want to drag. The reasoning behind the dragging was only too obvious. Seeing Margo again would require him to apologize to her for being a complete idiot.

How he was going to explain his behavior was definitely a cause for concern, because he wasn't exactly the type of guy to disclose his innermost secrets to a woman he only recently met.

Before he could dwell on his idiocy further, he was suddenly accosted by a woman carrying a microphone and smiling at him far too brightly.

"I've just been told by a helpful source that you are the deputy who was accompanying Margo Hartman when she was almost murdered." She shoved the microphone in his face. "Would you care to elaborate on what you were doing with her, and is it true that the two of you have been secretly dating for months now?"

"Uh . . ." was the only thing that seemed to want to come out of Brock's mouth, which was slightly amusing since he'd been known to win awards in the past for his excellent debating techniques.

His lack of eloquence didn't stop the reporter at all. Beaming a smile his way that showed practically every single one of her perfect teeth, she inched the microphone closer to his mouth, as if that might prod him into stringing together an entire sentence.

"What developments can you tell me about? Has the culprit been apprehended? Is it true Ms. Hartman suffered a gross disfigurement to her face and will have to give up live performances because she'll never look the same again? And if that is the case, are you considering breaking things off with her because she's not as beautiful as she once was?"

Stepping back from the microphone, Brock suddenly understood exactly why a woman like Margo, who seemed to have everything in life, would suddenly decide to jump into a car, turn her back on all her friends, family, and obligations, and simply drive away.

"Since we have an active investigation, I'm not at liberty to disclose much to the press just yet, except to tell you that Ms. Hartman was not disfigured in the least, and . . . we're not dating." Summoning up a smile of his own, one he hoped was just as bright as the one the woman had been sending him, he sent the reporter a nod and strode off, walking faster when an entire horde of reporters began to move his way.

Breaking into a jog when he heard what sounded exactly like the battle cry that signaled an attack of zombies in a movie, Brock steadily increased his pace when the horde started running after him. By the time he reached the hospital and made it to the safety of the back entrance where security guards had taken up positions—obviously in an attempt to keep the reporters and paparazzi away—he was breathing hard and sweat was streaming down his face.

After smiling his thanks to one of the guards, a young man who looked to be in his early twenties, Brock chugged down the entire bottle of water the guard handed him. "Any problems crop up with security?"

The guard rolled his eyes before he nodded to his partner. "Me and Hank have never seen anything like this. Those reporters have been trying just about anything to get into the hospital." He shook his head. "They set up a fake hit-and-run, hoping to distract us, and when Hank went to check it out to see if he could offer some help, I had like ten reporters and a few photographers rush me. I just do security because I'm saving up to move out of my mom's house, but I'm beginning to think I should find a different part-time job. Who knew Millersburg would turn into such a dangerous place?"

After spending the next ten minutes trading war stories, Brock realized he was deliberately delaying his return *into* the hospital. Knowing his apology to Margo was not going to become any easier the longer he put it off, he told the security guards to hang in there and turned for the hospital door.

He made it all of five steps before he was distracted by a female voice, a voice that held a distinctive note of haughty in it, mixed with a great deal of annoyance.

Turning, he found a woman rounding the corner of the building—one who was undoubtedly Caroline Hartman, Margo's mother.

Dressed in a white, fitted suit that hugged a figure that had unquestionably been well-maintained, and wearing heels that matched, the woman limped his way. She had not a single blonde hair out of place, her make-up seemed flawless, and Brock was fairly certain the overly plump lips currently pursed with clear aggravation were a direct result of visits to a plastic surgeon.

"I cannot believe you didn't have the foresight to call ahead and reserve us a parking spot here at the hospital, Mr. St. James," Caroline said as she limped ever closer Brock's way. "It's the end of June, if you weren't aware, which means the humidity is unbearable in this part of the country. I've taken to perspiring because of having to hoof it here from your office instead of being let off at the hospital door."

Brock switched his attention to his brother-in-law, who looked as if he'd raked a hand numerous times through hair that was sticking up on end. Ian was a man who never got flustered, was capable of repairing injured animals with the greatest of ease, never allowing the pressure of his job to rattle him. The very idea that he was looking rattled over simply having picked up Caroline Hartman at the airport had Brock swallowing a laugh.

"As you saw with your own eyes, Mrs. Hartman, the street to the hospital has been blocked, and since a spot was evidently deliberately saved for us at my clinic, that seemed the logical place to park. And while I know I've mentioned this a time or two, it's Dr. St. James, not Mr. St. James."

Caroline waved that away with a flick of a wrist, setting the numerous bangles she had on her arm to jangling. "You're a vet, not a real doctor. And in case you've neglected to notice, I'm wearing Jimmy Choos. They, as everyone knows, are not made for walking, and I've developed a blister."

"Jimmy who?" Ian asked.

"Jimmy Choo is a designer who makes the most divine shoes," a man who'd just appeared around the hospital corner said. "But as Mrs. Hartman mentioned, they're not shoes styled for walking."

For a second, Brock simply stood and stared as the man who had to be the stylist named Sebastian walked up to join Ian, pulling a large piece of luggage on wheels behind him.

That he was not what Brock had expected was an understatement.

The man was at least as tall as Brock and had shoulders that would have made a linebacker proud. He was wearing old jeans and Converse tennis shoes, and he had pulled his long black hair into what Brock thought might be called a man bun.

Catching the man's eye when he looked Brock's way, Brock shook himself and strode forward. "You must be Sebastian." He held out his hand, which the man immediately took, shaking it with a grip that was undeniably strong. "I'm Brock Moore, one of the men looking into Margo's case."

"Sebastian Welch," he returned. "I'm the stylist." He nodded to Caroline. "And that, I'm sure you've decided, is Caroline Hartman."

Brock turned a smile on Caroline, finding her doing anything but smiling back at him. "It's a pleasure to meet you, Mrs. Hartman."

"Of course it is, and just as an FYI, Margo is to be addressed as Ms. Hartman, never Margo. And now that our pleasantries have been exchanged, I really must insist you take me directly to my daughter. I've been *so* worried about her welfare, especially after seeing all the weirdoes roaming around the streets of this horrendous little town she's currently stuck in. What she was thinking, stopping here . . . well, I'm sure I have no idea. But rest assured, I'll be taking her away just as soon as the doctors allow her to leave the hospital."

Some perverse sense of stubbornness had Brock not moving so much as a single inch. "I'm sure you have to realize, Mrs. Hartman, that the town isn't usually filled with *weirdoes*. They're just here to get the story on your daughter."

Caroline rolled brown eyes. "I wasn't speaking about the reporters, Deputy Moore. I was talking about all those women walking around the town, the ones wearing dresses that look like they're at least a hundred years old, and shoes a woman with only the basic of fashion sense would never be caught dead in. And don't even get me started on those strange white caps they have on their heads."

"Those women are Amish, or some might be Mennonite, but they're not weirdoes."

Caroline took a single step toward him as her face turned pale, under what Brock was going to assume was a spray tan, and her eyes widened with disbelief. "There are *Amish* people living here—in the town where my daughter was shot?"

"Well, yes, but it's highly unlikely anyone in the Amish community was responsible for her being shot. They're pacifists, completely against violence, and tend to stick to themselves."

Caroline pursed her lips again. "I've seen stories on TV about people who left the Amish and claim Amish communities in numerous states are really secret cults where all sorts of horrors occur."

"That's not true," Ian said, speaking up. "The Amish aren't members of a cult, but of a religious calling, one that might seem different to most people, but one that's peaceful." He narrowed an eye on Caroline. "One of those Amish, a young woman named Sarah Yoder, was incredibly helpful in working with Brock to get your daughter to the hospital after she was shot. That should be enough to have you rethinking your position on everything Amish."

"And," Brock added, "Mrs. Hershberger, a Mennonite woman, made it a point to tell me her sister has assembled a home-cooked meal to deliver to Margo, which certainly isn't a sign of a weirdo, but of a caring woman hoping to provide a more edible meal to a complete stranger."

Caroline didn't bother to respond to Brock's or Ian's statements. Instead, she pulled out her cell phone, flipped through the touch screen, then began texting furiously to someone. Who that someone was, well, that was anyone's guess since she certainly didn't say.

Clearing his throat, Ian turned his attention to Brock. "Even though I've had just a . . . wonderfully delightful time of it fetching Mrs. Hartman from the airport, and then driving with her in a car she claims is nothing more than a golf cart with a body wrapped around it—for over an hour, I might add—I'm really going to have to get back to the clinic." Ian nodded to Sebastian. "It was a true pleasure to meet you, Sebastian, and I do apologize that we had to send the rest of your equipment and luggage on to your hotel because it wouldn't fit in my . . . golf cart of a car."

Sebastian smiled an easy smile. "No worries, Ian. I have an electric car myself, not that I drive it often since my clients are so determined to send their limousines for me, and, well, who am I to refuse their generosity? I'm sure my belongings will make it safely to that hotel, and I do thank you for coming to collect us." He tossed a nod

Caroline's way. "Having another guy around was . . . greatly appreciated."

Ian smiled. "I'm sure it was." He turned to Brock. "You'll give my regards to Margo?"

"Of course."

"Great. Then I'll see you later." With that, Ian turned and strode away, vanishing around the side of the hospital a moment later.

"He's a solid sort," Sebastian said before he looked at Caroline, who was still occupied with her phone. "Are you ready to go find Margo or do you need to finish that text?"

Caroline looked up. "I'm perfectly capable of texting and walking at the same time." Immediately proving she could do exactly that, she headed for the back entrance, her attention returning to her phone.

Sebastian fell into step behind her, pulling his wheeled luggage across the hot sidewalk.

"Do you need help with that?" Brock asked.

"I've got it, but thank you," Sebastian said. "And now, while we have a somewhat quiet moment, tell me, how is Margo really doing?"

Grateful that someone seemed to be concerned about Margo since Caroline certainly hadn't bothered to make that inquiry, Brock filled Sebastian in on Margo's less than life-threatening condition as they made their way to the elevator. Stepping into the elevator, he then explained what little details there were concerning what had happened to cause her that less-than-life-threatening condition while they rode the elevator to Margo's floor.

Caroline kept her attention firmly on her phone, checking her text messages and then texting someone what seemed to be an entire book in response. Looking up from her phone when the door dinged open, she stepped into the hallway, returning to her texting as they moved down the hallway toward Margo's room.

After being waved on by one of Margo's bodyguards, who said the other guard had gone out on his dinner break, Sebastian entered the room first, with Brock following behind. Caroline, however, stayed out in the hallway, her phone still in hand, apparently not in any great hurry to see her daughter.

Shutting the door after him when it became clear Caroline was occupied, Brock turned and watched as Sebastian abandoned his piece of luggage and snatched Margo, who'd been standing by the window even though the blinds were shut, into a hug. He immediately released her when she let out a yelp.

"Sorry, babe. I forgot for a moment you've been shot." Sebastian stepped back, holding her at arm's length. "Good heavens, girl, what have you done to yourself?"

"As you just mentioned, I've been shot."

"You know that's not what I meant." Sebastian

gestured to Margo's head. "That . . . What is that?"

"Are you going to totally freak out if I admit I bought a box of dye from a chain store and poured it over my head in a run-down, some might even say seedy hotel room?"

Brock wasn't certain, but he thought Sebastian turned a little pale. Before the stylist had time to respond to that apparently horrifying idea, though, Margo stepped around him. Then, to Brock's complete surprise, she smiled at him.

"Brock, thank goodness you came back."

"You're . . . happy to see me?"

Her smile dimmed. "More nervous than happy since I need to apologize to you. If you must know, I don't have much practice apologizing. But after you left I realized I'd behaved in a totally thoughtless, selfish, and I have to admit bratty way, and for that I'm really sorry."

"While I have no idea why Deputy Moore would have anything to forgive *you* for, darling," Caroline began, marching into the room, "especially because he didn't exactly do a very good job of protecting you given the fact you were shot in his presence"—she sent Brock a significant look before turning back to Margo—"we have no time to dwell on such unimportant matters. I've just had a little chat with the bodyguard outside your door and learned that two Amish women have been skulking around this hospital, trying to get approval to come visit you."

"It's probably Mrs. Hershberger and her sister," Brock began. "They want to—"

"We don't care what they want," Caroline interrupted, before she walked straight over to her daughter and took Margo's hand in hers. "I've been in contact with your father, and he's of the belief you're in serious jeopardy." She gave Margo's hand a pat. "You'll be relieved to learn he's making arrangements as we speak for you to be released from this silly hospital. Then we're going to fly directly home. I'll bring in help, which will allow you to recover in peace—or more importantly, in safety."

She lifted her head and nodded Sebastian's way. "Since the paparazzi seem to be out in full force, I suggest you, Sebastian, get busy and earn your exorbitant fee. You have about an hour to make Margo photo-ready."

chapter nine

Before she had a moment to voice a protest, Margo found herself sitting in an uncomfortable plastic chair as Sebastian set about what he claimed was "the impossible business" of making her photo-ready.

Glancing down at the suitcase Sebastian had opened on the floor beside her feet, Margo pressed her lips together to keep from grinning.

Sebastian took his work very seriously, and he'd brought enough product to style a hundred pop princesses. But according to him, or at least according to his mutters as he mixed up some mad concoction in a plastic cup, he didn't have the tools available to do a proper job of making her gorgeous.

Pausing mid-stir, he caught her eye. "You *are* allowed to wash your hair after I highlight it up a little, or a lot, aren't you?"

"One of the nurses gave me a waterproof bandage, and while I'd love to claim it's a huge bandage, it's . . . um . . . not. But she did say it was fine for me to shower, just as long as I don't get the stitches wet for a day or two."

"How many stitches did you have to get?" Sebastian asked.

"I'm too embarrassed to say, but not many.

Although, if you don't want me to pass out before you get me whipped into photo-ready shape, I'm going to suggest we put that kind of nasty talk—you know, anything to do with stitches—aside. Forever."

Sebastian exchanged a look with Brock that was filled with amusement. Opening her mouth to point out that it was hardly cool to mock a poor woman who'd lost her car in a lake, and then been shot, all in the same day, she found herself swallowing any words she'd been about to say when she caught sight of her mom.

Caroline, odd as it seemed, was behaving more neurotically than usual. She was currently crouching beside the window, peering out through the blind she was lifting up, and trying to text with one hand as she peered.

"Mom, what are you doing?"

Dropping the blind back into place, Caroline turned her head but didn't bother to straighten. "I'm texting your father about the latest developments."

Margo frowned. "You know, I didn't really think about it much, when you said you'd received a text from Dad and that he was making arrangements to get me released from this hospital. But now that I have . . . When did you and Dad start texting each other, because the last I knew, you two weren't communicating at all, as in nothing was shared between you."

Caroline shot a look to Brock and then back to Margo. "I don't think there's any need to discuss personal matters while strangers are in the room."

Brock smiled and began heading for the door. "I'll just go get everyone a coffee."

"You don't have to—"

"I'll have an iced café mocha, tall," Caroline interrupted. "And Sebastian, what will you have?"

Sebastian stopped mixing and tilted his head. "I have to say a nice non-fat Caramel Frappuccino sounds heavenly right about now. And if they have any scones—preferably raspberry—I'll take two. If they don't, I wouldn't mind a cream-filled donut, or three, and donuts that just happen to come from that little donut shop I saw on the walk through town."

"You're asking Brock to find you a *non-fat* Caramel Frappuccino, which even the most popular coffee chains balk at making, and you'd also like him to fetch you some donuts?" Margo asked.

Sebastian smiled and shook his head. "Since it would be very easy to turn your hair pumpkin orange instead of highly desirable blonde—with lighter highlights, I might add—I suggest you keep your far-too-honest observations to yourself, missy."

"And on that note, I'll just be off to the coffee shop, with a stop at the donut shop as well," Brock said, although he took a step toward her instead

125

of moving to the door. "What would you like?"

She grinned. "I wouldn't turn down a chocolate donut."

"Absolutely not." Caroline finally straightened and moved away from the window. "If you're going on another tour soon, you need to keep watching your calories. Your fans don't pay to see a plump Margo. They pay to see a fierce one, and fierce doesn't come with a paunch."

Before Margo could respond to that, Brock moved for the door, turning back to look at her once he reached it. "I'll bring you back a donut that's chocolate with . . . sprinkles."

Sending her a wink, he left the room.

"We cannot get out of this town fast enough," Caroline said before she immediately returned to the window, peeked out, and shook her head. "It gives me the creeps."

"I had that same reaction when I first landed here," Margo said. "But getting back to Dad . . . You two are talking again?"

"Of course we're talking," Caroline said, her attention still on whatever was happening below them on the street. "In fact, he's going to meet us here—at the airport, I guess—just as soon as he completes a business meeting he's holding in New York."

"Dad's coming here?"

"Of course he is. He and I have been very concerned that you were shot, and so he wants to be with you on the trip back to California to make certain you arrive there safely and without any other incidents."

Margo had the strangest feeling something was going on, something disturbing. What that something was, though, was anyone's guess.

Her mom and dad detested each other and had been separated for years. Because of that, Margo rarely saw Robert these days. But even before the separation, they'd never shared what anyone would call a close relationship. At times, Margo had actually believed her dad considered her more on the line of a pet than a daughter, which was why she'd never been bothered that she didn't get to see him much.

That he was pulling himself away from business—although everyone had always been annoyingly sketchy about exactly what type of *business* he was involved in—and was going to meet them in Ohio at the airport, suggested something bizarre was going on.

The sound of a drawer being opened and closed drew Margo out of her thoughts. Caroline had moved away from the window again, and was now opening and closing all the drawers in the dresser the hospital room provided for its patients.

Turning around, Caroline frowned. "Where are your clothes?"

"They're in my car."

"Why didn't anyone bring them in from your car for you?"

Margo winced when Sebastian began attacking her hair with a brush, waiting until he had some of the tangles out before she answered. "Didn't Brock tell you about what happened to my car?"

"I don't think you should call that man by his real name, Margo. He's not like us, and you know your father has never liked you to mingle with outsiders. But, yes, that deputy man did say something about an accident with the car, although I might not have been listening as well as I should." She tapped a finger against her chin. "I did tell you that one of my new doctors believes I may be ADHD, didn't I? Because of that, I can't be expected to process everything I hear."

"This new doctor didn't prescribe new medication for you, did he?" Margo asked slowly.

"Of course he did, but no need to worry. I took that medication today, and that means I can focus better, which also means I'm ready to hear all about that car accident. Should I assume no one could collect your clothes for you because your car's in a shop somewhere?"

"Didn't you tell Brock you were going to have Sebastian bring me clothes, which suggests you might have, at one time, known I'd lost all my clothes?"

Her mom waved a well-manicured hand in the air, wafting a strong scent of Calvin Klein

Obsession Margo's way as she waved. It was her perfume of choice these days, and one that, because her mother was never content with just one spritz, frequently left Margo with a headache.

"I might recall a bit about you losing your clothing, but I really had Sebastian bring you a new wardrobe because of the photo opportunities I knew the shooting would present. And because of that publicity, you, my darling, must look top-notch at all times. Although . . . did you tell me where your car is at the moment?"

"It's at the bottom of a lake."

Caroline cocked her head to the side and studied Margo for a long moment. Then she suddenly sucked in a sharp breath, hobbled across the room in her Jimmy Choos, and took Margo completely by surprise when she threw her arms around her. The scent of Obsession rushed immediately up Margo's nose, making in next to impossible to breathe.

"I didn't realize you'd run away because your emotional state was so bad." Caroline began smoothing her hand over Margo's hair, a move that rendered Margo momentarily speechless. It also sent Sebastian abandoning his brushing. With a huff of disgust, he stalked across the room, sitting down in the only other chair the room offered.

Drawing in a breath, which wasn't the brightest idea since it simply sent more Obsession traveling up her nose, Margo leaned away from her mom. "I didn't leave California because I was in a bad emotional state. I left because I was annoyed you'd taken it upon yourself, with Daphne's help, to arrange interviews *and* another tour for me."

"You don't have to lie to me, darling. I'm your mother, and I'm just so distraught that you didn't come to me and tell me you were suffering from depression. They have pills for depression—lovely, lovely pills—and those pills would have prevented you from running your car into that lake."

"What?"

"You were trying to end the pain that has evidently been hidden from the world for a very, very long time."

"Oh . . . no . . . You've found another psychiatrist, haven't you? As well as a doctor who obviously has you convinced you're ADHD."

Caroline stopped stroking Margo's hair, straightened, and frowned at her. "You weren't trying to kill yourself?"

"Since I've always been of the belief that God expects people to respect the life he's given them, no. I wasn't trying to kill myself. I was run off the road by what I'm hoping was just a careless driver."

"You know I don't like it when you bring up that troubling God business. It makes everyone uncomfortable, and besides, you know I don't believe in that nonsense. Quite honestly, there are times, Margo, when I just don't know where you came from, or how you managed to come around to believing such odd things."

Sebastian got up from his chair and began walking Margo's way, evidently of the belief Caroline was done with her fussing and he could get back to work. "Perhaps you were adopted."

Caroline sucked in a sharp breath and raised a hand to her chest. "What did you say?"

Sebastian stopped walking and tilted his head. "About what?"

"You said something about Margo being adopted, but you know that's not true, right?"

Before Sebastian could agree or disagree, Caroline turned to Margo. "You're not adopted."

"Okay," was all Margo could think to respond to that, right before Caroline whipped out her phone again and rushed from the room, an impressive achievement since she was wearing shoes that were probably still killing her feet.

"Someone's apparently mixed up their medication again today," Sebastian said just as the door opened again and Brock strode in, carrying a tray filled with covered coffee cups in one hand and a bag that had to hold donuts in the other.

"Is everything all right with your mom?" He set the coffee down on the tray table as he handed the bag of donuts to Sebastian.

"I'm afraid my mom might be in the midst of an episode."

Pulling a cup out of the tray, Brock frowned. "She has episodes?"

"She does, and to control those episodes, she's notorious for self-medicating, or over medicating, which has landed her in rehab more times than I can count over the years."

"There's a huge problem with prescriptions these days," Brock began. "I can't tell you the number of times I've been working an assignment and have discovered the crime would not have been committed if the offender hadn't been hooked on either OxyContin or a cocktail of other drugs." He busied himself with checking the writing scribbled on all the cups, pulling another one out of the tray before he handed it to her.

"I didn't know what drink to get you, but this is a white mocha, which should go well with the chocolate donut and sprinkles I'll get out for you next."

Accepting the coffee, she smiled. "It's perfect. Thank you." Taking a sip, she let out a sigh. "Delicious, and much appreciated." She caught his eye. "Can I hope this means you've forgiven me for behaving so unacceptably before?"

"You simply offered me a job, Margo. I was the one who overreacted, and for that, I'm sorry."

Before Margo could ask why he'd overreacted, there was a knock on the door. It opened, and two police officers dressed in blue uniforms walked into the room.

"Sorry about the interruption, folks." One of the officers stepped close to Brock and shook his hand. "We just wanted to deliver an update, but either someone"—he shot a smile toward Brock—"turned off his phone or it's run out of batteries. So we're delivering that update in person."

Pulling his phone out of his back pocket, Brock winced when he looked at it. "Out of battery."

"My charger is in my purse," Margo said.

Sending her a smile, Brock went to get her purse from the small closet while the two officers took a second to introduce themselves.

"I'm Officer Blakely, Ms. Hartman," the tall officer with brown hair and an earnest smile began. "And that's Officer Cook."

Officer Cook sent her a single nod.

"I'm a huge fan of yours, Ms. Hartman, just huge," Officer Blakely continued. "But since Deputy Moore has sent out numerous multi-departmental emails, letting everyone know you're to be treated as we'd treat any person passing through our town and not as a famous person, I'll save asking you for an autograph for another time."

Her pulse sped up just a touch at the very idea Brock had apparently been diligent about making certain she wasn't asked to play the role of pop princess on his watch. Ignoring that pulse since it would hardly be productive to dwell on such an unusual state, she smiled. "I'd be more than happy to sign something for you."

"What's the point of me making requests on your behalf if you're just going to ignore those requests?" Brock asked as he turned from where he'd plugged his phone into the wall.

"It's not going to kill me to give him an autograph, particularly since I'm going to assume he and Officer . . . Cook?" She glanced to the other officer, who nodded. "Are here about the investigation into my case."

Accepting what turned out to be a small pad of unused parking tickets, Margo took the pen Officer Blakely handed her and wrote out a quick autograph. Handing it back to him, she pretended she didn't see Brock roll his eyes, keeping her attention squarely on the officer who was now tucking her autograph carefully into his pocket. "So . . . any new developments?" she prodded.

Clearing his throat as he turned a little red in the face, Officer Blakely smiled. "A few, or . . . well, not really any developments of importance, other than there's a large group of locals down by the lake, trying to figure out how to retrieve your car. It seems that Ed, from Ed's Garage, has a plan."

"If it's too much trouble to get the car out of the lake, it can just stay there," Margo said. "I have other cars, and to tell you the truth, I don't really drive that much."

Brock moved to stand closer to her. "I think what you're missing here, Margo, is that this is one of those guy things. It doesn't matter if it's difficult to get your car out of the lake. The fun is seeing if it can be done."

"Guys don't like it when their fun gets taken away," Sebastian said before he sent a telling look to the cup he'd been mixing. "My fun, for instance, is rapidly fading away because the batch of color I just mixed up is drying out even as we speak. And if I'm forced to mix up another batch, I might take to sulking, and everyone in Hollywood knows Sebastian Welch is not fun to be around when he's sulking. So if everyone would be so kind as to clear out and let me work, I'd appreciate it."

Less than a minute later, the room was free of everyone except Margo and Sebastian, Brock having left with the officers to hear any other new information. Closing her eyes, she enjoyed the silence as Sebastian got started on her hair, and appreciated the fact he wasn't a stylist who needed to fill every minute with mindless chatter.

After he'd stuffed her head into a large plastic cap—which turned out to be an old-fashioned hair dryer cap complete with a hose that attached to a round machine and blew warm air over her head when Sebastian switched it on—Margo pushed one of her ears free of the cap when she noticed Sebastian seemed to be talking.

Realizing he wasn't talking to her, but to Brock, who'd returned, she strained to hear what they were saying over the noise of the dryer.

". . . and his ATM card has shown activity in West Virginia, which is getting a little too close to Ohio, if you ask me," Brock said. "Do you know anything about that Carl character?"

"I don't know much," Sebastian began. "It seems like everyone in Hollywood has a stalker or two, but it's really rare to have one of them shoot at their obsession. Are you sure Margo was an actual target? Or is there a chance this was all just a case of mistaken identity?"

"There were two attempts on her life, if you count the lake incident, which can't be discounted since no one ever came forward and claimed responsibility for it. Guilt normally pushes hit-and-run drivers into turning themselves in, or their relatives turn them in when they see unexplained dents on cars. But that hasn't happened. That makes me think she was a target and the shooting was deliberate."

"Then her parents are right to want to whisk her back to California, aren't they?"

"I wish that was the case, but I happened to overhear Caroline on the phone outside in the hallway. She was talking to someone named Daphne, and it sounded to me like she was firming up dates for either appearances or more concerts. It would be extremely difficult to protect Margo at a concert, and, in fact, I'm coming to the conclusion that the best option for her would be to go into protective custody. At least until we make some sort of conclusive progress on her case."

"That's the most ridiculous thing I've ever heard."

Turning toward the door, Margo found her mom marching into the room again, stopping when she reached Brock's side. Crossing her arms over her chest, Caroline lifted her chin. "Margo does not have time to go into protective custody. She's at the top of her game right now, and she can't afford to be knocked down the pop ladder just because some crackpot is roaming around out there." She spun around and set her sights on Margo.

"I've just been on the phone with Daphne, shoring up some dates for your international concert, and she was able to set things into motion much faster than I anticipated. We're leaving next week to do some pre-tour interviews in Europe. After that, we'll return to the States and you'll have a month or two to rehearse. Then you'll be hitting the stage." She smiled. "Isn't that marvelous?"

Quite a few words sprang to mind that described Margo's opinion about that, none of them *marvelous*. She was spared having to give a response, though, when Brock stepped forward.

"I don't think you're understanding the danger your daughter is in, Mrs. Hartman. Her life has been threatened twice in this week alone, which means she certainly can't be going on interviews. No one can guarantee her safety if she's constantly out in the open."

"Well, she's not going into protective custody," Caroline shot back. "I can delay the interviews, but she's going to have to come up with some fresh routines for the international tour. And for that she'll need a large studio, one I'm sure won't be available to her if she's sent off to some obscure motel room in some obscure town."

The loud clearing of a throat had everyone turning toward the door, finding none other than Mrs. Hershberger standing in the doorway. She was holding a pet carrier that seemed to be holding a duck, what with the orange bill poking out of the front grate. And she was in the company of a woman dressed exactly like her.

As her mother took to looking as if wolves had stepped into the room, and Sebastian took to looking the women up and down even as a clear trace of horror appeared in his fashion-conscious eyes, Mrs. Hershberger cleared her throat again. Taking a single step into the room, she looked Margo's way.

"Forgive me for eavesdropping, since that's not an acceptable thing to do, but I couldn't help but overhear Deputy Moore's concerns, and then . . . that woman's." She sent a jerk of her head Caroline's way. "Having said that, I think I may have an alternative solution. One that would see you well hidden away, but give you access to a large space—a barn."

Glancing at the woman next to her, Mrs. Hershberger traded a nod with that woman before she took a step forward.

"What I'm trying to say is this: I'd like to invite you, Margo Hartman, to come stay with me in my farmhouse on the edge of town, at least until the danger to you has passed."

As her mom immediately began arguing with that idea, bringing up the international tour and numerous other obligations she'd apparently arranged for Margo—without Margo's knowledge, of course—Margo found that strange buzzing noise returning to her ears. It was the same one she'd heard when she'd been with Daphne, right before she decided to flee from California.

Not allowing herself time to change her mind, she sent a nod of her own Mrs. Hershberger's way. "I would be delighted to accept your more-than-generous invitation, Mrs. Hershberger. When would it be convenient for me to move in?"

chapter ten

This was definitely turning into the strangest week Brock had ever experienced.

Five hours after Mrs. Hershberger showed up in Margo's hospital room, he was not, as he'd hoped he'd be doing, actively investigating Margo's case. He wasn't even looking for leads in his sister's case. Instead, he was sitting smack-dab in the middle of a luxury suite in the Hotel Millersburg, participating in what he could only describe as a staring contest with none other than Robert Hartman, Margo's less-than-jovial dad.

Robert did not have so much as an ounce of humor hiding underneath his perfectly tailored Armani suit, and he had a stare that was somewhat unnerving and set Brock's teeth on edge.

Because Brock was used to dealing with the dregs society had to offer, the fact that Robert Hartman was able to unnerve him did not give Brock confidence regarding the man's character. Nor could it possibly be looked at favorably that the man had not once inquired about his daughter's health. He had only demanded to know her whereabouts since Margo had gone missing.

It wasn't that she was really missing, at least not as far as Brock was concerned since he knew exactly where she was. But since he'd recently, as in only a few hours before, been asked to return to the FBI as an active agent, his boss believing it would not be a mark in the FBI's favor if Margo Hartman was injured again or . . . murdered, he was perfectly within his rights to not divulge Margo's whereabouts. A call to the sheriff, asking if he could take some personal time off without pay, had been granted, which left him available to keep an eye on Margo. That was a fortunate situation since she'd turned stubborn and was refusing to even consider the idea of going into official protective custody.

He was a little concerned that she might balk at having him protect her after he had what he knew was going to be an uncomfortable talk, disclosing the truth about his real identity, with her. He had a feeling that, with the way she'd so casually tossed out an offer of employment to him as her personal bodyguard, she might be a tad embarrassed to learn he held a law degree from Harvard and was a well-respected investigator for the FBI.

However, in his defense, it wasn't as if they'd known each other long. And he would have explained the FBI thing to her already if she hadn't decided at the drop of a hat to make another break for it. That break for it wouldn't have been nearly as successful if he'd hightailed it after her, no doubt drawing unwanted attention as he did that hightailing.

"I suppose what confuses me the most,"

Robert drawled, ending the apparent game of silence that had sprung up between them, "is how a man who works in law enforcement could misplace my daughter, a woman who is famous throughout the world and whom he'd been keeping track of rather diligently up until the time she disappeared."

"I was wondering the same—" Caroline's comment ended abruptly when her husband tossed a glare her way.

"It doesn't suit you to wonder," he bit out before he turned back to Brock. "So tell me. How is it that an esteemed FBI agent, one who seems to be on leave with his department, just happens to allow my daughter to slip straightaway from a hospital, and then not realize she's done so for over an hour—which, I have to say, gave her plenty of time to make her great escape?"

Leaning back in the armchair placed next to a gas fireplace, Brock crossed one ankle over the other. "Been doing some digging on me, have you, Robert?"

"It's Mr. Hartman, and yes, I've made some calls and discovered enough to know you're not exactly in Millersburg for the reasons the good folks of this town think."

"Why do you think I'm here?"

"I think you're on a case, but one the agency wouldn't sanction, and it has something to do with that sister of yours. The one who died."

"We'll leave my sister out of this, if you don't mind."

Robert leaned back in the chair he was sitting in and very deliberately crossed one ankle over the other, mimicking Brock's movement of only seconds before. "You asked who I thought you were, Brock, so I was simply answering your question."

Brock inclined his head. "It's Agent Moore."

Robert inclined his head in response. "Of course it is." His smile held not a glimmer of warmth. "Since we've now ascertained that you're not a small-town deputy, and you've more than likely ascertained that I'm not a man who cares to be trifled with, tell me your thoughts about where Margo could have gone."

"I told you, Robert," Caroline said. "That Amish woman, Mrs. Bergenstein—or maybe it was Haberdashery, or . . . something like that—offered her a place to stay. Margo, being difficult and obviously wanting to annoy me, told that woman she'd be delighted to take her up on the offer, and then, when I went outside to have a . . . well . . . take a little break because my nerves were getting the better of me, I came back a short time later and she was just gone."

"You went out for a smoke, didn't you?" Robert's voice held a distinct edge to it now, one that had Caroline getting up from the chair she'd been sitting in next to him and moving to the

143

window. Shoving back the curtain, she peered out into the descending dimness of evening until she finally turned and gave a bit of a shrug.

"I left my nerve pills in my suitcase, never imagining the man who picked us up at the airport wouldn't be able to fit our luggage in his teensy tiny car. That luggage got sent on ahead to this very hotel, since I was under the impression I'd be spending a few days in this town while Margo recuperated."

"I told you I was flying in," Robert said. "You shouldn't have bothered to even make a hotel reservation, let alone have your luggage sent here."

Caroline shot her husband a look that would have sent a weaker man cowering. Robert, however, didn't bat so much as a single eye. "You told me you were flying in after I arrived here and after I told you about what the strange—" She glanced to Brock, drew in a deep breath, and then looked out the window again. "I can't be blamed for the hotel reservation, Robert. You have to know it wouldn't have crossed my mind that you were going to involve yourself in this situation and get Margo released from the hospital sooner than anyone anticipated."

"But I can blame you for leaving our daughter to go out and have a smoke, or five."

Caroline shrugged again. "I thought having a smoke would be less attention-worthy than me suffering a nervous breakdown. And since it was you who was responsible for getting Margo released early, you bear some of the responsibility for her being gone. If she hadn't been officially released, she wouldn't have been permitted to waltz out of the hospital."

Not bothering to reply to what had been the most logical thing Brock had heard come out of Caroline's mouth so far, Robert settled back into his chair and returned his attention to Brock.

"Is there any truth to what Caroline said about the Amish woman, that she offered Margo . . . sanctuary, if you will?"

"I don't know if I'd go so far as to say it was sanctuary, but an offer was made. I'm afraid, though, I can't say with any certainty if she accepted that offer."

"Don't toy with me, Agent Moore. Did Margo, or did she not, run off to some Amish community?"

Since Mrs. Hershberger was Mennonite, not Amish, Brock had no qualms about shaking his head. "To my knowledge, she did not run off to an Amish community."

"How did she get out of the hospital without anyone noticing her?"

"I'm going to assume she just walked out."

"How do you know she wasn't taken against her will?"

"Because she left a note Sebastian found, telling

everyone she was going into hiding, and that no one should panic because she was fine."

Robert looked to Caroline. "Isn't Sebastian that stylist you're always paying too much money to dress you and Margo?"

Caroline nodded.

Robert's lips thinned to next to nothing. "Margo enjoys his company, so I would think you, *darling,* would have prevailed on him to talk some sense into her right from the start." He paused and regarded his wife for a long moment. "Where was Sebastian while Margo was making her great escape?"

A flicker of what almost seemed to be fear flashed through Caroline's eyes before she looked out the window again.

"From your lack of answer, I'm going to assume he was out having a smoke with you. So because of that, you'll no longer be using his services." Robert ignored Caroline's protest to focus his cold gaze on Brock. "Tell me how you think Margo escaped."

Since Brock had no intention of explaining what he thought had probably resembled a scene straight out of an old *I Love Lucy* episode, complete with a duck and a pop star dressed as an Amish woman, he settled for a shrug and a smile.

"While I have many thoughts on that subject, each one more outlandish than the last, I'm not free to disclose that information to you, Mr.

Hartman. It wouldn't do to have any unsubstantiated rumors out there attributed to a source who works with the FBI."

Narrowing his eyes, Robert leaned forward. "I would never leak anything to the idiot press."

Brock sent the barest hint of a nod Caroline's way. "You may not, but . . ."

"Point taken." Settling once again into his seat, Robert considered Brock for a long moment. "Can you assure me Margo's fine?"

"I can."

"And will she still be fine after the press finds out she's vanished again?"

"They won't know she's vanished again because Sebastian is going to spread it about that she went home to California, and"—Brock smiled—"he's going to drive around with a woman he claims he can style to look exactly like Margo. That means the paparazzi and reporters will clear out of Millersburg by tomorrow at the latest, which will allow us to concentrate on working Margo's case and get on with the business of figuring out who might be trying to kill her."

"That person is hardly likely to leave this town without trying to finish the job."

Brock shook his head. "Since it's highly unlikely that person is from anywhere near here, there's every hope he'll take off for California once he hears the gossip that Margo has returned home."

"You think it's one of her stalkers, don't you?" Robert asked.

"Don't you?"

Robert tilted his head. "But of course."

Knowing without a shadow of a doubt that the man sitting in front of him was hiding something, Brock sat forward, but was interrupted from questioning Robert further when a knock sounded on the door. When neither Robert nor Caroline moved, Brock got up, walked across the room, and opened it.

Agent James Colby was standing on the other side. Colby was one of the FBI agents who'd come to help with the investigation the media was now labeling "The Shooting of America's Sweetheart." The fact that he'd decided to pay a visit to the hotel instead of remaining out in the field was clearly a reason for concern.

"I'm sorry to bother you, Agent Moore." Colby lowered his voice and leaned closer. "And I'm sorry I just called you Agent."

"Mr. and Mrs. Hartman already know I'm with the FBI, although on *leave* from the FBI," Brock returned. "But what can I do for you?"

"It might be best if you step outside."

Telling Robert and Caroline he'd be right back, he stepped out into the hallway with Colby. Together, they walked to the stairwell, walked down the stairs, and moved outside, choosing a secluded spot in the back courtyard of the Hotel Millersburg.

"We've had some difficulties at the lake," Colby began.

"You couldn't get the car out?"

"Oh, we got the car out, but unfortunately, while this man named Ed was getting the car out, he drove his tow truck over the other crime scene we were in the process of photographing, the scene that had the tire tracks of the truck or SUV that ran Ms. Hartman off the road in the first place."

"Weren't photos already taken of those tracks?"

Colby rubbed the back of his neck. "Well, yes, they were, but someone misplaced that camera, and . . ." He shook his head. "I suppose there's every hope that it'll turn up again, but for the moment, we're in the midst of amateur hour."

"At least we were able to retrieve the car."

Colby winced. "We do have the car. There's just the little problem that someone made off with one of the suitcases we took from the trunk."

"You've got to be kidding me."

"I'm afraid not, and it might have been the suitcase that held a lot of Ms. Hartman's shoes, along with a few items we hadn't gotten around to logging at the scene."

Tension began settling in the back of Brock's neck. "Have someone start watching the e-sites, because you know those shoes will start showing up for sale."

"Unless someone is a huge Margo Hartman fan

and is just going to sit on her things for a while, admire them a bit."

Brock refused to sigh. "Definitely do not bring that idea up around her."

"Will do. And on a completely different note, Robert Hartman's been making some calls about you. He has some interesting friends, so watch your back."

"Interesting . . . how?"

"That's just it. No one seems to know, and that's never good. He's never attracted the attention of any law organization, but I did find out he embraces a bit of a deviant lifestyle, enjoying all sorts of nasty stuff. And he doesn't actually seem to have a job, using the pretense of business meetings and trips to enjoy his unusual amusements with little scrutiny."

"How's he pay for everything, then?" Brock asked.

"He has a daughter who has to be making bank. And I think his wife comes from money, but I'm not sure if he did or not. There's not much to be found on him or his family."

"Well, let me know if anything turns up on him. We can't arrest a man for being creepy, but I hope Robert and his wife decide to leave town sooner than later. They're a definite distraction from the real issue: Margo's safety."

Wrapping up their conversation a moment after that, Brock shook hands with Colby and watched as he walked out of the courtyard. Heading back into the hotel, Brock returned to Caroline's suite, hoping that while he was gone they decided to leave their daughter's best interest to the experts—and maybe even that their presence in Millersburg wasn't needed.

Unfortunately, he was not that lucky.

Waiting for him with drinks now firmly in their hands, Robert and Caroline immediately took to peppering Brock with more questions, leaving him with the distinct feeling they'd banded together in an attempt to trip him up.

When their attempts didn't succeed, Caroline grabbed her purse and stomped out of the room, going out for a *break,* if Brock wasn't mistaken.

Robert merely settled back into the business of staring at Brock without speaking.

"While this is an incredibly productive way for me to spend my evening," Brock finally said after a full minute of silence had passed, "I have entirely too much work waiting for me to play these types of games." He rose from the chair. "I would suggest you and your wife return to California. Your daughter is well protected, she apparently does not want you or her mother to interfere with her plans, and because she is an adult, you really have no say in what she does. If it's any consolation, from what I've learned about your daughter, she's intelligent, doesn't seem to be the overly impulsive type—"

"But you *don't* know my daughter, Agent Moore," Robert interrupted, setting aside his drink to rise to his feet as well. "You only met her a few days ago. Margo has been sheltered and pampered her entire life, so believe me when I tell you she's incapable of taking care of herself. She has three personal assistants who live in a separate house on her estate in California, but they only live there so they can be at her beck and call. She won't last more than another week out here in the wilds of Ohio. Because of that, and because I am a concerned father, I'm not leaving until she comes to her senses and comes back to me. Then, with my daughter in tow, I'll take her home to California, where, I can assure you, you won't be permitted to follow."

Brock forced a smile. "It's funny, but that almost sounded like a threat."

"I don't make threats, Agent Moore. Only promises."

chapter eleven

Stretching her arms over her head, Margo opened her eyes and found herself in a room painted an off-white, with a pair of translucent white curtains fluttering softly in the breeze blowing in from an honest-to-goodness open window.

She couldn't remember the last time she'd slept with a window open. And she certainly couldn't remember a time when what sounded like a real-live rooster greeted her day with the loudest crowing she'd ever heard in her life.

Swinging her legs over the twin-size bed covered with a soft and beautiful quilt Mrs. Hershberger had told her she'd created by hand, Margo looked down. She grinned at the nightgown her host had lent her the night before.

It was a long garment, made out of what she'd been told was calico material. Margo was sure she'd fit right in if they ever decided to film more episodes of *Little House on the Prairie*, a show she secretly adored and watched anytime she was up late at night and found it on obscure cable channels. The only thing she was missing was a nightcap, and even though Mrs. Hershberger had offered her one of those, Margo had politely declined. She'd never been one to like anything on her head, not even hats when it was cold—

unless she was trying to pull off a disguise, that is.

However, because her hair had sustained some unexpected damage due to the fact Sebastian didn't have time to properly remove his highlighting mixture before she made her second great escape, she knew she might have to revise her opinion about wearing hats in the not-too-distant future. It wasn't that all of it had fallen out, just a few hunks here and there. She was hoping the mixture Mrs. Hershberger had made for her the night before, one that had eggs, mayonnaise, and honey blended together would put her hair to rights, or at the very least, not allow any more hair to become parted with her head.

Bald was not a look she thought she could rock, especially since she had an unusually shaped head, something she'd never noticed until just recently.

If there had been any lesson to learn with the whole losing some of her hair business, it was that the stubborn streak she'd always known she possessed was not actually a good thing. Sebastian, bless his far-too-opinionated heart, had launched into a lecture about her wanting to skedaddle out of the hospital with Mrs. Hershberger, telling her it was not a good idea until he got every trace of the mixture he'd brushed into her hair removed. She, being stubborn, had refused to change her mind, and when he began to recite a long laundry list of everything that could go wrong if she left even a smidgen of mixture in her hair, she obviously missed the part about there being a good chance her hair could burn.

And while hindsight was a wonderful thing and might have prevented her losing some hair, Margo was still thrilled with the way *most* of the plan had turned out—especially since she'd been successful sneaking away from the hospital, the reporters, the paparazzi, and most importantly, her parents.

The success of that plan all came down to Mrs. Hershberger. She'd somehow managed to convince the staff to allow her into the hospital while carrying a duck, apparently appealing to their desire to please a pop princess by allowing her to visit with a duck Mrs. Hershberger claimed Margo was very fond of. It had been sheer brilliance on Mrs. Hershberger's part to stuff a spare Amish outfit in the very back of the pet carrier, knowing no one would bother checking it.

Letting the duck back out of the carrier after she had Margo dressed as an Amish woman, Mrs. Hershberger then sent Sebastian on a mission to distract Caroline longer, and as he walked out of the room, she gave the duck a bit of a shoo. That's when the fun had begun.

The guard who'd been watching Margo's door raced around with Brock, trying to catch the duck, and luckily for everyone involved in the plan, the duck was a great sport. She waddled

155

down the hallways as fast as she could, leading Brock and the guard away.

As soon as the coast was clear, Margo left with Mrs. Hershberger and her sister, hurrying down hospital's hallways and then through town in obscure anonymity. Before she climbed into Mrs. Hershberger's buggy and was driven straight out of town, Sebastian met them at the animal clinic. He handed the duck and carrier to Margo and told her Caroline was fit to be tied. Because of that, Sebastian stated rather firmly that he was off for the airport ASAP, stating most emphatically that he couldn't get back to California fast enough.

Mrs. Hershberger's going to so much bother to spirit her away had been a little confusing to Margo. But when she asked the woman about it, Mrs. Hershberger said it was her Christian duty to help those in need. Then she changed the subject, leaving Margo with the impression she wasn't disclosing the full truth.

Since Margo had been more than pleased with how the day ended, she'd left it at that, spending the rest of her evening charmed by the country atmosphere she'd been invited to enjoy.

When the rooster outside the window let out another crow, Margo got out of bed, taking a moment to stretch. Walking across the room after she felt more limber, she eased open the door because she wasn't sure what time it was. Tiptoeing down the wooden steps, she sniffed the air, smiling when the delightful smell of coffee met her nose. Hurrying into the kitchen, she found Mrs. Hershberger already standing in front of an old-fashioned stove, frying up some eggs.

"Ah, how wonderful. You're awake, and . . . looking very well rested." Mrs. Hershberger gestured to the simple plank table with the spatula she was holding. "Have a seat, help yourself to the pot of coffee on the table, and I'll get you some eggs and toast."

"You don't need to make me breakfast, Mrs. Hershberger. I do know how to make toast."

"Don't be ridiculous. You're my guest, dear, and as such, I'm expected to feed you. Given the scrawny look you have about you, you could use some fattening up, and that's exactly what I'm going to try to do."

Not wanting to admit to the very practical woman standing before her that her scrawny look was a direct result of spending hours with a personal trainer and sticking to the strict number of calories her dietician allotted for her daily consumption, Margo settled for sending the woman a nod. Then she found herself presented with a platter, not a plate, of food a mere moment later.

Joining her at the table, Mrs. Hershberger held out her hand, and together they bent their heads while Mrs. Hershberger delivered a simple blessing.

There was something comforting about that

blessing, as well as the simplicity with which it had been rendered. In Margo's experience, it often seemed as if public prayers were given as a way to draw notice, not for the true purpose they were meant to be—showing gratitude to God for the blessings a person was receiving.

With a quiet "Amen" after Mrs. Hershberger finished, Margo lifted her head, feeling much more at peace than she normally felt. Digging into the eggs, bacon, and potatoes heaped on the platter, she found she was absolutely starving. Setting about the business of enjoying an excellent meal, she finally blotted her lips with her napkin, set it aside, and found Mrs. Hershberger frowning back at her.

"Surely you're not finished yet, are you, dear?" Mrs. Hershberger asked with a telling nod to Margo's still somewhat brimming plate. "You've barely touched your food."

"I'm afraid I'll burst if I eat another bite, but do know that this breakfast was one of the best I've ever eaten."

Looking slightly appeased by that, Mrs. Hershberger lifted her coffee and took a sip, eyeing Margo over the rim of her cup. "Your hair turned out better than I expected, although it's . . . bright instead of being what I would think is a natural buttercup color."

Margo lifted her hand, ruffling the relatively short mop of curls she now sported.

"I'm afraid the brightness is another result of not getting Sebastian's concoction washed out as thoroughly as he instructed," Margo began. "But I do appreciate you cutting out the pieces of hair that got burned, especially since you shaped it so well. And I think the egg and honey mixture you made for me did the trick since I don't seem to be losing any more hair." She smiled. "Sebastian will be tickled about that. I think he would have fainted dead away if his highlighting blend had left me bald. Through no fault of his, of course."

Mrs. Hershberger took another sip of coffee. "He's a good man. Not many people in his position would have risked putting themselves in a situation where they were bound to draw anger. Your mother had to realize later that Sebastian went outside to join her only to delay her return to your hospital room. He'll lose a customer because of his decision to help you."

"He probably *will* lose my mom's business, but since I use his services more than she does, I'll make certain he's well taken care of, while also making certain my mother doesn't spread any nasty rumors about him."

The sound of wheels rolling over the dirt drive that led to Mrs. Hershberger's house suddenly drew Margo's attention. Not wanting to be caught in her nightgown, even with that nightgown covering more of her body than she normally covered, she got up from the table.

Waving her immediately back into her chair, Mrs. Hershberger started for the door. "That'll just be my sister, Anna. She always stops in for coffee before both of us begin our day, and she has numerous daughters, so you're fine." With that, Mrs. Hershberger walked out of the kitchen.

Picking up her own coffee cup, Margo took a sip—and then choked when Brock suddenly appeared in the kitchen, not Mrs. Hershberger's sister.

Striding immediately to her side, Brock gave her a brisk pat on the back. "Are you okay?"

Letting out a last cough, she raised now watering eyes to his. "I'm fine, but what are you doing here?"

Pouring himself a cup of coffee, Brock pulled out the chair beside her and took a seat. "I'm here to see you, of course." He took a sip and let out what sounded like a moan. "Oh, I needed that."

"Did you drive a horse and buggy here?"

"No, I just hitched a ride with Anna Hershberger. She drives her buggy every morning past the little carriage house I'm staying in."

"You're living in a carriage house?"

Brock nodded. "It's on Ian's property and the rent is reasonable considering he's not charging me to stay there." He took another sip of coffee. "I was standing out by the side of the road at the crack of dawn, waiting for her to drive by.

Luckily she saw me and stopped, although she did make me hide on the floor of her buggy."

"Why did she do that?"

"She was afraid someone might be watching me, so we were taking extra precautions."

"I'm not sure I understand why anyone might be watching you."

As Brock filled her in on what had happened since she'd last seen him, Margo found herself somewhat distracted from the conversation. That unusual situation was a direct result of Brock and his T-shirt. It was a perfectly ordinary T-shirt, one promoting an English band. But it fit him like a glove and drew attention to his muscles.

She wasn't a woman who'd ever noticed muscles on men that much before, being around muscular men so much because she spent hours at different gyms. But Brock's muscles, on the other hand, fascinated her, especially when he moved and they . . . rippled.

"Unfortunately, your father did discover that bit about me being in the FBI I just mentioned, which is why I sent that note around last night, explaining why I couldn't meet up with you then, and . . . Did you do something different with your hair?"

Shaking all thoughts of muscles away, Margo frowned. "Mrs. Hershberger had to cut it up for me because that stuff Sebastian used on it burned it. But did you just say you're *with* the FBI?"

"I thought you were taking that too well." He smiled a somewhat knowing smile. "Takes you a few cups of coffee to get going in the morning, does it?"

Since she certainly wasn't going to admit she'd missed the whole FBI business while gawking at his muscles, Margo settled for a nod before she narrowed her eyes on him. "So you *are* an agent with the FBI?"

"I am. And since I might as well divulge everything, get it out there in one painful minute, like when you have to rip off a Band-Aid, I also have a law degree that helped me get into the FBI in the first place."

"Where'd you get that degree?"

"Not online, if that's what you're thinking," he said with a grin. The grin faded when she crossed her arms over her chest and simply stared at him.

"Harvard."

For a second, she could only continue staring at him, until amusement bubbled up her throat, spilling out a second later.

As Brock watched her with what almost seemed to be concern in his eyes, Margo continued laughing, finally wiping her eyes with the sleeve of her nightgown as one last hiccup of amusement escaped.

"I offered to triple your salary, then told you money was no object, and wanted you to be my bodyguard."

Brock took a sip of his coffee. "You did, and I was flattered by it, although feeling flattered might have happened hours after you offered me the job."

"I thought you left so abruptly because I insulted you."

"No, that's not the reason. But since you and Mrs. Hershberger have to leave soon, there's no time to get into why I left after you made your job offer, especially since you clearly need to get ready for the day. I don't believe the Miller family would know how to react if you showed up at their house in whatever that is you're wearing."

"I'm going to the Millers?"

"I'm afraid so. Your mom remembers part of Mrs. Hershberger's name, and since she and your dad are refusing to leave town without you, I don't want to take the chance they'll figure out Haberdashery is really Hershberger and show up here to cart you off to California."

"They can't force me to leave."

"No, they can't, but since you were the one who decided to sneak out of the hospital, I'm going to assume you realize your dad isn't a man to take lightly. So unless you want to have a confrontation with him, we need to move you immediately. Since the Miller family has stepped up and volunteered to take you in, that's where you're going."

"Are they Mennonites like Mrs. Hershberger?"

"They're Amish, so you're going to find them more reserved."

"Amos Miller is a very kindly man," Mrs. Hershberger suddenly said, joining them in the kitchen with her sister, Anna, walking beside her. "They have a large family, so you'll be hidden in the sheer number of them, and they have a large barn if you want to go about the business of whatever it was your mother mentioned you needed a large space to accomplish."

"I think I'd prefer to take a few days off and just enjoy doing nothing," Margo admitted.

Mrs. Hershberger shook her head. "Doing nothing won't be an option at the Miller farm, dear. There's always a need for an extra pair of hands, so while they won't expect you to muck out stalls or help raise a barn, you might want to volunteer to feed the chickens, milk some cows, or take slop to the pigs."

"They have animals there?"

"It's a farm, dear. Of course they do."

Before she had a chance to remind everyone that animals were not her friends, she found her arm taken by Mrs. Hershberger. She was hustled straight out of the room, back up the stairs, and distracted from the thought of animals as Mrs. Hershberger and Anna went about the business of turning Margo into an Amish girl again.

Stuffing her into a heavy cotton dress, the sisters began throwing random Amish tidbits her way, explaining why they were closing her dress with straight pins, something Amish women evidently preferred over buttons, and even the fact that the white cap they pulled over her head was called a prayer cap. She was then handed a heavy pair of woolen stockings which she wrestled up her legs, before she shoved her feet into shoes that in no way resembled the designer heels Margo usually wore.

When they proclaimed her completely dressed, she pivoted around and smiled. "Will I pass for Amish?"

Instead of giving her the response she expected—at least a smile or two—the two women exchanged a look that was less than reassuring before they abruptly left the room.

chapter twelve

While he waited for Margo to get dressed, Brock pulled out his phone and checked his text messages. Scrolling down the list, he paused on the one he'd received from Agent Colby, asking him to call at his earliest convenience.

Stepping outside to the porch of Mrs. Hershberger's farmhouse, he placed the call, unsurprised when Colby picked up a second later.

"Hope I didn't wake you," Colby said.

"Hope you got at least a little sleep since I spoke with you last night after ten and you were still doing paperwork in your hotel room."

Colby laughed. "I'll catch up on sleep when things settle down. But I have good news, good news, and . . . bad news."

"Since it's barely the crack of dawn, hit me with some good news."

"Robert Hartman left town, was driven to the Akron/Canton airport, and boarded a private jet that belongs to Margo Hartman, not him. His flight plan was logged for New York, not California."

"And his wife?"

"She's still at the Hotel Millersburg."

"Was that the bad news?"

"Sorry, but no."

"What's the other *good* news?"

"Carl Franklin has been found."

Brock held out the phone, looked at it for a moment, and returned it to his ear. "Margo's stalker?"

"Yep."

"Was he caught in Millersburg?"

"See, this is what I would consider the bad news," Colby returned. "He was found in Florida, with a woman who is originally from Morgantown, West Virginia. That's apparently why he was *in* West Virginia, so I don't think he was responsible for shooting Ms. Hartman because . . . turns out he was getting married that day."

"You've got to be kidding me."

"Nope, not kidding, which means—"

"This is a whole different case than what we thought it was," Brock finished for him.

"Yep."

Blowing out a breath, Brock leaned against the porch railing, considering their options, of which there didn't seem to be many. "How long do you think we have to pursue an investigation before someone in the FBI decides she was shot accidentally by a random idiot?"

"If I were to hazard a guess, I'd say not more than a day or two, not even with potential evidence from that missing camera should we ever recover it, or if anything can be found out about that rifle still at the lab. Margo Hartman is certainly considered by most to be a national treasure, but she's in hiding, she has you, and unless we find something soon, everyone else on this assignment will get pulled. You'll still have the local authorities to help you, though, which is better than nothing."

"I suppose there is that." After making arrangements to meet with Colby and the other agents later, Brock ended the call. Turning from the railing, he found Margo stepping out of the door, the infamous duck waddling right at her feet.

She looked completely unlike herself. Her dress could only be described as a functional garment in that it did do an amazing job of covering her up from her neck to mid-calf. It definitely didn't have so much as a single piece of bling on it, something she'd had in abundance on the jeans she'd been wearing when he first met her, the ones Pudding had tried to rip straight from her leg.

She wore a white apron over the dress, and her outfit was completed by a white prayer cap that was a common sight in Millersburg on most days. Her hair had been scraped away from her face and secured with some kind of pins, although those pins didn't seem up for the job of holding her hair in place since tiny bright curls were already making their escape.

Looking down, he found her barefoot, the bright red of her toenails at distinct odds with the Amish look she had going on. "Where are your shoes?"

"They're right inside the door, along with the stockings Mrs. Hershberger wants me to wear. I had them on just a few minutes ago, but they're incredibly hot, so I pulled them and the shoes off. Believe me, I'm not looking forward to pulling those stockings up my legs again."

She began walking his way. "I don't have a choice but to wear them, because evidently it'll be a dead giveaway if my legs are bare." She stopped right beside Brock and lowered her voice. "I get them waxed, and apparently that would be a definite clue to someone I'm not really Amish."

Brock blinked. "I didn't even think about that."

"Neither did I, but now we know." She bent over, picked up the duck that had waddled beside her across the porch, and took Brock by complete surprise when she dipped her head and gave the duck a kiss on its head.

"You haven't made that duck into a pet, have you?"

"I have, and I've named her. Meet Gabby. Mrs. Hershberger told me she spoke with Jonas Yoder, and he was more than gracious in offering to allow me to keep the duck . . . forever."

"Hasn't anyone ever told you it's a really bad idea to name farm animals?"

"That's only if you intend to eat them. I would never consider serving Gabby up for a meal, so it's not an issue."

"Is it an issue that ducks aren't usually able to get the hang of being housebroken?"

Margo's nose shot straight up into the air. "Gabby would never be so rude as to . . . poop in the house. But you'll be relieved to learn I have a conservatory at my home in California, a lovely space that will be perfect for Gabby to roam around in to her heart's content. Not"—she gave Gabby another kiss on the head—"that I plan on returning anytime soon, but someday, after the crazy person is caught and after my mom agrees to stop meddling in my life and career."

Moving together to the steps, they walked down them before Margo headed to a grassy area. She set Gabby down and smiled fondly at the duck as it settled right into the grass.

"She's such a sweet girl," Margo said, sounding exactly like a proud parent, which had Brock swallowing a laugh. "And her wing is healing very well and it doesn't seem to bother her. Although"—she shook her head—"she hasn't tried to fly yet, which does worry me a little."

"I'm sure she'll make a full recovery, quite like you've done."

"I'm *not* looking forward to getting my stitches out."

Walking over next to her, he took her hand, which had her eyes widening a little and sent a jolt he hadn't been expecting traveling up his arm. "Getting stitches out is not a big deal. I've had it done numerous times. But since I don't want you passing out again, and talking about stitches could make that happen, I'm now going to expertly change the subject, distracting you from all thoughts of your very few stitches in the process."

"You're not supposed to tell a person you're changing the subject to distract them. You're just supposed to change the subject."

"You're very opinionated for an Amish lass, aren't you?"

Margo's eyes twinkled. "I don't think I'd care to have to wear these types of clothes every day, and I'm sure I am far more opinionated than the usual Amish girl. Having said that, there's just something very calming about living a slower life, isn't there?"

"I suppose there is at that." Brock squeezed her hand. "And while I wish what I had to say next was going to continue our chat in a calming way, I have to tell you some news. Do you want the good news or the bad news first? We have more good news than bad."

She didn't hesitate. "Bad news."

Brock tilted his head. "I would have never guessed you're one of those people who likes bad news first."

She wrinkled her nose. "You like to hear the good news first?"

"Sure, it makes the bad news more palatable."

171

"But if you hear the bad news first, the good news makes the bad news seem not so bad."

"Hmm . . . interesting point, not that I agree with you. But here's your bad news. Carl Franklin is married."

"And that's bad news because you're worried my feelings will be hurt that he's fickle and has decided he isn't in love with me after all?"

"No, it's bad news because he's in Florida, with his new wife, and was only in West Virginia to meet that new wife's family. And if we could return to the argument of getting good news first and then bad . . . that bad news I just gave you would have made a lot more sense if I had first told you Carl has been found, which is the good news, but that we learned he got married, which is the bad news."

"Or maybe you could have just phrased it differently so I could have understood exactly what you were saying in the first place."

"Maybe you should have had an extra cup of coffee this morning so you could keep up."

To Brock's delight, Margo flashed a grin his way. "Which would normally be a very good point because I'm not a morning person." She crossed her arms over her chest. "However, surprisingly enough, I'm wide awake and far too cheerful for this time of day. And that's after having the very rude crow of a rooster wake me up when the sun was barely peeking over the horizon."

"Not much of a country girl, are you?"

"No, I'm not. Although it's not nearly as bad out here as I thought it would be." She drew in a deep breath and slowly released it. "What was the other good news you mentioned?"

"Your dad went back to New York."

"And my mom?"

"She's still in Millersburg."

Margo bit her lip and trailed a bare toe over the top of the grass, heavy with morning dew. "I guess having one parent gone is better than nothing, and my father is the more difficult of the two, if you can believe that." She tilted her head. "Since I didn't get to see you last night, how did the meeting go with my father?"

"Not well, and quite honestly, I'm surprised he left town considering how adamant he was about staying here. I suppose if I had a daughter, though, and that daughter had attracted the attention of a killer, I'd be a little difficult to bear as well."

"Don't think for a minute that my father cares that much about me, Brock. He doesn't. He's a classic narcissist, only thinks about himself, and . . . No one knows this, and I don't really know why I'm telling you, but he only married my mom because she comes from money. *And* because he knew she'd be the sole beneficiary of her father's estate when he passed away."

"I have to admit I'm not surprised to hear that," he said, not bothering to add that at least he now understood how Robert funded his lifestyle, which also explained why he didn't actually need to be a man of business.

"He's not a good man, Brock, which is why I don't see him often. But—" She lifted her head when the sound of a motorcycle rumbled through the air.

Without hesitating, Brock turned, picked up Margo straight into his arms, then ran with her for the farmhouse. They met Mrs. Hershberger as she stepped out on the porch. She was holding a spatula in her hand, apparently the best weapon she had available.

"It's Dr. St. James," Mrs. Hershberger said.

Turning from the house, although he didn't set Margo down, Brock squinted toward where a cloud of dust was flying up a bit down the dirt drive.

"My goodness, he's brought out his motorcycle," Mrs. Hershberger all but whispered.

Ian had not ridden his motorcycle since Stephanie died, claiming it reminded him too much of a wife he missed more than anything. That he'd chosen to ride his bike out to Mrs. Hershberger's was definitely a reason for concern. Setting Margo on her feet, Brock moved off the porch to greet his brother-in-law.

Taking off his helmet, Ian dashed a hand across a face that seemed to be scratched up a little and grinned. "No need to worry that anyone followed me out here, Brock. I left the road and hit the fields. But that raspberry bush sure did take me by surprise."

He swiped at his face again with the sleeve of his leather jacket. "I might have to apologize to Mr. Wayne *and* help him replant a row of what I think might have been green beans. Got a little carried away on the rolling hills and was airborne before I noticed I was heading into a vegetable garden."

Noticing all the bits of leaves attached to Ian, along with clumps of what Brock was just going to hope was mud—though since Ian had been riding through fields, that might not be the case—Brock took only a single step closer to his brother-in-law. "Why are you out here?"

"You told me last night when you stopped by the main house that Mrs. Hershberger had offered Margo a place to stay at her farm. So, when I noticed you getting into Anna's buggy this morning while I was up feeding my cat, I figured you were coming out here since I know Anna likes to take breakfast with her sister every morning."

"Does your cat always need to be fed so early?"

"Unfortunately, yes, but that has nothing to do with why I'm here." Ian leaned forward and dropped his voice to almost a whisper. "Someone left a cryptic note on my front porch, probably last night, if I were to guess. And they used a typewriter, which is more than a little suspicious."

"Why didn't you just call me? I always have my cell phone."

Ian blinked. "Huh. That would have been an idea, although it wouldn't have been nearly as James Bond*ish,* calling you on your cell phone instead of racing my bike through the wilderness, knowing that time was of the essence, or . . ."

"The note would blow up?" Brock finished for him when Ian seemed to be struggling for an ending to his dramatic tale.

"Good one, Brock. Though that's a bit more *Mission Impossible*, if you ask me."

"Which is an excellent point, but speaking of *Mission Impossible*, did you bring the self-exploding note with you?"

"Ah, right, the note." Sticking a hand in the pocket of his jacket, he pulled out an ordinary-looking piece of paper and handed it to Brock. "See, it's been typed out with an honest-to-goodness typewriter. That was a mistake, if you want my less-than-expert opinion, because typewriters aren't that easy to find these days."

"Unless you're living in a town where people still drive horses and buggies and don't subscribe to the electricity idea." Brock unfolded the note.

"There is that," Ian muttered.

Smiling, Brock turned to the note, his smile dimming as he read it aloud. " 'Answers to your questions may be found at the library.' " He lifted his head. "What answers, and to what questions?"

A trace of sorrow flickered through Ian's eyes. "At first I thought it might have something to do with Stephanie. But then, if you'll read on, the instructions say we need to track down a certain article that can be accessed on microfiche."

"I didn't even know microfiche was still around."

"Not everyone has the budget the FBI does to update old files."

"True." Brock returned to the note. "*The Millersburg Journal*, August 14, 1993." He frowned. "What answers could anyone expect us to find from a local newspaper article? And again, what questions would either you or I even have from that time?"

"We'll never know until we plan a covert operation to the library."

Laughing, Brock shook his head. "You do remember you're an animal doctor, don't you?"

"For now. But check back with me after we investigate the microfiche."

Brock laughed again. "I don't know, Ian. This might be a huge waste of our time. But we certainly can't ignore a lead, even if we have no idea what that lead is for, so I'll meet you at the library later today. I have to see Margo settled first, though."

Ian lifted his head before he nodded toward the porch. "She seems pretty settled from where I'm standing."

Turning, Brock set his gaze on Margo, who'd sat down on the wooden swing hanging on the porch. Gabby was sitting in her lap and Mrs. Hershberger was sitting at her side.

"She does seem to be comfortable here, strange as that might seem considering she's from an entirely different world." Brock turned back to Ian. "Unfortunately, she can't stay here because Caroline Hartman heard Mrs. Hershberger's offer of sanctuary. Even though Caroline comes across a little ditzy, I think there is a slightly sharp mind mixed in with all the prescription medicines she seems to enjoy. Because of that, she very well might remember Mrs. Hershberger's real name sometime in the future."

"Where are you going to put Margo, then?"

"Amos Miller has evidently stepped up and offered her a place with him."

Ian's brows drew together. "I didn't know you were personally acquainted with Amos Miller."

"I'm not. In fact, I've never met the man, but Mrs. Hershberger reached out to him yesterday and arranged everything. She obviously realized Margo needed to go deeper into hiding and took it upon herself to organize the particulars."

"She is definitely very good at organizing things," Ian agreed. "It's one of the reasons Stephanie insisted on hiring her, even with Mrs. Hershberger having no idea how to use a computer. Stephanie didn't let that minor detail stop her from bringing the woman into our practice, especially not after she learned Mr. Hershberger had passed on, leaving his wife of forty years. She was lonely and had an empty house on her hands, what with her children having lives of their own."

"Stephanie was annoyingly thoughtful at times."

Nodding, Ian tucked his helmet under his arm. "She was indeed. But getting back to Amos Miller, have a care with him, Brock. He's not partial to outsiders, sticks to the Amish, and he rarely even travels to town. It's strange that he'd be the one to offer to take Margo in, and I'm not sure how long he'll be content to let her stay, what with her being a pop star and all."

"I don't think Mrs. Hershberger would have reached out to him, if she thought there was going to be a problem."

"You're probably right. And on that note, since I do need to make my rounds soon, and then meet you at the library, I have to get going. Ten okay to meet there?"

"I should be able to make that. I have permission to take some personal time from the sheriff's department, but I still want to be seen out and about around town. It might draw too many questions if I suddenly disappear, and this way, once word spreads that I'm on temporary leave, everyone will think I've got something horrible wrong with me, or . . ."

"You've suffered a devastating breakup with America's favorite pop princess," Ian finished for him. With that, and with amusement once again in his eyes, Ian walked around Brock and headed for the porch.

After taking a moment to say hello to everyone, including Anna Hershberger, who'd moseyed out to the porch as well, Ian turned around, headed back to his bike, put his helmet on, and sent Brock a nod. "I'll see you later."

As Ian roared down the dirt driveway, Brock walked to the porch. Mrs. Hershberger was standing by the steps, shielding her eyes from the morning sun with her hand as she watched Ian speed away.

"It's a blessing to see that man on his bike again." She turned and made her way back into the house with her sister following, leaving Margo with her duck on the swing.

When she patted the spot right beside her, Brock didn't hesitate to join her.

"Why did your brother-in-law give up his bike?" was the first thing she asked.

"Ian used to ride with my sister, and he's said many times that it's just not the same without her." Brock released a breath. "*He's* not the same without her."

"Is that why you left the FBI, to help him?"

"I was only on a temporary leave from the FBI, Margo. And while I did want to be around Ian as he tries to adjust to life without Stephanie, strings were pulled to get me on as a temporary deputy so I would have a reason to snoop around Millersburg."

"Because . . . ?"

"My sister's death was ruled a suicide, but I'm not convinced that's what happened."

Reaching out, Margo laid a hand on his arm. "Then you did the right thing by coming here. But I do hope you know you're not to blame, nor is Ian, if your sister *did* commit suicide." She patted his arm, just once. "My mom has threatened to kill herself numerous times over the years, and what I've come to realize is that, in her case, it's a cry for attention. For some people, though, it's a cry for help, or a way to escape the anguish they suffer because of mental illness."

"I wouldn't blame myself, although Ian might, if we discovered Stephanie really did take her own life. But I will blame myself if she was killed and I missed something that could have prevented her death, some clue she might have given me on the frequent chats we shared over the phone."

"And what will you do if you never find the answer to what happened?"

"I'm not ready to think about that just yet," Brock said, surprised he'd admitted that out loud, and to a woman he barely knew.

As if sensing he'd disclosed more than he was comfortable disclosing, Margo gave his arm another pat. "If it makes you feel better, I'm not ready to think about where I want to go from this point in my life either. Being shot does tend to have a person reevaluating, and while I know that I want to keep singing, I'm just not certain I want to continue with all the nonsense that goes along with being America's Pop Princess."

"Those near death experiences are certainly good for helping a person get their priorities straight."

Margo's lips curved. "I'm fairly certain I didn't have a near death experience since I was only diagnosed with a flesh wound."

"I'm sure it was an extremely painful flesh wound, though, which we shouldn't fail to acknowledge."

Margo grinned. "Calling it extremely painful might be a stretch since I do only have a few, as in very few, stitches. But stitches aside, while it's just the two of us, I'd like to tell you how much I appreciate you looking out for me." She placed her hand over his. "You don't owe me anything, but I left you to face my parents after I took off from the hospital, and I know that was asking a lot. So thank you for that, and thank you for continuing to offer me your protection."

Not nearly comfortable enough with her yet to explain questioning his ability to protect her, Brock considered his response. He was spared any response at all, though when Mrs. Hershberger and her sister walked out of the house and rejoined them.

With both ladies looking what could only be described as determined, and directing that determination his way, he had the strangest feeling his day was not going to go as planned.

Stopping directly in front of him, Mrs. Hershberger cleared her throat. "Anna and I"—she tossed a glance at her sister, who sent an encouraging nod in return—"have decided it would not be in Margo's best interest for you to accompany us to Amos Miller's house today."

"What?" was the most eloquent response he could come up with to that.

Mrs. Hershberger didn't bat an eye. "Amos does not mingle well with the *English*, and that means it's going to be difficult enough for him to adjust to the idea of having Margo around, let alone having to deal with a man who is . . . intimidating."

"I'm not intimidating."

Margo patted his arm again. "You are, Brock. There's no getting around that. Although, intimidating, especially considering your chosen profession, is a good thing." She smiled. "Attractive even, most women would say."

"What would you say?" he heard come out of his mouth before he could stop the question.

Thankfully, Mrs. Hershberger, after she exchanged what almost seemed to be a rolling of the eyes with her sister, cleared her throat again, loudly. "There'll be none of that flirting business between the two of you, if you please. This is hardly the time, especially since Anna, Margo, and I need to get on the road. Amos will be expecting us soon."

"I can't just let you go off with Margo without protection."

"She'll be more successful hiding among the Amish community if you're not around," Mrs. Hershberger countered. "She looks absolutely nothing like her normal sassy self, and she'll be safe. We won't let anyone get near her, and we're very good at spotting outsiders if anyone would dare come snooping around the Miller farm."

"I can't abandon my vow to protect her and simply leave her to her own devices."

"You're more than welcome to come visit her, but you'll have to come through the fields and by horse or bicycle. Do not even consider coming by motorcycle, which would certainly get everyone riled up on the Miller farm. You'll also have to visit at night."

"You want me to ride a horse, or even better, a bike, through unmarked fields, and . . . at night?"

"You're an intrepid sort," Mrs. Hershberger said with a lift of her chin. "I'm sure you'll figure out a way to get there that won't see you lost or . . . injured." She nodded to her sister. "Since the morning is wasting away, shall we get going?"

Anna's only response was another nod.

"But I came in Anna's buggy," Brock had to point out.

Frowning, Mrs. Hershberger tapped a finger against her ample chin right before she smiled. "Nellie."

"I'm afraid I don't know anyone named Nellie," Brock said.

Less than ten minutes later, he was sitting astride Nellie, a somewhat chubby horse that was barely taller than a pony, but a horse Mrs. Hershberger assured him could hold his weight with ease.

"Now, don't forget," Mrs. Hershberger cautioned. "Nellie is a little deaf, which is why I wanted to have her checked out by Dr. St. James, and which is why I'm so appreciative that you can do me the favor of riding her into town. That will save Dr. St. James the bother of making arrangements to see her, so he'll be appreciative as well, I have to imagine."

"I'll be sure to collect that appreciation from Ian when I meet up with him at the library in a few hours."

Mrs. Hershberger narrowed her eyes. "Why are you going to the library?"

Collecting Nellie's reins in his hand, Brock smiled. "Ian wants me to help him on a quest."

Glancing to Margo, Brock couldn't help but

notice that she seemed to be trying hard not to laugh. When she realized he was looking her way, she sent him an absolutely delightful grin. "If you only had a sword, Brock, you could brandish it now as you go off on this quest to the . . . library, meeting your fellow knight, Sir St. James."

Returning the grin, even though he thought riding a chubby horse as though off into the sunset hardly went with the intimidating appearance the ladies had only recently been remarking on, Brock saluted Margo with an imaginary sword. Then he nodded to Mrs. Hershberger and Anna—who seemed to be exchanging satisfied looks—and prodded Nellie with his knees, which sent her plodding into motion and trudging slowly down the drive.

chapter thirteen

While she didn't remember much about the ride in Mrs. Hershberger's buggy the day before because she'd been keeping a sharp eye out for anyone following her, Margo had a feeling she would never forget the horror of the buggy ride she was *definitely* not enjoying now.

The road leading from Mrs. Hershberger's farm to the Miller farm was filled with tourists, which was, at least according to the two women riding in the buggy with her, a common occurrence every weekend in summer.

The fact that these tourists didn't seem to have much respect for sharing the road with horses and buggies, nor the people in those buggies, had Margo pressing her lips together as tightly as she could. She hoped that would stop her from giving the tourists a piece of her mind as they zoomed around Mrs. Hershberger's buggy time after time after time.

A horn suddenly blared behind them, which had her practically jumping out of her skin. Then as a pickup truck zoomed past a second later, teenage boys yelled something toward the buggy that Margo assumed wouldn't have made their parents proud.

"Aren't you afraid someone's just going to run

right into you?" Margo asked, grabbing hold of the seat and hanging on as tightly as she could as she watched another car come directly at them as it passed a buggy on the opposite side of the road. Thankfully, the car swerved back into its lane before it reached them, but there hadn't been much room to spare.

"God watches out for us," Anna suddenly said, taking Margo by complete surprise since she'd spent the entire morning so far in silence. "And if someone would run into us, we look at it as being God's will, although we might not understand why such a thing would happen. We simply accept it, and know it's not up to us to question his will since he has bigger plans for all of us. Plans that aren't always revealed, at least not at first."

Shifting on the seat as she let that settle into her mind, Margo found the idea of God's will and God's plan to be an interesting one. Having only recently admitted to herself that she'd definitely fallen from the faith she'd once embraced, set aside because of the obligations of a hectic life, Margo allowed herself a moment to simply enjoy being with women who seemed to have a deep and abiding faith. One that just . . . was.

They hadn't taken to trying to push their beliefs on Margo, but had only stated what they believed as truth, as if that truth was such an integral part of their lives there was no need to preach about it all the time. Instead, they led by example.

"It won't be too much longer now, Margo, although the Millers live quite a distance down this lane," Mrs. Hershberger said just as Anna, who'd chosen to drive this morning, steered the buggy off the paved road and onto a dirt track that led them toward a grove of trees. "You might want to loosen the hold you have on poor Gabby, dear. She's looking a little ruffled."

Releasing fingers that she hadn't noticed were digging into the feathers of her duck, Margo smoothed a finger down Gabby's neck. "Sorry about that, girl," she said, earning what she assumed was an affectionate nibble from Gabby in response. Drawing in a deep breath as her nerves began to settle, most likely because they were no longer on the main road, Margo lifted her face to the sky, enjoying the warmth of the sun when it flickered through the trees they were under and slid over her cheeks.

Butterflies fluttered through the air while bees buzzed from one wild flower to the next. She'd never been one to visit the country often, thinking she was more of a city girl. But now that she was in the country, truly experiencing it for the first time, Margo couldn't help but feel as if she'd somehow come home, especially since her current surroundings seemed to feed her very soul.

The sound of a barking dog in the distance had a little of that sense of peace disappearing. "Do they have . . . dogs?"

Reaching over and patting her knee, Mrs. Hershberger nodded. "They do, but I've met their dogs, and they're friendly."

"That's what everyone said about Pudding, but she tried to rip off my leg."

"I'll have a talk with Amos about keeping the dogs away from you."

"That might be for the best."

Anna leaned forward and leveled her gaze on Margo. "Have you always been afraid of animals?"

"I'm not sure if I've always been afraid of animals, but they've never seemed to like me, especially dogs." She smiled at her duck. "Gabby likes me now, though, so I might be making progress."

"Animals can sense fear," Anna began. "But dogs are pack animals, so if you show them you're the dominant one, they'll stop trying to rip off your leg. At least, most of them will."

Margo lips curved. "How . . . reassuring."

"Just keep that advice in mind while you're with the Millers," Mrs. Hershberger said as she gestured up ahead. "There's the house now."

Squinting against the morning sun, Margo found a large farmhouse sitting at the end of the drive. It was two stories, painted a gleaming white, and it had a wraparound porch that beckoned a person to sit on one of the many chairs scattered around. Large trees lent the yard a great deal of shade, and a red barn could be seen in the distance.

Every window of the farmhouse seemed to be open, although the plain white curtains on one of those windows took that moment to twitch, almost as if someone was standing on the other side watching the buggy approach, but hadn't wanted to be noticed.

Switching her attention back to the front porch, Margo saw a man there. He had a long beard, was wearing a straw hat, and was standing perfectly still, leaving Margo with the impression he was bracing himself for what he was about to face.

"Now, Amos Miller is a good and honest man," Mrs. Hershberger said in a quiet voice. "But he's not used to people like you, Margo, so go easy on him."

"I'll be on my best behavior."

"Good girl."

Having no recollection of the last time someone called her a girl, but finding it charming, Margo exchanged a smile with Mrs. Hershberger as Anna brought the buggy to a stop. To her surprise, Amos stepped from the porch and came to the buggy. He presented her with his hand, helping her down before he turned and did the same with Mrs. Hershberger and Anna.

"It's good to see you, Amos."

"And you as well, Faith, and"—he inclined his head—"Anna."

"I didn't know your name was Faith," Margo said.

Mrs. Hershberger nodded. "It is, and while I know this might seem curious to you, the Amish don't use titles like Mr., Mrs., or Miss. They prefer using first names."

Margo frowned. "But everyone always seems to call you Mrs. Hershberger."

"That's because, while I was born Amish I married into the Mennonite community. We do prefer to call each other by our first names when we're at our community gatherings. But when we're out in the world, it doesn't bother us to be addressed more formally if you will. Once I began working for Dr. St. James, it was easier for everyone to address me as Mrs. Hershberger since we have three women by the name of Faith who work in the animal clinic." She nodded to her sister. "Anna married into the Mennonite community as well, but she still prefers to be addressed by her given name at all times."

"As do I," Amos Miller said, inclining his head in Margo's direction.

Margo inclined her head to him in return. "Then that is exactly what I'll call you, Amos, and you must me call Margo."

"Margo," he repeated before he sent her nod, then turned and sent a nod to the house where a large number of people were coming out the front door, all of them dressed in Amish clothing and all of them staring her way.

A woman broke away from the crowd and moved forward, her steps tentative as her gaze never seemed to leave Margo's face.

"Allow me to present my wife," Amos began. "This is Esta. Esta, this is Margo Hartman, our guest for a while."

Esta walked slowly down the porch steps, her gaze still on Margo's face, although she had yet to speak a single word. Reaching the bottom step, Esta hesitated, then, with what seemed to be tears in her eyes, reached out a hand toward Margo. Her lips trembled, she whispered, "Welcome home," and before Margo could say a single word, or take the hand Esta was holding out to her, the woman let out a small sob, turned, and rushed away.

"Oh . . . dear, I was hoping that wouldn't happen," Mrs. Hershberger said before she drew in a deep breath, squared her shoulders, then turned her attention to the people still standing on the porch. "Don't be shy. Come say hello to Margo."

Margo soon found herself surrounded by the rest of the Miller family, their greetings having her swallowing all the questions she had regarding what had just happened with Esta, especially why the woman had welcomed her *home.*

As the names began to blur, a loud quack reminded Margo that she'd abandoned Gabby

193

to the seat of the buggy. Turning around, she smiled when a girl of about fourteen hurried over to scoop Gabby straight up into her arms, then hurried back to Margo and handed her the duck.

"*Dat* told us you might be coming with a duck, and that the duck is allowed to stay with you instead of sleeping in the barn." She wrinkled her nose. "That's strange, but we're not supposed to—" Suddenly, exactly like her mother had done but without all the drama and whispers of welcoming Margo home, she turned and dashed away.

"Don't mind Hannah," another girl said, this one about sixteen, if Margo were to guess. "She's not been around *English* much, so I'm afraid she's a little excited. I'm Katie."

Since Margo had dealt with excited fans who did far stranger things than running away from her over the years, she brushed Katie's concerns aside. "Hannah's fine. Don't worry that she's offended me."

Katie inclined her head. "Thank you. And since I'm sure it must be uncomfortable standing out here with all of us staring at you, would you like to come with me and take a tour of the house? That will allow you to get to know us better, but without the staring."

"That would be wonderful, Katie. But I do think it might be better if Gabby stayed with your other ducks, or at least in the barn. She's still recovering from a wound, so I do want to make sure she's in a safe place. But I don't want to abuse your hospitality by keeping her in the house."

"I'll take her to a pen," a teenage boy said, moving up to join them. After introducing himself as Samuel, he took Gabby, tucked her under his arm, and when the duck didn't bother to quack even once, any worries Margo had about letting her go off to the barn disappeared.

Turning around to tell Mrs. Hershberger she was going on a tour, Margo found that woman walking in the direction Esta had disappeared with Amos and Anna. Knowing there was little chance she'd be of any help since she had no idea why Esta had fled in the first place, she fell into step beside Katie and walked up the steps to the porch. Moving through the front door, she stopped after she crossed the threshold and glanced around.

All the breath suddenly seemed to steal straight out of Margo's body when yet another distinct feeling of déjà vu swept over her.

She'd been here before. Or at least she thought she had.

Forcing feet that wanted to stay stuck to the floor into motion, she wandered further into the house, moving down the hallway and into a room that was obviously where the family came to be together.

Prickles of alarm began trailing up her spine when she noticed a black wood burning stove, the prickles a direct result of having *known* that black stove would be positioned exactly next to a large window *and* have a rocking chair pulled up beside it.

Forcing down the sense of panic that was threatening to overwhelm her, she glanced around the rest of the room, her attention settling on a small chair obviously meant for a child. There was a rag doll perched in the chair . . . a rag doll exactly like the one she'd had since childhood.

A throbbing began at the base of her neck and traveled to her forehead as she stood there, unable to look away from the doll. It was an unusual doll because it had no face, which was exactly what was so unusual about her own doll.

She'd never seen another doll like hers, and had even once questioned where her mom had gotten it since it was her most precious of childhood toys. Her mom had claimed not to remember, and to this day complained about how much Margo was attached to her doll and never left home without it, not even when she went on tour.

That doll, named Martha, provided Margo with a sense of peace whenever she was feeling out of sorts.

Swallowing past the lump that had developed in

her throat, Margo took a single step toward the doll. "Whose doll is that?"

Whispers behind her made her turn. Katie, Hannah, and another sister Margo thought might be named Miriam were now huddled together. They were speaking in a language she didn't understand, but thought sounded almost like German, and their eyes were wide as they stopped their whispering and stared back at her.

"Whose doll is that?" she repeated.

"I don't think that's a matter we need to discuss yet," Amos said as he stepped into the room with Mrs. Hershberger and Anna on either side of him.

Lifting her chin, Margo crossed her arms over her chest. "I'm sure you believe that would be for the best, but with all the strange circumstances I've been involved with lately, I'm really going to have to insist on getting some answers. So . . . tell me about that doll."

chapter fourteen

By the time Brock got Nellie back to Ian's animal clinic, he was in a surprisingly great mood.

There was just something hilarious about riding a horse that couldn't hear and couldn't see very well, either, something Mrs. Hershberger had neglected to mention. She also hadn't bothered to say a thing about Nellie passing gas. A lot.

A man simply couldn't hold on to his dignity while riding a gas-passing, deaf, and practically blind horse through town.

Climbing off Nellie's back, Brock gave the horse a pat, earning what sounded exactly like a snort in response. Grinning like he hadn't grinned in ages, he led Nellie around to the back of the clinic and handed her off to one of the techs Ian employed. Taking a moment to give the woman a quick rundown on Nellie's problems, he paused when she shook her head.

"I'm not sure why Mrs. Hershberger gave you this particular horse to ride, unless you've done something to annoy her. Mrs. Hershberger knows Nellie doesn't like to move faster than a plod, and Dr. St. James was just out at Mrs. Hershberger's farm the other day to check on Nellie's condition. He diagnosed her with a weight problem and a slight case of cataracts. Other than that, and being lazy, of course, Nellie's fine."

"Mrs. Hershberger claimed she needed to have Nellie's hearing checked."

"Nellie doesn't have a problem with her hearing. She's just obstinate and only listens when the conversation revolves around oats."

The moment the word *oats* left the tech's mouth, Nellie's ears perked right up and she let out a whinny as her tail took to swishing.

Smiling, Brock left the tech with a word of thanks for looking after a horse that evidently had relatively little wrong with it, except attitude, and walked toward the animal clinic. As he walked, he couldn't help but wonder if there'd been an ulterior reason for Mrs. Hershberger giving him Nellie to ride. She would have known her horse would take forever to get Brock back to town, leaving him no time to double back and check on Margo at the Millers', which . . .

Shaking his head when he realized he was acting far more paranoid than he usually did, because there were obviously no mysteries surrounding Mrs. Hershberger or Amos Miller—a man known throughout the town as reclusive, certainly, but not dangerous—Brock headed into the animal clinic. He came right back out when he learned Ian had already left for the library.

Because Brock didn't spot a single reporter in town, he was able to enjoy a stroll down the sidewalk, appreciating the idea that not one person holding a microphone in his or her hand tried to accost him. That circumstance was a direct result of the brilliance of one stylist named Sebastian.

He'd texted Brock the night before, only an hour after he'd landed back in California, to tell him he already had plans in motion to have everyone believing Margo had returned to California as well. Those plans had concluded with photos being sent to Brock a few hours after Sebastian's first text of a woman who looked exactly like Margo, tooling down Hollywood Boulevard in a convertible. The photos, along with numerous articles speculating why Margo was back in California had already hit the wires which was certainly providing Brock with the distraction he needed.

Nodding to a gathering of some rotary club members who were posing for a picture right outside the library, Brock made his way inside and went directly to the reference desk. He got directions to the room where a microfiche projector really *was* stored, and after thanking the librarian, he headed toward the basement.

Pulling open the heavy door that led to the storage room, he found Ian already sitting in an old-fashioned leather chair, scrolling through newspaper articles. Dragging another chair over to join his brother-in-law, he leaned forward, his gaze on the screen.

"Find anything?"

Instead of the denial he was expecting, Ian nodded and blew out a breath.

"You're not going to believe what I found. Take a look at this."

After Ian scrolled back to the beginning of the article he'd been reading, Brock exchanged seats with him. Leaning closer to the machine since the writing was incredibly blurred, he read the article, going through it two times to make sure he'd absorbed everything before he turned to Ian.

"Why do you think someone wanted us to read an article that's over twenty years old and concerns three Amish children who disappeared from this town?"

"Why do *you* think someone did?" Ian countered.

With a squeak of rusty hinges, Brock leaned back in the chair. "I'm not sure, nor am I sure why, according to the article, it took the Amish over a week to alert the authorities that three of their children were missing—stolen straight out of their beds, from what was reported."

"That's just how the Amish are, Brock. They really don't like to involve outsiders in their business. They would have wanted to look for the children first, but when they apparently couldn't find them, they turned to the police as a last resort."

"But why would someone send us here to

discover that? Or more importantly, who would send us that note in the first place?"

"I've been thinking about that *and* the thing you mentioned about there being so many old-fashioned things in this town, like the typewriter used to type out the note. That thinking led me to the obvious answer about who sent us the note, although I'm not sure why just yet. Anna Hershberger."

"Why would you think it was Anna?"

"Because she drives past my house every morning before the sun even fully comes up. It would have been an easy thing for her to slip out of the buggy and put that note on my door. She also is more likely to have a typewriter on hand, or knows someone who does, since the Amish and Mennonites aren't known to keep PCs hooked up in their houses."

"Why would Anna Hershberger want us to know about three Amish children who'd gone missing so long ago?"

"Why does Margo Hartman look like the spitting image of Sarah Yoder?"

"What does that have to do with anything?"

Ian frowned. "I'm not sure it does. It's just weird, although . . . Did I miss something in the article about who the missing children belonged to?"

Skimming the article again, Brock shook his head. "It doesn't mention their names."

"That's probably because the Amish don't like to see their names in print or have their pictures taken." Ian flipped the page of a notebook he'd apparently been taking notes in, wrote something down, then lifted his head. "Margo hasn't mentioned anything to you about being adopted, has she?"

"I'm not sure where you're going with this, Ian, unless . . ." Brock tilted his head. "You're not suggesting Margo may be one of these missing children, are you?"

Ian leaned back in the chair. "On a normal day, I wouldn't even consider such a thing. But you and I haven't experienced normal for a long time now, Brock. Since the Amish, along with the Mennonites, don't believe in involving themselves in other people's business, it must have taken a lot of courage for Anna, if she is the one who left me that note, to open up what may turn out to be a very large, very messy can of worms." His lips curved in the faintest of smiles. "It wouldn't surprise me, though, having worked with Mrs. Hershberger for so long now, if the sisters did resort to leaving us a somewhat obscure clue. That would allow them to not get overly involved in this mess, but also allow them to give us a push in the direction they wanted us pushed."

Brock frowned. "If Margo *was* adopted—and I'm not saying she was just yet—and if that adoption happened through questionable channels in this area, it would explain why Robert Hartman showed up in Millersburg and insisted he needed to get Margo out of town."

Ian nodded. "It would, and it would also suggest money was probably exchanged before a child was handed over."

Drawing in a deep breath, Brock slowly released it. "Now all that's left to do is prove our theory, although . . ." He smiled. "It just so happens I have the perfect source to interrogate—the pleasant and oh-so-charming Caroline Hartman."

Three hours later, Brock was almost ready to admit defeat because, unfortunately, Caroline Hartman was nowhere to be found.

He knew she was still in town because he asked the maid who'd been cleaning the rooms on the floor Caroline was staying if she'd checked out, and the maid told him Caroline's belongings were still strewn around her hotel suite.

Since Caroline didn't strike him as a woman who'd leave her things behind, Brock was certain she was somewhere close by, the question of the hour being where.

When his stomach let out a loud growl, Brock glanced at his watch, not really surprised to find that it was after two, but surprised that he'd somehow forgotten all about lunch. Since Caroline was hardly capable of packing up her things and getting out of town in the time it would take him to grab a quick bite, he headed down the street and turned into the Millersburg Diner.

After thanking the hostess who showed him to an empty table, Brock picked up the menu. But before he could make a decision, he was interrupted by Sharon Crawford, the owner of the diner.

"You here to eat? Or to find out more about what happened with that crazy lady earlier today?"

"I was here to eat, but . . . what crazy lady?"

"That mother of Margo Hartman's."

"She was here? How long ago?"

"About an hour, I'd say. She dumped a whole bowl of chowder on the floor. Didn't like the taste of it, or so she said." Sharon pursed her lips. "I've been thinking about pressing charges."

"Did anyone see her dump this bowl of chowder?"

"No, but I know she did."

"You can't press charges just because someone spilled chowder in your diner. Now, if she neglected to pay her bill . . . ?"

Sharon rolled her eyes. "She left fifty dollars on the table."

"That's certainly a reason for pressing charges, all right."

With the corners of her lips lifting just a touch, Sharon nodded. "Point taken. What can I get you to eat?"

After placing an order for a cheeseburger, fries, and a milkshake since it had already been a different sort of day, Brock waited until Sharon walked away before he pulled out his phone and checked his messages. After returning a few texts, he set aside his phone, allowing himself a few minutes to sift through everything rolling around his mind.

Millersburg was a sleepy town, not known for much excitement, unless a celebrity just happened to show up in town, so where would a woman like Caroline Hartman go?

There were a few churches, bakeries, and parks, places that probably wouldn't appeal to Caroline, which meant he was going to have to start with the shops. Caroline, when presented with such a limited range of activities, would surely choose the one where she might just find something she didn't possess, even though the chances of her finding anything remotely acceptable in a small Ohio town were slim.

Pushing aside all thoughts of Caroline when his burger arrived, Brock settled into the business of eating, enjoying every bite on his plate before he polished off his shake. After paying his bill, he walked outside, finding the idea of visiting all the shops not nearly as daunting now that he was no longer starving. Heading for the closest store, one that sold Amish furniture, he was just about to go inside when his phone vibrated in his pocket.

Moving into the shade so he could read the text he'd just gotten without the glare obscuring his screen, he read the message, blinked, read it again, then frowned.

His assistance was required by the Millersburg police department because they were experiencing a situation that they evidently thought he'd be the best person to handle.

Not bothering to text anything lengthy in return, just sending them a message saying he'd be there in five minutes, and not overly concerned that it was any type of major situation since those wouldn't have been handled through a text, Brock shoved his phone into his back pocket and headed for the police station.

Entering the building less than five minutes later, the first thing he heard was a very loud, very distinctive voice. Striding in the direction of that voice, satisfaction flowed through him since he knew without a shadow of a doubt that his search for Caroline Hartman had just come to an end.

He reached the open door that Caroline's voice was blasting out of, and took a good few seconds to absorb the scene unfolding in front of his eyes.

Caroline was sitting in a chair, her face flushed and her demeanor agitated as she shook a finger in the face of a police officer named Tony Hicks. He'd apparently had the misfortune of being asked to take a statement from the woman.

Tearing his attention away from the shaking finger—something oddly mesmerizing because it wasn't an everyday occurrence for anyone to shake a finger at an officer of the law—Brock lifted his head, blinked, and then blinked again. Caroline Hartman, a woman he was fairly sure never took a step outside unless she was perfectly made up, was a mess.

Her hair was standing on end, her cream-colored suit was smeared with mud, and the shoe she was dangling on the end of her toe, as if it had taken to hurting her, seemed to be missing a heel.

"I don't know why you aren't writing down what I told you about that woman from the restaurant," Caroline was saying. "She tried to get someone to kill me, and I demand that you go over there and arrest her right away. She's wearing one of those hideous diner costumes, with her name spelled out in embroidery, which is a trend that really should have stayed in the past—"

"What was the name on her costume?" Officer Hicks asked, his pen poised over a pad of paper, probably because he'd figured out the interview would end sooner if it looked like he was taking her very seriously.

Caroline gave a dismissive flick of her wrist. "I can't be expected to remember details like that, but how many women can be found in a town wearing a diner-girl outfit?"

"Excellent point, Mrs. Hartman." Officer Hicks scribbled something down on the pad, then raised his head and smiled when he caught sight of Brock. "Ah, Deputy Moore, I see someone tracked you down even with it going around that you're taking some personal leave time from the department. You can color me . . . relieved." With that, Officer Hicks got up from the chair, thrust his pad of notes Brock's way, then practically bolted from the room, a word of thanks drifting back over his shoulder.

Taking the seat Officer Hicks had just vacated, Brock pulled the notes the man left behind closer and took a moment to read the description of Caroline's complaint. He lifted his head when he was done.

"You're claiming someone tried to kill you?"

"It was the woman from the restaurant."

"That woman already told me you made a scene there earlier, something about a bowl of chowder you intentionally dropped on purpose, I assume on the floor."

Caroline's face began to mottle. "I didn't drop the chowder on the floor. It was that woman, the one in the diner. She walked right past me, gave a swipe of her hand, and the next thing I knew, the chowder went flying through the air."

"What possible reason could she have for doing that?"

"She evidently had a problem with the fact I complained just a teensy bit about the service. To get back at me, she called someone. And, before you start questioning the validity of that, *I know* she called someone because I saw her on the phone, and fifteen minutes after that, I realized I was being followed."

Rubbing a hand over his face, Brock considered Caroline for a moment, not exactly certain how he should phrase what needed to be said. Clearing his throat, he leaned toward her. "I hope you won't take offense at this, but I have to ask. What medications have you taken, or forgotten to take, today?"

"I haven't forgotten my medications today, nor have I taken more than the prescribed amount of any of them. That means I didn't imagine someone was following me, and I certainly didn't imagine that someone tried to run me over with their truck."

The hair on the back of Brock's neck stood up. "Someone tried to run you over with a truck?"

"That's what I've been trying to tell everyone. It happened in a back alley behind the hotel."

"What were you doing in a back alley?"

"Trying to get away from that person I knew was following me."

Brock would have loved to say he had a feeling Caroline was lying, or at least exaggerating her story, but he was very much afraid she wasn't.

Someone had tried to run her over, just like someone had succeeded in running Margo off the road. But why had someone done that . . . or more importantly, who?

"Can you describe the truck?"

Caroline rolled her eyes. "It was a truck. It was big, maybe black, or . . . blue, and . . . Did I mention it was big, and it was smelly, like what the air smells like in California during rush hour traffic?"

"Did you see who was driving it?"

Shuddering, Caroline shoved some hair out of her eyes. "It had those dark windows, tinted they call them, and after I heard whoever was in the truck start revving up the engine, I didn't stick around to take notes. I took off running, broke the heel straight off my shoe when I tripped, and I thought I was going to be dead when I landed on the pavement." Caroline shuddered again. "I would be dead, too, if someone hadn't come out of the hotel to empty a big cart of trash, which scared that truck away."

"Did that someone from the hotel help you, then?"

Caroline released a snort. "Of course not. It was just a maid, wearing those over-the-ear head-phones. She was singing really loudly, and didn't even see me lying on the road. Not that I'm surprised she didn't see me. This is a horrible town, where I think horrible things happen all the time, and I can't wait to get out of here."

"Why didn't you leave with Robert?"

"It's no secret that Robert and I are estranged. There was no reason for me to leave with him. Besides, I'm not leaving without Margo."

"Why did Robert leave, then, since he claimed to me he wasn't going to leave without her either?"

Caroline gave a dismissive wave of her hand. "He's got business up in New York, and he doesn't like to put off matters like that. I told him I would stay here and look after things, and since we can tolerate each other for only a very, very small amount of time anyway, he apparently decided that time was up. So he left town."

She inspected a nail that seemed to have broken. "I've been toying with the idea of leaving as well, especially now that it seems someone wants to kill me." She looked up. "I think it's probably the same person who wants to kill Margo, and since he can't find her, he's turned his attention to me."

"Why would anyone do that?"

"How should I know? I'm not the expert on these things. But speaking of these things, shouldn't you be taking more notes or having me fill out a few forms so charges can be pressed against somebody?"

"I'm not exactly certain who you want to press charges against, Mrs. Hartman. You don't know who was driving the truck, and I'm not convinced the owner of the diner was behind the plot to run you down, although we will send someone over there to speak to her later."

Caroline pursed her incredibly plump lips before she rolled her eyes. "Fine. Then if it wouldn't be too much bother, I'd appreciate it if you would escort me back to my hotel. At least that way, if someone tries to run me over again, you'll be there to witness it and believe me."

"I didn't say I didn't believe you, Mrs. Hartman." Brock got up from the chair and waited as she did the same. "I'll look into the matter of the truck. But before I do that, I'll walk you back to the hotel. That'll give us time to have a little chat, especially since I have something of importance I need to discuss with you."

"You've come up with a plan to convince Margo she needs to flee from this community of weirdoes and come home with me?"

"Well, no, not exactly. But we should wait until we get away from here to speak further."

Caroline gave a knowing nod. "Someone could be recording us, couldn't they?"

Since he was more concerned with Caroline pitching a fit when he finally got around to asking her questions he doubted she was going to enjoy being asked, he merely gave her shrug. That shrug was apparently taken as a yes, because she nodded again, stuck her nose in the air, and marched for the door.

The effect was a little lacking since she was wearing only one shoe and limping, but that didn't stop her from marching all the way through

213

the police station, out the door, down the front steps, and onto the sidewalk.

Heading in the direction of the Hotel Millersburg, Brock was just beginning to enjoy the quiet that had sprung up between them when Caroline suddenly decided to break that silence.

"Do you think Margo will come to her senses soon and abandon this ridiculous plan of hers, the one that has her hiding in the middle of all the"— Caroline glanced around and dropped her voice to barely a whisper—"Amish people?"

"Since I'm not at liberty to discuss your daughter's current location with you in the first place, I can't answer that. I would, however, caution you to have a bit of discretion about what you say and where. You never know who might be listening, as *you* just recently mentioned, and I'm sure you wouldn't want to be responsible for saying something that could lead the person who seems to want to harm Margo directly to her."

"We know who's after her. That Carl guy . . . the stalker."

Having completely neglected to realize Caroline would have no knowledge that Carl had been cleared, Brock braced himself for the worst. "We've learned that Carl isn't the one responsible for the misfortunes Margo has experienced lately."

"Misfortunes? My daughter was forced into a

lake and then later shot. I think those experiences are a bit more than misfortunes."

"You're exactly right, and I apologize if I gave the impression I don't take what happened to Margo seriously, because—"

"What do you mean, you've discovered Carl isn't the one responsible, and why, in heaven's name, wasn't I informed of this information earlier?" Caroline interrupted.

"You've been a little difficult to track down today."

"Surely you don't expect me to believe you were deliberately trying to track me down earlier. I overheard one of the men at the police station say they were going to reach out to you because they found me . . . difficult."

Because Caroline had stopped walking, and because they were now attracting a lot of attention, probably because she'd started almost yelling, Brock took hold of her arm, ignored the fact she immediately tried to pry his hand off her, and prodded her into motion again. He summoned up a smile and sent it along with a nod to all the people they passed who were now definitely staring their way.

"I *was* looking for you," he began, wincing when Caroline started hitting him every few steps with the broken shoe she was still holding. "But I admit it wasn't to discuss Carl, because he's unimportant to my investigation now that he's been cleared of any involvement in Margo's case."

Caroline lowered the shoe. "Then what did you want to talk to me about?"

Steering her over to a small park that sat in the middle of town, because there really was no putting off the inevitable any longer, he picked out a bench that was off by itself and got Caroline settled on it. Joining her, he took a moment to collect his thoughts, drew in a deep breath, and opened his mouth.

"I don't know how else to ask this but to simply get it out there, so . . . Is there any possibility that Margo was . . . adopted?"

For a moment, Caroline looked as if she'd been slapped in the face, but she recovered quickly with a smile that reminded him of a smile an aging beauty contestant would make.

It was a perfect smile, showing just enough teeth, but the effect of it was ruined when he looked past the smile and into her eyes. They were glittering with something . . . disturbing.

Reaching out to give his arm what he assumed was supposed to be a playful tap, Caroline inclined her head and batted long lashes his way.

"Of course Margo wasn't adopted, and I have a birth certificate to prove it."

chapter fifteen

Margo couldn't help but think she'd been doing a lot of running away lately.

First she'd run from California and all the madness that made up her life. Then she'd run away from the danger that was stalking her, as well as from her parents. And now, well, she'd run out of the Miller home and was definitely coming to the conclusion that the whole running thing had become rather disturbing.

She was now sitting by the side of a pond, an idyllic setting if there ever was one, dipping her bare toes into the cool water as Gabby swam around in the shallow end. Her thoughts, on the other hand, no matter the sereneness of her surroundings, were less than calm.

Something was wrong, really wrong. And yet no one—not Amos Miller, nor his wife, any of the Miller kids, or the Hershberger sisters—was willing to say what that something was.

Margo knew that at least some of those people had some answers. But when she decided that Katie, who seemed like a logical girl, would be the most likely to spill some of those answers if she just applied the right amount of pressure, Amos sent Katie off on some errand. She'd not been seen again.

Now, with the sun moving across the sky and the day settling into evening, Margo was hungry, annoyed . . . and more confused than she'd ever been in her life.

"I've brought you a picnic."

Looking toward the voice, Margo felt her heart give an unexpected lurch when Brock walked into view, swinging an old-fashioned picnic basket, an ancient dog ambling beside him. Since that particular dog had been visiting Margo on and off for the last two hours, and had not so much as bothered to growl at her, preferring to lick her instead, she was more than happy to have the pooch join them. She didn't really have any say in that matter anyway because the dog plopped right down beside her, dropping its head on Margo's lap.

"If you keep this up," Brock began, stopping beside her, "you're going to turn into one of those crazy animal people, with ducks, dogs, and the next thing you know, goats, following you around."

"I don't think I'll ever warm up to goats. A goat tried to eat the bottom of my shirt when I went to a petting zoo when I was all of about seven." She shivered a little. "I was traumatized, my nanny was traumatized, and we couldn't get out of there fast enough. I've never been back to any type of zoo since."

With his lips curving right into a smile, Brock

set down the picnic basket, opened it, took out a red-and-white-checkered tablecloth, and whipped it right over the grass. Holding out a hand to her, he waited until she moved the dog's head off her lap, then helped her to her feet, allowing her to use him for balance as she swished her feet through the pond water, shaking off the bit of algae that had attached to her toes. Walking with her over to the checkered tablecloth doubling as a blanket, he waited until she got settled on it, and then got down to the business of unpacking the goodies stored inside the basket.

The thought flashed to mind that there was something downright charming about a man serving a woman a picnic. Add in the fact that this particular picnic was being held by the side of a pond, with a dog right up against her again, and a duck now waddling out of the water in a clear attempt to see if there were any goodies for her as well, and Margo was fairly certain she'd somehow ended up smack-dab in the midst of her own personal romance novel.

Not that Brock had actually done anything to give her the idea he was romantically interested in her. Although bringing a woman food, and food in a picnic basket, and bringing that food when the woman was starving to death . . . well . . . that could be a sign there was at least a little romantic interest there. But she'd never been around a guy like Brock before—a normal guy, or at least somewhat normal—so she really had no idea what he was thinking.

"While I would love to take all the credit for this basket, I have to tell you that although it was my idea to bring you a meal after I heard about the difficult day you've had, I didn't get to the Millers by car. That right there is why I was left to the mercy of all the women in the house to help me assemble a meal." Brock grinned as he sat down beside her, gesturing to the feast that was now laid out in front of them. "As you can see, we'll be eating well this evening."

Taking the plate he handed her, Margo, instead of being disappointed that he hadn't been responsible for the meal, found it refreshing that he'd owned up to that. So many of the men she'd gone out with over the years tried to impress her through exaggeration. Brock, on the other hand, seemed to be capable of impressing her by just being himself, which was such an unexpected twist that she felt as if she'd traveled into uncharted waters and had no idea what to do next.

Lucky for her, Brock seemed to have no hesitation about what to do. He went about the business of filling up her plate, handing her silverware, and then pouring her a glass of lemonade from a bottle that had honest-to-goodness condensation dripping down the side of it.

Pouring himself a glass, he took her by surprise

when he asked if she thought they should say grace.

It was such an appropriate question, one she didn't hesitate to answer with a nod. Feeling a true sense of gratefulness for a meal laid out before her for the first time in what felt like forever, Margo bowed her head as Brock said grace. As he spoke simple words of thanks, the weight that had settled in her heart that day eased just a bit.

"I haven't said a true grace in a long time," Brock said after he finished the prayer and raised his head.

Margo touched her lemonade glass to his. "I know exactly what you mean, but that felt . . . right."

A comfortable silence settled over them as they ate, broken every now and then by Gabby when she quacked for additional pieces of the cracked corn someone had included specifically for her. The dog, apparently named Henry according to the worn tag on his collar, wagged his tail every time a morsel was tossed his way. After they had stuffed themselves with chicken, creamy potato salad, some type of bean salad, and shoofly pie for dessert, Margo insisted on cleaning up, saying it was only fair since Brock had brought the food.

By the time she had almost everything packed away, evening had definitely fallen. Crickets had come out to chirp their song, and bugs that lit up the night—Brock told her they were called lightning bugs in this part of the country—entertained Margo with a flickering glow.

"Why do they flicker?" she asked, smoothing out the skirt of her dress.

"I suppose the polite way to put it would be to say it's their version of dating."

Blinking, and then feeling her lips twitch at the amusing thought of bugs dating instead of what they were really doing, a subject she certainly wasn't going to bring up, she stopped smoothing her dress. "Yes, well, moving on to a completely different topic, if you didn't get here by car, how did you get here?"

"I rode Nellie back from the animal clinic."

"You're kidding."

"I wish I was kidding, but no, I'm not. You see, Mrs. Hershberger doesn't normally *take* Nellie to the animal clinic to be looked over."

"She doesn't?"

"No, never, because, it turns out, Nellie doesn't like it there. And because she's a slightly ornery creature, Ian always makes a trip to Mrs. Hershberger's farm if anything is ever really the matter with her. That right there is exactly why I'm sure Ian will be having a word or two with Mrs. Hershberger over the little deception she pulled today. Although according to Mrs. Hershberger, she's pleading complete ignorance of any plot I may believe she's hatched against me."

"Why would Mrs. Hershberger be hatching a plot against you?"

"No idea, but why else would she suggest I ride a horse into town that doesn't haven't anything wrong with it, under the pretense that there was something wrong?"

"That is strange, almost as strange as when she claimed ignorance about some questions I had earlier. But before we get into that, since you mentioned that Nellie was ornery, why in the world would you have chosen to ride her out here? Doesn't Ian have any vet techs who could have returned Nellie to Mrs. Hershberger?"

"He does, but when I stopped off at the animal clinic to see if Ian had any ideas for how I was supposed to get to you without the benefit of my Jeep or even his motorcycle, I'm afraid he jumped all over the idea of me riding Nellie over to get to you."

"Maybe you should have reconsidered coming to visit."

Brock shrugged that aside. "We have stuff to discuss."

"We do?"

"I'm afraid so."

Not wanting to dive into that stuff since there was every chance it was going to ruin the sense of peace she'd only recently found, Margo leaned toward him. "Tell me more about the horse. What exactly did Ian do to convince you to ride a less than prancing stead what has to be a few miles into the country? Far be it for me to be the voice of reason here, but I'm sure, given that degree from Harvard you have, you could have come up with a better travel plan."

"In all honesty, I was hoping to take one of Ian's other horses. You know, real horses, ones that aren't chubby and cantankerous. But once I heard how ornery Nellie was being, and after Ian asked me if I could do him the very great favor of bringing Nellie back to Mrs. Hershberger, I didn't have it in me to say no." He grinned. "I wasn't gracious about it, though, something Ian made certain to point out after he reminded me that he'd been relatively gracious with the favor I asked of him—picking up your mom from the airport."

"She was probably more poorly behaved than the horse."

"That's exactly what Ian pointed out to me." Brock took a second to wipe his fingers on a napkin. "So, after being talked into returning Nellie, I rode her out here rather than to Mrs. Hershberger's place, keeping to the forest as much as I could and feeling very much like a true frontiersman. But then Nellie somehow seemed to figure out I wasn't riding her to her farm, and that's when things got a little sketchy."

"Sketchy?"

"She turned into a bucking bronco for a while there, but I won the day in the end. I'm not saying

I didn't get tossed from the saddle a few times, but I made it here, and in relatively one piece, discounting a bruised backside and some scratches where I might have landed in a blackberry bush. I'll feel fortunate indeed if one other patch of plants I landed in turns out not to be poison ivy. But since I'm not itching just yet, I think I'm good."

"And Nellie?"

"Well, Nellie and I will never be what anyone could call friends now, but she's currently eating oats in the Millers' barn. I have no intention of ever riding her again, which I'm sure she'll be just delighted about as well, so that's that. And here I finally am, ready to hear what happened to you today."

"How did you know where to find me?"

"Mrs. Hershberger told me, while also telling me she hadn't abandoned her promise that you'd be protected at all times. Apparently you've been watched by one or more members of the Miller clan ever since you came out here by the pond."

"That's a little . . . alarming, and for lack of a better word, creepy."

"Yes, well, you have evidently been marked for murder, so in their defense, it was an unavoidable necessity." He smiled. "I'm hoping the picnic helped your mood, though. I heard you've been more than annoyed."

"I have been, although before we jump into the

reasons behind that, I would like to thank you for the picnic. It was a very sweet gesture and was certainly the highlight of my day."

Brock smiled. "I'm glad. We'll have to do it again sometime, and hopefully not to cheer up your dismal mood or chase your annoyance away."

"That would be nice."

"It would be, and now on to matters that aren't so nice. Even though I have a few things to discuss with you about your mom, I think it might be best if you go first. Tell me what sent you out here, where I understand you've spent the entire day by yourself."

Taking a deep breath, Margo collected her thoughts before she launched into a long, detailed account of what had made up her day, most of it centering on what had happened that morning.

She told Brock about Esta and how weird it had been when she whispered something about welcoming her home and then fled. She moved from there to the strange sense she'd had when she walked into the Miller farmhouse, and how everything had seemed oddly familiar. When she got to the part about the doll, her voice quavered just a little, coming to a stop when Brock reached out and ran his hand down her arm. His touch, curiously enough, gave her the strength to continue her story.

"I almost fainted dead away when I saw that faceless doll sitting in the chair, and then everyone started acting really bizarre when I asked them who the doll belonged to and where it had been purchased."

"And what exactly was so special about this particular doll?" Brock asked.

"I have one exactly like it. Her name is Martha. She's a raggedy old thing and she doesn't have a face. The doll at the Millers' house didn't have a face either. It was sitting in this little chair, like it was special, or . . . I don't know how to explain it, but it was . . . disturbing, and no one would talk to me about it."

She was not exactly reassured when Brock moved closer to her, took her hand in his, gave it a squeeze, and suddenly looked a little too intense as his gaze locked with hers.

"How long have you had Martha?"

"I've always had her. She goes with me whenever I'm on the road, but . . ." She bit her lip. "I think she's probably lost to me forever since she was in the Mini Cooper, which is, as I'm sure you'll remember, sitting on the bottom of the lake."

"It's not," Brock countered. "That's one of the things I was going to tell you. The Millersburg dive team found it, and then they swam down the towing cables that Ed, of Ed's Garage, provided them. After attaching those cables, Ed somehow managed to work his magic and pull the car from the lake with his tow truck."

"They have a dive team in Millersburg?"

"I think you might be missing the main point of all this. They got your car out of the lake."

With her lips curving at the corners, Margo shook her head. "It's been a long day, and yes, the car . . . out of the lake, and . . ." She tilted her head. "Did they retrieve my luggage?"

"They did, although I'm afraid there was a little mishap. One of the pieces went missing."

"Did it sink as they were towing out the car?"

"Someone stole it."

A tingle of what felt exactly like tiny little spiders began crawling up her back. "I suppose I shouldn't be surprised, especially with the popularity of eBay and the lure of making some easy money. Do you know which suitcase went missing?"

"I'm hoping you'll find it good news that it was the one that held your shoes in it, since I get the impression you probably have a lot more of those at home."

"I have to admit that I do have way more pairs waiting for me at home than I should. And as odd as this may sound, this isn't the first time someone has stolen my shoes." She blew out a breath. "I once found a pair of Ugg boots of mine that went missing at my gym up for sale on an e-site. It gave me the willies and a queasy stomach when I saw that someone purchased them for over a thousand bucks."

"We already have people watching the e-sites for your shoes."

"I wouldn't want them back, although the Christian Louboutin strappy sandals were really cool, but thinking of some thief running his hands over them." She shuddered and then froze when she remembered what else had been packed in that particular suitcase.

"My doll, Martha, was in that suitcase."

"Are you sure about that?"

"Of course I'm sure. It's a special suitcase, one made specifically for shoes, and I use one of the separated compartments to provide Martha with more protection when we travel."

Blowing out a breath, Brock looked out over the pond, settling into silence for a long moment before he turned back to her. "I keep getting the strangest feeling—you know, the ones that just won't go away—that we're missing something, and all this must have some sort of common thread."

"A common thread?" Margo repeated.

"Yes, something that will tie everything together with a big red bow. The theories running through my thoughts seem incredibly far-fetched and unlikely, yet they keep coming to mind, time and time again."

"Maybe they'd get out of your head if you spoke

them out loud, like how you can get a song out of your head if you belt it out instead of allowing it to turn into an earworm."

Taking hold of her hand, something Margo couldn't claim she didn't enjoy, Brock simply held it as he looked out over the pond again. Content to leave him to his thoughts because she had a feeling he was guy who enjoyed quiet to figure things out, Margo closed her eyes and allowed the sounds of the night to flow through her.

When Brock squeezed her hand a few minutes later, she opened her eyes and found him watching her.

"Any luck puzzling out that common thread?" she asked.

"I'm not sure."

"Why don't you tell me exactly what you're thinking?"

"I'm not sure that's a good idea."

Margo blinked. "Why not?"

"Because there's a very good chance that if I do that, you're going to think I've lost my mind."

"People who have lost their minds aren't normally concerned about people believing they've lost their minds, so I don't think you need to worry about that."

A ghost of a smile played around the corners of his lip. "An excellent point, so having said that, I'm just going to get all of this out there as fast as I can."

Brock squeezed her hand again, drew in a deep breath, blew it out, and then met her gaze with his.

"I don't think you were born Margo Hartman, and I don't think your parents are your biological mom and dad."

Whatever Margo had been expecting him to say, that had never crossed her mind, and for a minute, she thought she'd misheard him.

"I'm sorry, but . . . what?"

"Oh, I'm making a complete mess of this, aren't I?"

"I would have to agree."

"Okay, let me try again." Brock leaned closer to her. "Over twenty years ago, in this very town, three Amish children disappeared from their beds, never to be seen or heard from again . . . until *you* somehow managed to find your way home."

chapter sixteen

The last response Brock expected from Margo after disclosing such life-changing information was a little laugh, followed by another little laugh. Before he knew it, she was practically howling as she dashed a hand over eyes that were beginning to water.

Wondering if maybe he should have approached the subject a little differently, especially since Margo clearly hadn't gotten the message he'd wanted her to get, Brock leaned back on his elbows and simply waited for Margo's amusement to run its course.

Sucking in a gulp of air, and then soothing a hand over Gabby's head since the duck had started quacking the moment Margo began laughing like a hyena, she finally let out a last hiccup of amusement. Wiping her eyes again, this time with the apron she just then seemed to realize she had at her disposal, she moved Henry's head gently away from her leg where the dog had taken to snoozing, the moving not disturbing him at all. Getting to her feet, she stepped from the tablecloth to the grass.

"That was hilarious," she began. "Exactly what I needed on what has got to be the strangest day of my life. I *really* enjoyed the dramatic tone of your voice when you told the part about the missing children."

"Ah . . ." was his brilliant response to that, a response Margo didn't seem to hear since she began strolling for the pond, stopping at the very edge of it and dipping a toe into the water. Turning back to him, she flashed a smile.

"I know I'm dressed the part of an Amish woman at the moment, which must have been your inspiration to make up such a tale. But can you really picture me as Amish in real life?" She shook her head and continued before he could answer, which was fortunate since he still had| no idea how he'd messed everything up so horribly, or how he was going to get the conversation back on the right track.

"I'm the complete opposite of an Amish woman." She lifted the hem of her Amish dress, pulling it up to about her knees as she lifted a leg and nodded toward it. "I have my legs waxed, indulge in spray tans, have my hair highlighted and styled on a regular basis, and I love fashion."

"Hmm . . ." was all he could get out this time before she plowed on with the differences between her and the Amish. And while he would have loved to have been able to say his "Hmm" was a result of him trying to formulate an eloquent response, it was more likely due to the fact his attention was now firmly directed to the riveting sight of her legs.

It was almost as though he'd never seen a woman's calf before, or the intriguing turn of an ankle, or maybe it was because she was almost completely covered up, which drew attention to her bare legs, the woolen stockings she'd been avoiding putting on that morning nowhere to be found.

". . . add in the idea that I have personal assistants who run all my errands for me, and I don't know how much more removed I could be from the Amish. I even have one assistant, Fauna, who ordered a BeDazzler specifically to add bling to some of the designer jeans I own after I mentioned I wished they had a little more sparkle to them." She looked down and gestured to the less-than-fashionable outfit she was currently wearing. "I can't imagine not having a different look every day. That right there proves I'm far too shallow to be Amish. I also don't like animals, love flashy cars, adore diamonds, and I have a completely frivolous career, one that doesn't seem to have a lot of substance to it."

That had him pulling his attention from her legs. Getting to his feet, he walked over to join her, reaching out to take hold of her hand. "Why would you think your career as a singer doesn't have a lot of substance to it?"

Margo wrinkled her nose. "I'm not exactly sure why I just said that, since it's not something I've really considered before, but . . ." She bit her lip. "I'm not saving any lives, haven't invented anything that will advance civilization, and I don't feel as if I really do enough to earn the exorbitant amount of money I make, which makes my career seem frivolous."

"I think you're selling yourself short. Your music provides people with an escape, while your concerts, what with all the attention to detail I understand goes into each show, prove you work incredibly hard to make certain your fans enjoy your performance and feel as if they've gotten their money's worth for the price of a ticket."

"It's just entertainment, Brock, not a cure for cancer."

"Art in all its forms, be it music, sculpture, literature, or commercial fiction, is a medicine for the soul, Margo. You should never forget that. You've been given a true gift, and I would imagine you're doing exactly what God wanted you to do with that gift—sharing it."

Tilting her head, she considered him as the seconds ticked by until she finally smiled. It wasn't the professional smile he'd seen her summon up at will, but a genuine one. It was soft and sweet and left him with the distinct urge to pull her close and never let her go.

"Thank you for that, Brock. It's nice to hear a different perspective, and one I hadn't really thought about." She gave his hand a squeeze. "There certainly does seem to be something about this place that has me looking at my life differently."

"Which is never a bad thing, but I don't think you need to dwell too long on the idea that you have a frivolous career. I've seen some of your performances."

She immediately arched a brow his way. "Should I assume you've been perusing YouTube since I know you've never been to one of my live performances since you didn't recognize me at first?"

"Which I think you found delightful, even if you're not admitting that."

Margo narrowed her eyes on him before she grinned. "You're right. I did like it that you didn't know who I was, a situation that rarely happens to me these days. It was refreshing."

"I still felt like an idiot when I found out how famous you are. It's not like I'd *never* heard of you."

"You just weren't a fan."

"Something that has since changed after watching those clips from YouTube, which you were right about. I did Google you and then watch quite a few of your performances." He smiled. "You sing some catchy turns, which have now, thankfully, replaced that ringtone you have on your phone that kept repeating itself over and over in my mind."

"I'm thinking about changing that to a duck call."

"Which is certainly a cause for concern, but getting back to your concerts. Tell me this, how did you manage to walk across the stage in those boots you wore on the last day of your national tour, let alone dance in them?"

"It was not without difficulty, and I fully blame Sebastian for those boots in the first place. He's great at styling me to look fashionable, but I'm pretty sure you'd never see him in six-inch heels." She nodded to the pair of sensible, rubber-soled shoes Mrs. Hershberger gave her that were lying abandoned in the grass. "Those, I'm sad to say, are like fluffy clouds for your feet. It's really too bad they don't make stylish shoes that comfortable, but that right there is another argument against the idea I could possibly be Amish. I would never abandon style for comfort for long. And that attitude I know came directly from my mom, Caroline."

The mention of her argument regarding the Amish left Brock wondering again how he'd managed to allow his disclosure to go so horribly, horribly wrong. Knowing he had to at least try to get that turned around, he kept hold of Margo's hand and led her back to their picnic spot. He waited until she took a seat directly beside a still-snoozing Henry before he joined her.

Watching as Margo settled Gabby into her lap, he leaned back on an elbow, using the time it took her to place Gabby exactly right to rethink how he should disclose information that could very well change her entire world.

Unfortunately, nothing came to him. Because of that, when she turned his way with a look on her face that could only be described as expectant, he had absolutely no words at his disposal.

"So where were we?" she asked, clearly not experiencing the problem with words he was.

Thinking it might be a little abrupt to begin this tricky conversation again with a *you're not exactly who you've always believed* comment, he settled for "We were talking about your doll."

"A subject I don't think I want to discuss further since poor Martha will soon be put up for sale, along with a bit about me having owned her at one time. Then the tabloids will put out all sorts of speculation as to why Margo Hartman was so attached to a doll with no face."

"Why *were* you so attached to that doll?"

"I don't know. Maybe because I'd had it forever."

Seeing an opportunity to direct the conversation where he need it to go, he leaned toward her. "Why do you think everyone started acting so strange back at the Miller house when you questioned them about the doll they had there, the one just like your Martha?"

Margo bit her lip, seemed to give his question consideration, then drew in a sharp breath. Her eyes turned the size of saucers before she leaned closer to him, the action almost having them touching. "Maybe someone in the Miller family stole my suitcase and they were acting so weird because I showed up at their house, told them I had a doll just like the one sitting in their house, and . . . What if that doll was actually Martha, and I just didn't realize that at the time?"

"Was that doll exactly like your Martha?"

Margo suddenly seemed to deflate. "You know, that doll might have had a different color dress on, something I didn't realize until just now. But, why would the Millers have acted so strangely, and . . . ?" She held up a hand. "I don't want to hear they acted that way because they think I'm one of those missing Amish children, who just happened, because of an encounter with a duck of all things, to stop by Millersburg, the scene of a long-ago crime."

"But what if you *are* one of those children?"

Margo reached out and touched his arm. "I don't really know how to go about saying this because it's rather sensitive. But, since you're being so tenacious, is this really about me, some missing Amish children, and a mystery that's never been solved? Or is this just a way for you to avoid something you may have learned about your sister today?"

"Why would you think that?"

She withdrew her hand. "Sometimes people

try to distract themselves from their own problems by turning their attention to someone else's problems. I just thought maybe, with that note Ian drove out to you today, that you'd learned something disappointing. And because of that, you're focusing on slightly deranged theories to explain the weirdness that's going on in Millersburg right now."

"I'm afraid that note wasn't about Stephanie, although I think Ian was hoping it was a clue about her at first. He's desperate to find answers that might allow him to find a sense of peace, but that note had nothing to do with Stephanie. Quite honestly, if it had, it would have been the first lead discovered about my sister."

"You haven't found any leads?"

"Nope. I only have my instincts which say she didn't commit suicide, just like the instincts Ian has as well."

"Have you ever considered talking to someone *besides* Ian about Stephanie?"

Stretching out his legs, Brock frowned. "I've spoken to the local police about her death, as well as to some fellow members of the sheriff's department and my associates with the FBI. But I've never really talked *about Stephanie* to anyone but Ian. Not since she died."

"Maybe that's why you haven't made much progress. Maybe because of your emotions you're so focused on certain details, or certain scenarios you've thought up about how she could have died, that you're missing the obvious."

"I don't think that's true at all."

"Perhaps not, but humor me. Tell me about her. How exactly did she die?"

Turning his attention back to the pond, Brock watched the lightning bugs flicker off and on. "She was found hanging from a rafter in an old barn just outside of Millersburg. Her death was ruled a suicide by the local authorities. But as I said before, I'm not convinced that's what happened. However, the reality is, as I implied earlier, that I'm no closer today to discovering the truth than I was months ago when I first arrived in Millersburg. And with every passing day, her case gets closer and closer to going cold forever."

"Were you close to her?"

The corners of Brock's mouth curved. "I was. She was younger, the typical pest of a little sister while we were growing up. She used to insist on joining in with all the neighborhood football games, at the same time insisting we didn't treat her like a girl." His lips quirked into a smile as memories traipsed through his mind. "She never knew this, but I always had a talk with the guys, made sure they knew if anyone tackled her, hurt her, or made fun of her, they'd be sorry."

"She knew you did that," Margo said with a touch of a laugh. "We girls always know stuff like that. Not that I had a brother, but if I did, I'd want one exactly like you. A brother who'd protect me no matter how bratty I was, or how annoying I could be at times."

"I didn't do a very good job of protecting Stephanie in the end."

"How old was she when she died?"

"Stephanie was almost two years younger than me, so she was twenty-nine when she died. Had just turned twenty-nine, in fact."

Margo tilted her head. "Hmm. So she was definitely an adult, married, had a career, and yet you feel her death was *your* fault?"

"I've made it my career to protect people, Margo. In fact, I've tried to do that my whole life. I failed Stephanie, even if it does turn out she took her own life, which I still highly doubt. I should have known something was wrong. I didn't, and because of that, I failed her."

"That's ridiculous."

"I've failed you as well. In case you've forgotten, let me remind you that you were standing right next to me when you were shot. I certainly didn't prevent the shooting, and I don't have a clue who could have pulled the trigger. That's failure at its finest."

Margo waved his comment aside. "Again, ridiculous. Since it seems relatively clear the shooting was not caused by one of my stalkers, it's a complete mystery to *everyone* who'd want me dead. That right there is why my being shot is not your fault. You can't protect people from a threat no one knows is pursuing them. So, stop being so hard on yourself."

"I don't deserve to be anything but hard on myself—not until I find some answers about what's going on in Millersburg, and what really happened to my sister."

"Maybe someone in this town has made it a point to deliberately bury any and all leads about your sister."

"How so?"

Margo shrugged. "It's a weird town, Brock, and it has a definite weird vibe to it. Something is wrong here. You know it, I know it, and probably everybody knows it, but nobody seems to know what that something is. That just goes to show you that sometimes secrets remain secret and loose ends remain loose. Or you've been missing the obvious because of your closeness to the case."

For a second, he simply sat there, feeling as if someone had just bounced a two-by-four off his head.

Margo was right.

He'd been so focused on trying to find clues that would fit a motive for a murder—such as obsession, jealousy, or greed—he'd failed to see the obvious.

All the weirdness surrounding Millersburg could very well be . . . connected.

The vanishing Amish children, Stephanie's death, Margo arriving in town, her distinct resemblance to Sarah Yoder . . . and a doll that had freaked Margo out and had caused everyone in the Miller family, along with the Hershberger sisters, to act in a way that could only be described as suspicious.

Forcing his gaze to meet Margo's, he nodded. "What would you say if I told you I think we may have traveled to this place, at this exact point in time, because God is allowing us an opportunity to answer questions that have been left unanswered for a very long time, *and* right some very dark wrongs that occurred in this very town?"

Margo blinked, blinked again, and then her lips began to curve. "I would think . . . sure? Why not?" And then, she began inching straight away from him and straight off the tablecloth they were still sitting on.

Laughing, Brock pushed up to his feet. "I'm not crazy, Margo, although I realize I might sound like it." He held out his hand, and wasn't really surprised when, instead of taking it, she handed him the duck.

Tucking Gabby into the crook of his arm, he waited until Margo got to her feet before he smiled. "It's all related, Margo. You, my sister, those dolls, Mrs. Hershberger taking such an unusual interest in you, and then . . . there's your mom."

"What does my mom have to do with anything?"

"She has answers, I know she does. But she's not cooperating with me. That's why we're going to go and pay her a little visit, and the sooner the better I say."

Margo took Gabby back and then put her on the ground when she began to quack, the quacking stopping in an instant as the duck waddled back to the pond. Turning back to him once Gabby hit the water, Margo brows drew together. "You're not still going on about me being some long-forgotten, missing Amish girl, are you?"

"That right there is what you need to ask your mom. But, until we track her down, and given your obvious skepticism, I think it might be best if I don't say another word about you being a missing Amish girl—even if, well, I'm pretty sure that's exactly who you are."

chapter seventeen

By the time Margo fished Gabby out of the pond, requiring her to wade into the murky waters since Gabby apparently didn't want to leave, evening had turned to night on the farm.

Handing the duck over to Brock since she definitely didn't want Gabby to take off for the water again, Margo wiped the muck the pond had left on her feet the best she could on the grass. Walking over to where she'd left her clunky shoes, she slipped them on her feet and lifted her head.

"Can I hope you came to your senses about that Amish conspiracy theory you seem to be clinging to while I was fetching Gabby?"

Instead of providing her with the answer she wanted to hear, Brock whistled for Henry, handed Gabby back to her, tucked the handle of the picnic basket over his arm, and then smiled. "I told you, I'm not discussing that particular subject until we're with your mom. But not to be difficult, I must point out that it's probably more likely that an honest-to-goodness Amish woman would proclaim she's been off *fetching* a duck than a woman who's . . . well . . . not."

"You've obviously lost your mind." Lifting her chin, Margo marched away from him, having to stop just a little way into her march because she had no idea where the path leading back to the farmhouse was. She hadn't even thought about bringing a flashlight with her, which made finding her way in the darkness a little tricky.

A beam of light suddenly flashed just before Brock strode up beside her. To give the man his due, he didn't say a single thing about her not knowing where she was going. He just took hold of her arm, turned her around, and started forward, whistling what almost sounded like a Barry Manilow song under his breath.

"I would have never taken you for a Manilow fan," she said as they walked into the forest.

"Love Manilow, as well as Sting, All That Remains, The Cars, and The Doors. You gotta love The Doors."

With that, Brock launched into a rousing discussion about what bands he thought were great and which ones he thought were overrated. By the time they reached the farmhouse, she knew he hated disco, loved the Rat Pack, and was still iffy on whether or not he was a supporter of tribute bands.

"I mean, they're not the actual bands, so it's tough to go to a club and listen to them unless they're really, really good," he said, coming to a stop.

"I don't think I've ever heard a tribute band before, but that's probably because it's not a good idea for me to just show up in public." She smiled. "Tends to draw, well, mobs." She nodded to the farmhouse where there wasn't a single light on. "It doesn't look like anyone is still up. Do you think I should knock on the door?"

"I'm not sure." Brock flicked the flashlight over the porch. "But Mrs. Hershberger seems to be waiting for us. She's sitting in the rocker over there."

"There's a part of me that hopes Mrs. Hershberger will tell me everyone's sleeping. But there's the other part of me, the one that knows my rushing away from the house earlier was not my finest hour, that needs me to go inside and apologize for my behavior."

Brock moved closer to her. "While I'm sure you think you might have overreacted, from what you told me, you had some valid reasons for running off. It's not exactly normal behavior for a woman to burst into tears like Esta did when she first saw you. And, I would have been freaked out as well if I'd seen another faceless doll that looked exactly like one I had, if I was the doll-owning type that is."

Before she could say anything to that, she caught sight of Mrs. Hershberger walking toward them.

"Ah, there you are. I was getting worried."

"How long have you been waiting for us?" Margo asked as she set Gabby down in the grass and moved to meet her. She was taken by complete surprise when Mrs. Hershberger pulled her into a strong embrace and held her tight for a long moment.

"I'm so sorry, my dear Margo. This was all my fault." She released her hold on Margo, stepped back, and then smoothed a stray piece of Margo's hair away from her face.

"It was *my* fault, Mrs. Hershberger. I reacted impulsively and I shouldn't have run off." She nodded to the house. "Are the Millers still awake?"

"No. But I don't believe it would be wise for you to speak to them just yet anyway. Esta is not in a good way right now, and I should have listened to Amos in the first place. He cautioned me against meddling in this nasty business, but I pressed him, convinced I was doing the right thing."

She tucked Margo's hand into the crook of her arm, and turned her toward where her sister's horse and buggy stood waiting. "I had Anna take Nellie and leave the buggy so you, Brock, and I could leave the farm tonight. I can drive you to my home, where I'm sure Brock will insist on guarding you all night. Or I can take you somewhere else. It's the least I can do after all the trouble I've caused."

Turning to ask Brock where he wanted Mrs. Hershberger to take them, Margo found him looking at his phone, then texting a response to someone before he tucked it into his back pocket and walked up to join them. Gabby waddled at his feet.

"That was an associate of mine, Agent Colby." He turned a smile Mrs. Hershberger's way. "You waited for us."

"I couldn't very well have left, not with the mess I created." Mrs. Hershberger blew out a rather resigned-sounding breath. "I knew better than to meddle; it's simply not our way. And yet I justified that meddling by convincing myself everything was lining itself into place. I'm afraid instead I've just made matters worse."

Brock shook his head. "I'm sure you haven't. But since I've just had word from Agent Colby that Margo's mom is in a bit of a state at the Hotel Millersburg, if you wouldn't mind dropping us off there, I would appreciate it. And you can tell us more about why you were meddling in the first place during the drive there."

Not leaving anyone time to voice an argument or ask questions, Brock headed for the buggy, then turned around as Gabby suddenly started putting up a fuss. Striding back to where the duck was standing, he picked her up. But instead of taking her to the buggy, he headed for the barn.

"Where are you going with my duck?" Margo called.

"She's going to have a nice rest in the barn, in

the nice stall little Hannah Miller showed me earlier, and she's going to love it. So there's no need for you to worry."

"But she's not from this farm. She's from the Yoder farm, and what if she gets lonely and misses me?"

Brock, annoyingly enough, did not bother to respond to that, but vanished from sight into the darkness, reappearing a short time later.

Cocking an ear, Margo listened for any quacks of distress, but only the sound of crickets came back to her.

"She's fine, has already settled in, and tomorrow, if it'll make you feel better, we'll come get her and take her over to the Yoder farm so she can visit her family."

"But what if she decides she wants to stay with them?" Margo asked, climbing into the buggy as Brock helped Mrs. Hershberger up.

"Then you'll wish Gabby the best, and leave her to live a long and happy life with her own kind," Brock said, walking around the buggy to climb up right beside her.

Mrs. Hershberger finished lighting a lantern that hung beside her on the buggy and picked up the reins. With a click of her tongue and a flick of her wrists, she got the horse moving down the dirt lane.

"That's good advice, that is." Mrs. Hershberger turned to nod at Brock. "I should have taken advice like that before I got everyone involved in this mess. I don't know what I was thinking. I was raised Amish, then married a man who was Mennonite, and I have been told all of my many years on this earth that we are to mind our own business and live our lives apart from mainstream society." She shook her head. "I chose not to embrace that idea, involving myself in matters that should not have concerned me. But worse yet, involving others in those matters, like Esta Miller, who is now suffering greatly from what I put into motion."

"Those *matters,* as you call them, concern the children who went missing from this very town over twenty years ago, don't they?" Brock asked.

Before Margo could remind him that he'd said he wasn't going to bring up that business until after they had a chance to speak to her mom, Mrs. Hershberger sat forward.

"So you found out about them, did you?"

Brock sat forward as well and raised a single brow at Mrs. Hershberger. "I don't know why you'd be surprised about that, especially since I've been coming to the conclusion that you and Anna are responsible for leaving that note for Ian."

Shaking her head in a sad sort of way, Mrs. Hershberger released a sigh. "We shouldn't have left that note. We only did so because we thought if someone could be pointed in the right direction, maybe we'd finally get some answers, and maybe, just maybe, the poor mothers who lost their sweet babies would be able to put the worries they've been holding close to their hearts all these many, many years to rest."

Margo's ears began to fill with that odd buzzing noise she was almost becoming used to, having experienced it so often lately. Clearing a throat that had gone remarkably dry, she forced words out of her mouth she didn't really want to force.

"So there really *was* an abduction of Amish children from this town?"

Mrs. Hershberger glanced Margo's way, then pressed her lips tightly together, for all of five seconds. "I've vowed not to concern myself further in this matter, dear, but you have a right to know why Esta Miller behaved so strangely with you today. She lost her sweet Rebecca all those years ago, the girl stolen straight out of her bed in the very farmhouse we just left. And even though I thought I'd explained myself well to Amos and Esta, centering around the idea I didn't think you were Esta's daughter, Rebecca, I apparently didn't explain well enough. I thought for certain that mentioning your resemblance to Sarah Yoder would put any false hope aside, but . . ." Her voice trailed off and she took to settling into silence, lost in thought.

"But I wasn't adopted," Margo said softly, reaching out a hand to touch Mrs. Hershberger's arm. "My mom has pictures of me from when I was a newborn, and she had someone put them into those fancy scrapbooks for her. She has pictures of me being bathed as an infant, and sitting on Santa's lap when I'm not even a year old, and . . . well, the pictures go on from there."

"You might not be one of the missing children," Mrs. Hershberger said with a small inclination of her head. "But Esta was hoping you'd turn out to be her missing daughter. I'm afraid the disappointment in seeing that you don't resemble any of her children, but that you do bear a remarkable resemblance to the Yoder children, was too much for her. She wasn't ready to deal with what she sees as a loss of hope, and that's why she ran from you and then refused to explain that the doll you saw belonged to her daughter, Rebecca."

"I only wanted an explanation because I have a doll just like hers. It doesn't have a face, which I've always found weird. So when I saw that doll at the farmhouse, I was curious."

"Amish dolls never have faces, dear, just like the Amish don't want their pictures taken, believing their images are not meant to be captured."

Something that felt very much like fear crept through Margo's veins, brought on by information that almost seemed to lend truth to what Brock had been saying. Finding herself incapable of stringing another sentence together as her thoughts turned into one big jumble, she was spared any response at all when Brock spoke up.

"Do you know why Sarah Yoder or anyone in her family hasn't bothered to try to come see Margo? It's apparently become common knowledge throughout the Amish community that Margo bears a striking resemblance to Sarah, and Sarah saw Margo herself."

Mrs. Hershberger gave the barest hint of a nod. "The Yoder family seems to have decided it isn't their place to meddle in this, Brock. I'm sure, though, if legitimate leads concerning the case come to light, they will step forward at some point. Until then, I think they're of the belief that it would be better for them to simply wait and see."

Then, as if she'd just that moment decided a wait-and-see attitude was the attitude to embrace, Mrs. Hershberger refused to say another thing about the missing children. She spent the remainder of the buggy ride talking about how young ladies shouldn't neglect to realize when a fine man came into their lives. Her less-than-subtle and incredibly unexpected attempts at matchmaking left Margo's face rather warm, while leaving Brock suspiciously shaking on the seat beside her, pretending an interest in the scenery that couldn't really be seen since it was pitch black outside.

Relief was the most prevalent emotion she felt when Mrs. Hershberger pulled up in front of the Hotel Millersburg—although that relief turned to amusement when Mrs. Hershberger, after Brock and Margo had climbed from the carriage, turned her matchmaking attentions to Brock. She encouraged him in a very grandmotherly fashion to make certain to take Margo out for a nice meal, because it was everyone's job to fatten up "that poor girl." With that, and a wink sent Margo's way, she flicked the reins, wished them a pleasant night, and trundled off down the street.

"And here I thought the day couldn't get any stranger." Brock took Margo's arm. "Now, remember, you're not supposed to be Margo right now. You're an Amish woman, but keep your head down because we don't want anyone to recognize you."

Dropping her chin, Margo allowed her shoulders to slump, and then walked behind Brock a little as he moved into the hotel, not bothering to stop at the front desk but moving directly to the elevator and pushing the button for Caroline's floor.

Once the door closed, Margo raised her head. "Do you know, I've just realized I never questioned a single thing about who this Agent Colby is, or what kind of state my mom's in, or why an agent is with her in the first place."

"Which I, for one, was relieved about, because I

wasn't sure how you'd feel learning the FBI is more involved in this case now that we've uncovered the bit about the missing children. Your mother is in a state because I sent an agent to watch over her, and apparently she doesn't like that."

"You requested that an FBI agent look after my mom?"

"It was more of a case of watching her to make sure she didn't do anything suspicious, or leave town until I got the answers I wanted from her, but . . ."

"You think my mom has done something . . . criminal?"

"Well, that depends on if you're one of those children who was abducted, and if she knew anything about it."

The elevator stopped, dinged, and the door opened, but Margo didn't move a muscle. "You didn't already bring this whole business up with my mom did you?"

"Not exactly, although I did ask her if you were adopted. But that didn't go over very well, because after she assured me she had a birth certificate to prove you were her daughter, which I thought was a strange way to phrase a response, she just stopped talking except to tell me she wanted to go back to her hotel. I left her here, had Agent Colby come over to watch her, and that's all I know at this point."

Even though her mom annoyed her on a

frequent basis, and Margo had driven straight out of California what seemed like years ago because of that annoyance, Caroline was still her mother. Because of that, and because she knew her mom would be beside herself by now with an FBI agent watching her, Margo squared her shoulders and stepped out of the elevator. Unfortunately, before she could march more than a few steps down the hallway, she had to stop and wait for Brock to catch up with her since she had no idea what room her mom was in.

Gentleman that he was, Brock didn't even crack a smile as he took her arm, walked her down the hallway, and stopped at the very end, right in front of a door where a man about Brock's age sat in a chair. He looked exactly like he'd been dealing with Caroline all evening.

His short brown hair was rumpled, he had dark circles under his eyes, and because he was currently rubbing his temples, it was clear he'd had one of *those* days.

"Sorry it took us so long to get here, Colby."

A smile of clear relief flashed across his face at Brock's words. "I'm just glad you're here, but . . . traffic wasn't bad, was it?"

"We came by horse and buggy."

Looking past Brock, the man's eyes widened as he got to his feet, flashed a grin her way, and then leaned closer to her and lowered his voice. "Love your work, Ms. Hartman."

"This is Agent James Colby, Margo," Brock said quietly, and after exchanging greetings with her, Agent Colby went to the door, put a key card in it, and then stepped aside.

"Mrs. Hartman is currently taking a bath and singing Elvis songs, which is an improvement over what she was doing two hours ago when she ordered every dessert on the room service menu and ate those desserts until . . . well, it wasn't pretty."

Armed with that disturbing information, Margo thanked the man and stepped through the door, finding a charming suite complete with a sitting room, separate bedroom, and a door in the bedroom that apparently led to the bathroom.

A horrible rendition of "Love Me Tender" was drifting through the bathroom door, so after she sent Brock to a chair in the sitting room, she moved to that door and gave it a rap.

"Who is it?" her mom belted out in a singsong way that wasn't exactly reassuring.

"It's me, Mom. Let me in."

"Margo, honey? Is that you?"

"Since I'm fairly sure I'm the only one who calls you Mom, yes, it's me, your daughter, here to have a mother-daughter chat."

"Did you bring wine?"

"No, I did not bring wine, and in case you've forgotten, I don't drink. So why would I have brought wine?"

"Because I, your mom, love wine, but no one will bring me any, even though I called and asked room service to bring me up a bottle or two hours ago. They never did."

Vowing that she would definitely be leaving the staff at the Hotel Millersburg a hefty tip for that courtesy, Margo jiggled the doorknob, blinking when she found the door was unlocked. "Are you decent?" she called through the door.

"I'm in the tub, so not really," her mom called back. "I do have bubbles in the tub with me, though."

Thanking God for that small favor, Margo opened the door. Her mom was reclining in a tub full of bubbles with her blonde hair piled into a messy knot on top of her head. Caroline's gaze was trained on the door, and as soon as she focused in on Margo, her eyes turned about as large as the platters Mrs. Hershberger had served breakfast on, a meal that seemed as if it had occurred years ago instead of hours.

"What have you done to yourself?" Caroline whispered. "You've let those weirdoes pull you right into their cult, haven't you?"

"Mom, this is my latest disguise." She smiled and twirled around. "It's good, isn't it?"

"Disturbing would have been the word I would have chosen, but . . ." Her eyes narrowed on Margo's head. "What happened to your hair?"

Margo raised a hand, realizing that the prayer

cap had slipped back to the middle of her head, exposing the bright platinum color her hair had turned after her unfortunate hair incident. "Just a little coloring problem, but I've always wanted to see if I could pull off the Marilyn Monroe thing."

"You can't, and why is it short?"

"All I'm going to say in explanation is that those warnings you always see on hair coloring products really do need to be taken far more seriously than we do."

Caroline opened her mouth, but before she could get out even a word of the lecture Margo knew she was about to begin, a cell phone sitting beside her on the ledge of the over-sized tub began to ring. Leaning over to read the screen, Caroline's forehead puckered before she leaned back and smiled Margo's way.

"It's your dad. Would you be a darling and see what he wants?"

Talking to her dad was the last thing she wanted to do after the day she'd had, but knowing he, just like her mom, would continue calling back until someone answered, she walked across the bathroom and picked up the phone. Sliding her finger across the front of the touch screen, she brought it to her ear.

"Hi, Dad."

For a second, there was no response, but only for a second. "Margo? What are you doing with Caroline's phone?"

"She's in the tub and asked me to answer for her."

"Are you both still in Millersburg?"

"We are."

"I'm very disappointed in you, Margo. You should have confided in me from the start regarding your true plans, instead of pulling off a ruse behind my back. Nevertheless, there's not been much harm done, and I'll be returning with the jet to the Akron airport tomorrow. I'll send your mother a text as to what time I want both of you to be there. And Margo, don't even think about disappointing me again by not showing up. You won't like the consequences. I can guarantee you that."

"I'm not sure meeting you at the airport tomorrow is feasible at this point. The FBI has come to Millersburg, and I think they may want to question Mom."

"About what?"

Ignoring the fact that her dad's voice had turned as cold as ice, Margo swallowed, considered what she was about to say for all of a second, then opened her mouth. "They seem to think Mom might have some information that could assist them in solving a cold case that happened over twenty years ago. A case, from what little I understand, concerning some abducted Amish children, one whom some people seem to believe is . . . me."

Silence was her dad's only response to that, but as the silence continued, Margo realized he'd hung up on her.

Frowning at the phone for a second, Margo looked back to see Caroline watching her warily. Returning the phone to the ledge of the bathtub, Margo pulled over a small vanity stool, took a seat, and simply considered her mom for a long minute.

"You really need to change out of that hideous dress, darling," was the first thing Caroline opted to say as she lifted a leg and scrubbed it with a loofah. "It's beginning to freak me out."

"A lot of things are freaking me out at the moment, Mom, the least of which is this dress."

"I really don't think I'm in the mood to have a serious mother-daughter discussion, especially without wine."

"I'm not ordering you wine, and I'm going to have to insist on the mother-daughter thing."

"You were far more fun when you were a child and I got to act like the parent," Caroline muttered before she soaped her other leg with the loofah.

"That's because I was probably six. Explain to me why Brock Moore seems to believe there's a very good chance I'm adopted."

Caroline pressed her plump lips together, kept them that way for a few seconds, then smiled as if she'd come up with the perfect explanation. "Because he's unhinged, dear. That sad state of affairs is because of his sister—or, er, maybe it was his mother—dying."

"He's not unhinged. Try again."

"If you were adopted, you'd look nothing like me."

"I don't look anything like you. Or Dad either, for that matter."

"We share the same hair color."

"Because you get Sebastian to color it every few weeks."

Caroline lifted her chin. "I'm a natural blonde."

"You're not. You have brown hair. I saw a picture of you once over at Grandmother's house, before she died."

Narrowing her eyes, Caroline bit her lip, and then smiled again. "You take after your grandmother. Everyone always remarked on that."

"No one ever remarked on that. And you have dark eyes, and so does Dad, but mine are light. Explain that."

Sinking down into the bubbles, Caroline shrugged. "You know I've never been very good at that science stuff."

Leaning forward, Margo met her mom's gaze. "I really didn't want to believe, or really even consider, the idea that I might be adopted, but the more you avoid the topic, the more I'm forced to consider it."

"You're not adopted."

"I'm not sure I believe you."

"I told Agent Moore that I have a birth certificate to prove I didn't adopt you."

"And while I should find that reassuring, I have to wonder if that birth certificate was bought and paid for to allow you, when necessary, to pull it out and prove you didn't adopt me."

With her face beginning to mottle, Caroline sank deeper into the bubbles. "I really don't like the way you're implying I've done something wrong, Margo."

"I'm not implying anything, Mom. I'm pretty much saying I think you're lying to me about whether or not I'm adopted."

Caroline slid down another inch. "I resent these unfounded accusations you keep throwing at me. For the last time, we didn't adopt you. I was turned down from all the adoption agencies, something to do with the number of times I'd been in rehab. Because of that, I was afraid I'd never be able to have a child, which was why Robert arranged to buy one for me." She smiled. "So you see, because we bought you instead of adopting you, I haven't lied at all."

chapter eighteen

"You're an FBI agent, right?"

Looking up from the *Vogue* magazine he'd been reading, a copy that must have been Caroline's but had Margo's face splashed across the front cover, Brock found that particular cover girl stomping his way, her color high and her eyes a little . . . scary.

"I thought we'd been over the fact that I'm an FBI agent," he said slowly, setting aside the magazine.

Margo stopped directly in front of him. "Maybe I should have phrased that differently." She cleared her throat and held out her hand. "Since you're an FBI agent, you have to have a gun, so I'd like to borrow that gun . . . *please*."

Sitting back in the chair, Brock considered her for a long moment. "You want to shoot your mom?"

"Don't be ridiculous. I would never deliberately shoot someone. Maybe fire off a shot toward the ceiling, or . . . bathtub . . . to make that person see some reason, but that would be strictly an accident."

"I'm not giving you my gun."

"So you *do* have a gun."

Trying to ignore the fact that Margo Hartman

was incredibly adorable when she was in a temper, Brock crossed his arms over his chest. "I plead the Fifth."

"I was wondering when the attorney in you would come out, but fine, don't give me your gun." She moved to another chair and sat down, leaning forward. "Tell me, how do you normally get criminals to talk?"

"I see we've moved on to thoughts of torture, have we?"

Her lips thinned. "Caroline's gone silent and I need more answers."

"I don't think torturing her, or shooting her, will actually get her to talk."

"We won't know until we give it a go."

Swallowing the completely inappropriate laugh he longed to release, Brock settled for a single nod instead. "There is that. However, since I am beholden to a vow to serve and protect, not shoot a woman who's being stingy with her answers, how about if we start with you telling me what's wrong?"

"I'm *not* adopted."

Brock blinked. "You're . . . not?"

Slouching down in the chair, Margo folded her hands over her stomach. "Nope, I'm not adopted, at least according to . . . Caroline. Instead, I was . . . purchased. For a steep price, I have to imagine—exactly like one would buy a puppy, or a . . . boat."

Brock allowed himself a few moments to absorb that information. It wasn't that he was overly surprised by the idea Robert and Caroline would bypass traditional adoption procedures and fork out money to secure a child. But because they'd secured a child who'd more than likely been abducted, that put a whole new spin on the situation.

Rising from the chair, he headed through the bedroom for the bathroom, stopping when Margo suddenly darted in front of him, blocking his way.

"You need to let me handle this, Margo. A serious crime might very well have been committed, and I have to proceed with that in mind."

"If that's code for *go and wait while I, the big, strong, FBI agent deal with Caroline,* you can forget it. I've obviously been lied to my entire life, and I deserve to be there if she decides to talk, not that I think she will. She's clammed up, probably because she admitted Robert warned her to never disclose that I'd been purchased. Caroline may be a little ditzy at times, but she knows better than to deliberately go against Robert's wishes."

"That's why I need you to stay out here, at least at first. Since she's in the tub, she's not going to be expecting me to come into the bathroom, which will give me the advantage. If I run into any problems or if she just starts talking, I promise you, I'll let you join us. Fair enough?"

Blowing out a breath, Margo nodded, although it was more of a grudging nod than an enthusiastic one. Sending her a smile, Brock stepped around her and moved to the bathroom, opening the door as quietly as he could.

A blast of cold water hit him directly in the face before he even had a chance to shut the door behind him.

Holding up a hand to disperse the stream of water that seemed to be aimed directly for his mouth, as if Caroline was trying to drown him, Brock leaned to the right, blinked water out of his eyes, and found Caroline, who was dressed in a hotel robe, wielding a shower jet. Her aim, unfortunately, was spot on.

"Turn . . . off . . . the water," he managed to get out, moving a foot forward, but then stopping when the water suddenly stopped pelting him in the face.

Taking a second to swipe at his eyes, Brock found the water turning off was a direct result of Margo having stepped into the room. Strangely enough, she was holding a bright red high-heeled sandal in her hand. Glancing to Caroline, Brock saw what looked exactly like horror in the woman's eyes.

"Put the shower head down, Caroline, or I swear the Manolo Blahnik gets it."

Caroline held out a hand. "Not the Manolo Blahnik. You know that's one of my favorite shoes."

Margo ran a finger over the leather. "It's a very soft shoe, isn't it? Must feel like slipping your foot into butter when you put it on, but I don't think it'll feel the same if it gets submerged in, say . . . the toilet?"

"You wouldn't," Caroline breathed out.

Smiling the smile Brock had certainly come to realize was not a good sign, Margo looked at the shoe in her hand, then, calm as you please, broke off the thin heel. Completely ignoring the hiss of disbelief Caroline uttered, she then chucked the shoe, along with the heel, into the toilet bowl. Dusting her hands together, she caught Brock's eye and sent him a wink.

Right there, in the middle of the bathroom, as Caroline started to shriek, Brock realized his life might never be the same again. He'd somehow, much to his surprise, managed to become completely fascinated with a woman who was clearly one of the most unusual women he'd ever met.

"I noticed that you brought a lovely pair of Prada sandals with you," Margo said. "Shall I have a turn at them next?"

Caroline lifted her chin. "I don't think it's a good idea for me to say anything else before I talk things through with Robert."

Margo hitched up the wattage of her smile, turned on her sensible shoe that squeaked as she stomped over the wet bathroom floor, and disappeared through the door. Returning only a few seconds later, and dragging a suitcase behind her, Margo flipped it open. Without so much as a blink of eye she began chucking shoes straight into the filled tub.

By the time the fifth shoe sailed through the air, Caroline was white as a ghost and completely willing to fork over a few answers.

With a nod to the door, Margo marched out of the room again, leaving Caroline behind.

"Her father is going to be furious with me." Caroline padded her way on bare feet after Margo.

"He's obviously not my father," Margo called.

"Of course he is," Caroline called back as she stepped into the bedroom.

Having no idea what was going to happen next, but knowing it probably wasn't wise to leave Margo alone with Caroline for even the shortest span of time, Brock joined the women as they entered the sitting room. He took a seat beside Margo on a small couch. Caroline sat in the chair by the fireplace.

"Start talking," Margo said the moment Brock sat down.

Caroline smoothed back her hair before she shrugged. "I really don't know what more there is to say."

"You could start by telling us where you and Robert found Margo," Brock began.

"I had nothing to do with the details. Robert has always taken care of anything of a difficult nature for me. You should schedule a meeting with him."

Smiling, Brock inclined his head. "Oh, I think we'll be scheduling something with him, but it's not going to be a meeting."

"And are you going to be scheduling something along those lines for me?" Caroline asked slowly.

"I'm afraid so, but what that something might be, well, that depends on how cooperative you are in the next few minutes."

"Jail?"

"That's a possibility, although I'm going to assume you have a more than capable attorney on speed dial. He should be able to plead you out to a lesser charge than kidnapping."

Caroline's mouth dropped open. "Kidnapping? I didn't kidnap anyone. We simply paid a lot of money for a child, and I never heard a word about any kidnapping. From what I understood, the children came from mothers who'd decided to give them up. But they were attractive mothers, ones who were certain to produce good-looking children."

Margo shot straight up from the couch. "You wanted to make certain you got a good-looking child?"

Sinking back against the cushions of her seat, Caroline frowned. "No one would have believed I would give birth to an ugly child, Margo. I mean"—she gestured to herself—"look at me."

Grabbing hold of Margo around her middle as she actually lunged toward Caroline, Brock lifted her feet off the ground, hauled her over to a chair well away from Caroline, and set her down. "Stay."

"I don't like being told what to do."

"Clearly. But we won't get the answers we need if you resort to hair pulling."

"How did you know I was going for her hair?"

"Because you already took care of most of her shoes."

Margo smiled. "It's so weird how well you get me, and we haven't even known each other that long."

He returned the smile. "It's weird all right, and probably should be considered a little closer, but . . ."

"Now is not the time," she finished for him.

"Exactly." Turning back to Caroline, Brock found her studying her nails, looking rather bored. Walking back to the couch, he sat down, and simply waited until Caroline looked up before he continued.

"Were you and Robert incapable of having children of your own?"

Caroline's forehead immediately puckered. "We

never tried that. I never wanted to have a child of my own, not with the damage pregnancy can do to a body. I had no intention of losing my shape for the sake of having a baby. Besides, Robert and I don't enjoy what anyone could call an . . . intimate relationship." She shook her head. "That was one of the main reasons we decided to adopt, but I just didn't know there'd be such scrutiny into our lives by the adoption agencies. That scrutiny, and my occasional stays in rehab, made it next to impossible for us to be approved."

Margo let out a snort. "Yes, frequent drug and alcohol use is normally a deterrent to adoption agencies deciding if a person is capable of caring for a baby."

Caroline went back to studying her nails.

"Tell me about Robert's part in this," Brock said. "I'm surprised he would have gone to such lengths to have a child, what with his obviously narcissistic nature."

"Oh, Robert didn't want a child at all." Caroline looked up. "He only agreed to the idea after I threatened to expose a few of his . . . deviant behaviors to all our friends." She smiled.

"Robert is incredibly careful of the image he projects to the world. And since he wanted to protect that image, while making certain he still had access to that lovely fortune my parents possessed, he did what he had to do to get me what I wanted."

She tapped a finger against her chin. "I was very specific in what I wanted. A blue-eyed—or I said I'd settle for green-eyed—blonde-haired little girl. Not a baby, mind you, since diapers are not my thing, but a little girl who was already two or three years old and needed a good and privileged home."

Brock's temper, one he'd been carefully holding in check, ratcheted up a notch. "And Robert took those specific specifications, and what? Had Margo abducted?"

"I don't know anything about abduction," Caroline said. "Robert has contacts, some legitimate, some not. I'm sure he used those contacts to find a child, but I know Robert wouldn't have personally dirtied his hands with an actual abduction. He's much too fussy for that."

"Tell me about Robert's *not so legitimate* contacts."

"I think I need a glass of wine first."

"We're not in the middle of a cocktail party, Caroline," Margo snapped. "The last thing we need at the moment is for you to have wine."

"I don't like you calling me Caroline."

"And I don't like knowing you bought me like one of your pairs of shoes."

Caroline leveled a cool look on Margo, then deliberately turned her head and settled her attention on Brock. "Robert's family is riddled

275

with black sheep, and I imagine he used one of them to find what I wanted. I don't know any names, though. Robert and I only married because it was convenient for us to do so. My parents were threatening to cut me out of their will if I didn't settle down and abandon my wild ways, and Robert was there to provide me with a way to convince my parents I was heeding their demands. In return for marrying me, he got to enjoy the finer things in life my fortune could provide, and I got to enjoy inheriting my father's entire estate after he died, something that would have been in question if I hadn't married."

Uncertain whether he should continue his questioning while Margo was in the room, especially since the answers to his questions were becoming more and more sordid, Brock glanced Margo's way and found she didn't seem overly distressed. She looked more along the lines of furious. Deciding that fury was going to allow her to deal with the disclosures much better than despair, he drew in a breath and turned back to Caroline.

"Tell me how you got Margo."

"We went to New York City and picked her out."

"You picked me *out* or picked me *up?*" Margo's voice had turned glacial.

"There were three children to choose from, and we were offered first pick. I'm sure that offer cost us a pretty penny, but you should be thankful for it, Margo. I adored you on sight. You were exactly what I wanted and were the prettiest of the bunch, although a bunch might not be the best way to describe it. Again, there were only three children presented to us, two girls and one boy." She sent what almost seemed to be a look of fondness Margo's way. "You were gorgeous even back then, and I had to have you. Plus, you looked similar to the baby pictures I'd found in a scrapbook that I bought in one of those quaint used bookstores, so that was what sealed the deal for me."

"I really *am* one of those missing Amish children, aren't I?"

"You're not Amish. Not anymore. And from what I was told, I saved you from a freakish life surrounded by weirdoes. Robert explained to me that the Amish have a habit of shunning young women who find themselves in a pregnant way without the benefit of a husband. Your mother was apparently one of those women who'd been shunned and had been struggling to live hand to mouth, which is why I think, maybe, she might have agreed to sell you. If she hadn't done that, and if we hadn't bought you, well, you would have grown up an outcast, staying in the Amish world. That would have been your lot in life, Margo, so I'll thank you to stop being so judgmental."

Margo got to her feet and lifted her chin. "How much did you pay for me?"

"I'm sure you'll be relieved to learn you were quite expensive, darling. You cost me well over two million dollars."

Any hope that they were dealing with a small-time operation vanished for Brock in a split second. Over two million dollars for one child meant someone had thought out every detail of the abductions, and they had done so for profit—big profit.

Getting to his feet as well, Brock moved to stand in front of Margo. "Will you go ask Agent Colby to come in? He should still be out in the hallway, and I'm going to need his help."

"You're going to send him after Robert?"

"Since the cold case of three abducted Amish children just became decidedly warmer, I'll have the luxury of calling in an entire FBI team to begin a more active investigation. But I need Agent Colby to see Caroline secured."

"Secured?" Caroline all but spat. "What do you mean, secured?"

"A man who would have no qualms about paying for a child who'd been abducted is not a man who's going to react well when he learns his wife just sold him out," Brock began. "We'll get you to a secure location, and I'm sure you'll want to contact legal counsel. We'll go from there."

"I won't go to jail, will I? Not after I've cooperated?"

"That's not up to me to decide."

Caroline turned to Margo. "You have to help me, darling. I'm your mom, and I've done what I've done to make certain you were given every advantage in life."

"And I'm grateful for those advantages," Margo said quietly. "I love my career, enjoyed the private education your money provided me, and I've been given opportunities most people only dream about. However, now that I know the truth, I can't help wondering if you ever really loved me, or just thought of me exactly like you think of your shoes. I'm pretty, people are envious of me, and I'm certainly the reason so many people provide you with so much attention. The mom of Margo Hartman—the woman responsible for pushing her to super stardom." Her lips thinned. "You must be so proud of your accomplishment."

Margo turned and walked out the door.

"I *did* make her a star," Caroline whispered. "And because of that, she owes me."

"She doesn't owe you anything. Your selfishness ruined the lives of numerous people, and that's why she'll not step in and save you."

"I didn't know about the abductions."

"Would that have mattered?"

Her silence was an answer in and of itself,

and left Brock shaking his head. "That's what I thought."

Walking to the door, he met Colby as he entered the room. After explaining that Caroline needed to be taken into custody, Brock moved into the hallway and found Margo waiting for him.

"Are you all right?"

Looking at him with eyes bright with unshed tears, she shook her head. "Not really, but I will be, just as soon as I find my way back to my family . . . my real family."

Taking hold of her hand, he squeezed it, and together they walked out of the hotel and hopefully toward resolving a piece of a mystery that had been left unsolved for far too long.

chapter nineteen

The sound of a diesel engine rumbling from somewhere outside stirred Margo from sleep. Pulling the pillow over her head, she staunchly pushed aside the idea it was probably time to get up, not really ready to face another strange day just yet, if ever.

When she'd left the hotel with Brock the night before, she'd finally gotten to experience a ride with an Uber driver, the only Uber driver in Millersburg from what Brock told her.

Being driven down the street by a man dressed in what appeared to be pajamas, and while obeying every posted speed limit sign there was, no doubt because Brock was in the car, had lifted Margo's spirits. When they'd finally arrived at the little carriage house that was situated a bit past Ian's house, the sense of panic that had threatened to overwhelm her from the moment she'd realized the truth of her birth, had turned into determination to discover the whole truth once and for all.

Brock wouldn't hear of her doing anything else but getting some sleep, so after providing her with a toothbrush, toothpaste, and one of his old T-shirts, he'd shown her to the guest bedroom and wished her good night.

A blast of a horn honking interrupted her thoughts. Shoving aside the pillow still over her head, Margo opened her eyes and looked around.

Cheery yellow curtains hung from the one window the room offered, and one wall had little wooden plaques with motivational sayings painted on them, like *Love the Life You're Living* and *Stop Wishing. Start Doing.* Squinting, she tried to see what a plain white plaque said, catching something about fearless on it. When she couldn't make out the words from where she was, she stretched, threw aside the covers, swung her legs over the edge of the bed, and got up.

Yanking up the sweatpants she'd borrowed from Brock, she padded across the floor on bare feet. Stopping in front of the plaque, she took a moment to read it, and then felt unexpected tears spring to her eyes. Wiping those tears away with a dash of her hand, she read the words again.

The phrase "do not be afraid" is written in the Bible 356 times.

That's a daily reminder from God to live every day fearless.

Having no idea if that was true—but not actually caring since it seemed as if that particular message had been waiting on that particular wall just for her and was exactly the message she needed to hear—she reached out and touched the words, lingering over every one. When she felt their power settle into her very soul, she turned and moved to the window, pushing aside the curtain so she could enjoy the view of a new day spreading over the meadow right outside the carriage house.

The idea that it was a new day seemed a little daunting since she knew what she was going to have to face. But remembering the words she'd just read, she drew in a breath and released it.

"I'm not Margo Hartman," she whispered, not really surprised when those words left a bitter taste on her tongue.

Before she could think about all that went along with not being Margo Hartman, the rumbling from the truck that had originally awakened her drifted through the window and drew her attention.

Twitching the curtain just a little to hide herself from view, her attention settled on a tow truck idling in the driveway. The driver's side door opened when Brock suddenly strode into view and waved at the man behind the wheel.

The sound of the engine died as the man got out. He was dressed in a sleeveless T-shirt that brought attention to his tree-trunk-sized arms. He had a ball cap on his head, and a big, bushy dark beard, reminding Margo of a man who'd missed the fact that the whole bushy-beard fashion thing had already been laid to rest. That, in Margo's mind, had been a very good thing.

The man walked right up to Brock and clapped

him on the back, apparently telling him quite the story since he kept gesturing with his hands every other second, laughing and then clapping Brock on the back again.

Noticing that Brock had already showered—his hair seemed to be wet and he was wearing a different T-shirt and a darker pair of jeans—she turned from the window and made her way down the short hallway to the small bathroom she'd used the night before.

Stepping out of Brock's sweats, which wasn't tricky to do since they were so large they slid right down her legs, she slapped on a new waterproof bandage Brock had considerately left out for her three whole stitches, and then stepped into the shower.

Ten minutes later, feeling much better and smelling like Irish Spring, a soap she'd seen commercials for on TV but had never tried, she wrapped the large towel she found in the cabinet under the sink more securely around her. Then she practically jumped out of it when someone knocked on the bathroom door.

"I have clothes out here for you," Brock called through the door. "And I'll have breakfast waiting in the kitchen after you get dressed."

Her knees turned a little weak on the spot. A man who would bring her clothing and make her a meal was a man a girl didn't find every day.

"Where'd you get the clothes?" she called back.

"Ian picked them up for you from a discount store this morning that opens at the crack of dawn. He dropped them off before he went in to do rounds at the animal clinic. I hope you like Nirvana."

"As in the old grunge band?"

"Ian's what one would call a frugal shopper, and apparently Nirvana T-shirts were 50 percent off."

Margo's lips quirked into a grin. "I *love* Nirvana."

"That's the spirit. I'll be in the kitchen."

Unable to find a brush, Margo settled for scrunching her hair a few times with her fingers and slid a wisp of lip balm she found in the medicine cabinet over her lips. Making sure her towel was securely wrapped around her, she hurried back to the guest bedroom, finding a plastic bag with a pair of jeans, a Nirvana T-shirt—black, of course—flip-flops, underwear, and a bra sitting on the bed.

Not allowing herself a moment to picture Dr. St. James picking out panties and a bra for her, because that was far more embarrassing to think about than she cared to at the moment, she hurried and got dressed. As she left the guest bedroom, her bright pink flip-flops made distinctive flopping sounds as she moved down the hallway.

The tantalizing smell of coffee hit her before she reached the kitchen, and when she did step into that room, she found herself completely charmed by the atmosphere Brock had seemingly created just for her.

The country table was set with a tablecloth and mismatched dishes, and a bunch of wildflowers, like some of the ones she'd seen from the bedroom window, were stuck in an old mason jar sitting smack-dab in the middle of the table.

Turning her attention to Brock, she found him flipping pancakes, looking completely at ease, as if manning a stove was an everyday occurrence for him.

"You can cook," was all she could think to say.

He flashed her a smile. "I can, and I love it. So I cook whenever I'm home, preferring that to eating out all the time."

"Well, that's great." She tilted her head. "Why aren't you married?"

Brock's smile turned into a grin. "I know, right? Obviously, I'm a catch."

"And modest."

"That too."

After sliding a pancake onto a blue plate that almost matched the color of his eyes, Brock took the plate to the table and set it down, right before he pulled out a chair and waited for her to allow him to see her seated.

On knees that had unsurprisingly taken to turning weak again, she allowed him to do just that. Then she smiled her thanks as he whipped open a folded towel that had been placed next to her table setting and drew it over her lap, a towel that might have been a hand towel from the bathroom.

Trying to maintain a sense of cool while sitting down to breakfast with the most intriguing man she'd ever met, who'd made her breakfast with his own hands, was just not going to happen. With heat rising in her checks, she bent her head after Brock joined her at the table and took her hand, enjoying the sense of peace that settled over her when he said grace. Then he squeezed her hand and they began to eat.

Breakfast was uneventful, with Brock keeping the conversation centered on inconsequential things like ducks, and dogs, and how interesting it was that animals weren't trying to maul her as much as when she first arrived in town.

"I think that has something to do with Gabby," Margo said. "Ever since she and I saved each other in the lake, I don't feel as uncomfortable around animals. And since Anna Hershberger told me animals can sense a person's fear, I'm hoping that because I'm not as nervous around them now, they'll stop wanting to attack me."

"That would probably make you like animals more."

After clinking coffee cups, they continued eating with an easy banter springing up between them. All too soon, though, reality edged ever closer.

She took her last sip of coffee as Brock polished off his eggs. He lifted his head and caught her eye. "You think you're ready for this?"

"It depends on what *ready* you're talking about."

"I think we should go out to the Yoder farm, the place you were shot and where Sarah Yoder lives."

"One of the missing children was abducted from that farm, weren't they?"

"I think you already know the answer to that."

Blowing out a breath, Margo lingered at the table, almost as if she was incapable of forcing herself from the chair. "Do you know that when I first got to town, after I took Gabby to the animal clinic, I went shopping?"

"I do because I was trying to follow you, but you saw me."

She smiled. "I did see you, and . . . wow, that seems so long ago, when in reality it wasn't. But I bought a quilt, one that turned out to have been made by Sarah Yoder. That's weird, now that we suspect she might be related to me, isn't it?"

"It is, but I'm not that surprised, considering all the other weird things we've encountered lately. And speaking of weird, or something downright unexpected, I forgot to mention what happened with your car."

"Someone stole it, just like my luggage?"

Brock laughed. "No, surprisingly enough, it was not stolen. Ed Johnson, the mechanic who pulled it from the lake, just stopped by here a little while ago. He somehow managed to get your car running again."

"I don't remember asking anyone to get the car running again. I thought it would just be ruined."

"I'm sure most of the interior is, but Ed apparently enjoys a good challenge. Because of that, and because he also didn't want to see what he called a prime piece of machinery go to waste, he took it upon himself to tinker with your car. And he got it up and running."

"Why did he tell *you* that?"

Brock settled back in the chair. "Probably because even though everyone believes you've left town, they might also believe some of the gossip that had you and me linked as a couple."

"Ah, how quickly I forgot about the tabloids, but I'm not surprised they'd take an interest in you. You have that *bad boy, I'm dangerous, don't mess with me vibe* about you. That kind of vibe sells scads of papers, so you'll probably find photographers hounding you for a while."

"I suppose I could have worse things thought about me." He got up from his chair, walked over to Margo, and pulled her to her feet. "If you're not ready for this, Margo, we don't have to go to the Yoder farm today."

"Have they been told we're coming?"

"They haven't. I wasn't certain what you'd want to do, or even if you'd want to go visit them after a good night's sleep and then thinking on things, so I didn't send them word we might be coming out."

"Do they know about me?"

"Sarah couldn't have missed your resemblance to her when she helped me get you to the hospital, so I'm sure they've had their suspicions ever since."

"But she never came around again. Why wouldn't she have come around?"

"You heard what Mrs. Hershberger said. The Amish don't believe in meddling. They didn't even bring in the police until a full week had passed after their children were abducted all those years ago. From the way I understand it, they truly do believe everything happens in God's time and if it's God's will. So maybe they're just waiting for you to go to them."

"Should I change back into those Amish clothes?"

"Since that plan didn't exactly work out as we hoped, I don't think you should. And, besides, you need to meet the Yoders as you, not as a woman dressed in a way that's so unfamiliar to you and will hardly let you be comfortable while you're meeting them."

Drawing in a deep breath, Margo nodded before slowly releasing it. She took a few minutes to help Brock clean the kitchen before she went and brushed her teeth, trying to quiet nerves that felt like they were attempting to claw themselves out of her body.

After climbing into Brock's Jeep a short time later, she appreciated that he didn't fill the ride with conversation, but allowed her to simply sit with her thoughts as the few miles it took to get to the farm sped by.

Turning the Jeep down a two-lane dirt road, Brock eased off the gas as Margo drew in deep breath after deep breath, feeling distinctly light-headed the closer they got to their destination.

A team of horses pulling a plow in the distance caught her attention, and it suddenly hit her that the man driving the plow could very well be her . . . dad.

Not quite ready to deal with that, even though it had been her choice to come here today, Margo turned front and center, keeping her gaze deliberately focused on the dirt lane.

It was too much to comprehend—the horror that might have happened all those many years ago, and at this very farm.

Were the cornstalks they were passing a part of who she really was?

Could these people who farmed this land and lived in the big white house now appearing in the distance really be her family?

Swallowing past the large lump that had developed in her throat, Margo swallowed again when Brock brought the Jeep to a stop and the reality of the moment closed in on her.

Brock leaned toward her, touched his forehead to her forehead, and took one of her cold hands in his.

"You're not alone, Margo. I'll be here with you the entire time."

When he squeezed her hand, and then whispered a prayer, asking God to watch over her, everything she knew in her world shifted.

It no longer mattered that she wasn't really Margo Hartman, or that she was some famous woman who lived a life most people envied. It only mattered that some of the wrongs that had affected innocent people were soon to be righted.

It also mattered that she was finally recovering the faith she'd fallen from, realizing that God had simply been waiting for her to return, and that he was more than willing to welcome her back with open and loving arms.

As that truth settled into her soul, Brock sat back, got out of the Jeep, and moved to open her door. Stepping down to the ground, he took her hand, and they turned to look at the house.

It didn't surprise her at all when a flash of memory struck from out of nowhere. In fact, it would have surprised her more if it hadn't.

Closing her eyes, she allowed the memory to fully form. She pictured a long hallway that greeted a person right past the front door. To the right of that hallway, there'd be a flight of stairs with a wooden banister, and the air inside the house would smell like freshly baked bread. A sense of peace permeated the entire house, brought about by the very people who lived there.

"Deputy Moore, we weren't expecting you."

Turning toward that voice, Margo couldn't breathe.

A woman was walking toward her, a woman who looked remarkably like Margo, and a woman she knew without a doubt was Sarah.

Sarah . . . her sister . . . her twin.

As Margo's knees started to give out, she stumbled. But Brock was right beside her and caught her, drawing her up and then keeping her pressed against his side.

"Did you know she was my twin?" she whispered.

"I had a feeling she might be, but I didn't know how to tell you."

Forcing air into lungs that wanted to remain constricted, Margo swiped at the tears dribbling down her cheek. Moving out of Brock's safe embrace, she lifted her chin and caught and held the gaze of her sister—a sister she hadn't seen or even remembered for over twenty years.

"Sarah, it's me . . . *Martha.*"

As she said a name she hadn't expected to hear coming from her mouth, everything began spinning right before her eyes. And then her world went black.

chapter twenty

"I gather she had no idea we're twins?"

Following Sarah down a hallway and into a large room that was obviously the family gathering place, Brock laid Margo on a couch with a quilt folded over its back. Straightening, he shook his head. "No one mentioned anything about her being your twin, not even Mrs. Hershberger, although I'm convinced she realized exactly who Margo was five minutes after she first saw her."

Sarah moved closer to the couch and looked down at Margo. "I'm sorry I didn't stay at the hospital, but . . . I just wasn't ready to believe she was really my sister."

"I could always bring someone out to do a DNA test on both of you, Sarah. But I think the evidence we have now points to her almost certainly being your missing sister."

"Of course I'm her sister."

Turning his attention from Sarah, Brock found Margo watching them, her face somewhat pale underneath the remnants of her spray tan. But her eyes were clear and . . . curious.

"I think I called myself Martha before I passed out."

"You remember your name?" Sarah all but whispered as she edged just a bit closer to Margo.

"That's my real name?"

Sarah nodded. "It is."

Wrinkling her nose, Margo struggled to a sitting position. "That's my doll's name."

Sucking in a sharp breath, Sarah plopped right down beside Margo on the couch.

"You still have your doll?"

"Well, technically, she got stolen, but up until a few days ago I had her. How do you know about my doll?"

Sarah smiled a smile that, because Brock had seen it so many times on Margo's face, made his mouth drop open.

"I have a matching doll to your Martha, although my doll is named Sarah. Our mother told me a long time ago that you and I, being twins, had these funny little things between just the two of us. Naming our dolls after ourselves was one of them." She blew out a breath, and then, almost tentatively, she reached out and took hold of Margo's hand, looking at it for a long moment. "We used to hold hands all the time."

A single tear trailed down Margo's cheek. "I'm sure we did a lot of things all the time, Sarah, and would have done much more if we hadn't been separated."

Tears began trailing down Sarah's cheeks as well. "I knew you were out there somewhere. I've felt you for years, but no one ever really believed me."

"What do you mean, you *felt* me?"

The faintest of smiles flickered across Sarah's face. "When we were little, we always knew what the other was thinking and feeling. I've had little jolts for years, feelings of excitement, happiness, and even sadness, and I knew they were coming from you."

Margo bit her lip. "But why haven't I felt you, then?"

"Because you didn't remember me. The memory of you was kept alive for all of us because you lived here, with us, were part of our family. Our prayers have included you in them for over twenty years. You, on the other hand, were stolen away from us. I have to imagine your memories of your time here faded over the years, as memories are known to do unless they're cherished and brought out every now and again."

"I must have been really young when I was taken since I'm twenty-three now and Brock said I was abducted in the early 1990s."

"You're twenty-five, almost twenty-six."

"What?"

"You're twenty-five," Sarah repeated.

Margo's brows drew together. "Are you sure about that?"

"Positive."

"Why would Caroline Hartman, the woman I thought was my mother for the past twenty-odd years, lie about my age? I thought I was twenty-three."

"At least you have an explanation as to why you seem really mature for your age," Brock said, pulling up a chair and taking a seat in front of the sisters.

"And," Sarah added, "since you were abducted, I imagine this Caroline Hartman person wasn't certain how old you were. You and I were premature at birth, probably because we were twins, and we were really tiny for our age."

When the distinctive beeping of Brock's phone went off, he excused himself for just a moment, walking out of the room to check his messages.

The messages weren't ones he wanted to see, but they also weren't exactly a surprise. Deciding he'd check back with Colby after he was certain Margo was okay and not overwhelmed, he walked back into the family gathering room. He smiled when he saw Margo and Sarah sitting even closer together on the couch, talking so quickly it was evident they couldn't catch up fast enough.

"Is everything all right?" Margo asked, looking up as he walked farther into the room.

"It's . . ."

"More bad news?" she finished for him.

"It's not unexpected news," he said slowly.

"And . . ." Margo and Sarah said together.

The single word *and,* at least in Brock's mind, proved without a shadow of a doubt that the two women watching him were definitely twins. They'd been reunited for less than an hour, but they thought remarkably alike, their faces were almost identical, and they even had the same mannerisms, an observation they went about proving when they tilted their heads at identical angles and at exactly the same time.

"Robert Hartman has disappeared, as have old files I had Agent Colby request from the Millersburg police department. Those files concerned the original investigation notes after the abductions."

A crease settled in the space directly above Margo's nose. "What does that mean, the files have disappeared?"

Taking his seat again, Brock shrugged. "It could mean a lot of things, but I'm hoping it only means that, because of the number of years that have passed since the abductions took place, they've simply been misplaced."

"And if they haven't?"

"Well, that *could* mean we've got an inside job. If that's the case, it'll get messy, and it'll add a whole different level of danger to this situation." He sent her a nod. "That means you won't be leaving my sight anytime soon."

Returning the nod, Margo smiled. "Duly noted." She leaned in toward her sister. "I need you to tell me everything, starting with the family." She paused. "Where is everyone? I thought Amish families were supposed to be large. But I'm going to just admit right here and now that what I know about the Amish could fit in my little finger."

"I don't think I'll be able to tell you everything about the Amish in the span of an afternoon, but the most important thing you need to understand about us is that we're just people. We laugh, we cry, we love, and we're not nearly as different as everyone thinks. We embrace a simpler life; there's no question about that. But we do so to make our lives more about what God expects from us than what we expect from God."

"I suppose I never thought about the Amish like that," Margo admitted. "Tell me what your parents are like . . . what *our* parents are like."

"*Dat*, or Dad as the *English* say, is a gentle soul. He's a quiet man but has a sense of humor if you look for it. *Mamm*, or Mom, is definitely the tougher of the two, but I think she had to be to survive the tragedy of losing you." Sarah shook her head. "She has an almost unshakable faith, and that faith, I believe, is what allowed her to release the anger she felt after you disappeared. Turning her rage over to God allowed her to live her life without bitterness. Her sadness never completely disappeared, though, and I know to this day she prays for your well-being every morning and every night."

"Have they been told about me, that I've returned to Millersburg?"

Sarah nodded. "I told them after I got home from the hospital the day you were shot." She took a moment to pat Margo's hand. "I suspected the moment I saw you, when you came to return the duck, that you were my sister, but then you were shot and everything turned strange."

"Why didn't you come visit me at the hospital and tell me everything?"

"*Dat* and I agreed it would be too much for you to take in at that particular time. We didn't know how serious your injuries were, and we didn't want to take the chance of interfering with your recovery." Sarah's lips began to curve. "There was also the chance you wouldn't believe us if we burst into your hospital room, claiming you as our long lost Martha. Why, you would have thought we were crazy."

"Why did Mrs. Hershberger come, then?"

"From what Brock has told me, Mrs. Hershberger apparently recognized you right away at the animal clinic. We had no idea she was planning to go to the hospital, though, even after she told me she wanted to confirm your identity." Sarah smiled. "She's been very vocal about the fact she thought you should be told, but *Dat* held true to his own beliefs and refused to go see you."

"He was right not to come," Margo said. "I wouldn't have believed the story. Now, however, with the way everything has unfolded, I know this is the truth. I know I'm one of those missing children, and . . . I'm ready to meet my real parents."

"I'm afraid that meeting will have to wait just a little longer. *Dat*'s out in the fields and *Mamm* isn't home. She's spending the day with Esta Miller."

Shifting on the couch, Margo glanced at Brock and then back to her sister. "Did you know I met the Millers? That I was supposed to stay with them until what we thought was a stalker could be found?"

"It was a mistake for them to agree to take you in, but no one could have known how Esta would react, or that she thought you might be . . ."

"Rebecca," Margo finished for her.

"You know about Rebecca?"

"Only that she was abducted as well. Considering I recently learned that my parents—well, I think I'll just refer to them from this point forward as Robert and Caroline Hartman—paid two million dollars to take me home with them, I have to imagine Rebecca and the other child who went missing landed in fairly affluent homes."

Sarah raised a hand to her mouth. "Your abduction was because of . . . money?"

"That's the theory we're just now beginning to consider," Brock said. "Since Caroline Hartman doesn't seem to have any qualms about turning

301

on her husband as she's being questioned by the FBI, the other agents on the case and I are hopeful we'll have some success finding the other two missing children in the foreseeable future."

Sarah's nose wrinkled exactly like Brock had seen Margo's do on numerous occasions.

"Aren't you a deputy in the sheriff's department?"

"That's a little tricky to explain. I've been on leave with the FBI for the past several months, taking up a temporary role as a deputy sheriff here in Millersburg. That role has allowed me to travel freely around the county while I looked into a case that's of a distinct personal nature to me."

"A personal case?" Sarah repeated.

"Yes. I came to Millersburg with the hope of discovering information about how my sister, Dr. Stephanie St. James, really died. That investigation has gone nowhere lately, although"—he blew out a breath—"it has crossed my mind a time or two, strange as it sounds, that there may be a link between Stephanie's death and the abductions, even given the time that passed between those two tragedies."

Sarah rose to her feet. "Perhaps this is the time God intended for you to find some answers, Brock. But I do hope you'll do what we Amish do and simply wait for a sign from God." She reached out, took hold of Margo's hand, and pulled her sister up beside her. "However, this should be a joyous time. So I'm going to insist we set aside our concerns for the moment and revel in the unexpected blessing we've been given, the blessing of Margo finding her way home. Which means, I should show you your home."

"You two go on ahead," Brock said. "I'll wait for you here."

"Don't be silly," Margo and Sarah said at the same time, laughing right after they said it.

Unwilling to disappoint them, and curious to hear what might come up while Sarah gave Margo the tour, Brock nodded. He stayed a few feet behind them, though, as they began walking around the house, wanting Margo to be able to enjoy the experience with her sister.

Sarah continued chatting as they climbed the stairs. "You have other sisters and you have brothers. Daniel, Elizabeth, and Emma no longer live here, all being married with homes of their own. Then there's Isaac—he's sixteen—Grace is fourteen, and Aaron is the baby at twelve."

"I have . . . seven siblings?"

"You do. How many siblings do you have with your other family?"

"I grew up as an only child," Margo said as they reached the second floor and continued down the hallway. Margo slowed her pace as she looked around, then stopped entirely when she came to one of the bedrooms. Pushing open the door, she turned and looked at her sister. "Did this use to be . . . my room?"

"It *was* your room, and you used to share it with me."

Margo took Sarah's hand again, and together they walked into the room, sitting down side by side on one of the twin-size beds.

"I didn't want to stay in here after you were taken, so *Dat* and *Mamm* moved me to the room next to theirs." Sarah fell silent for a moment as she looked around. "We were all sleeping, you see, and no one heard a thing. Then, I've been told, there was a loud banging on the front door. It was Amos Miller. He was frantic because one of his children had woken up sick, and that's when they realized Rebecca wasn't in the house."

"And that's when I was discovered missing as well?" Margo edged closer to her sister.

"I think it was. I don't really remember that night, it was so long ago. But *Dat* and *Mamm* still discuss it every now and then, although not as much as over the first ten years you were missing." She released a sigh. "It was a horrible time back then, and then we learned Harley King had gone missing as well, and that's when I think everyone realized evil had come to visit Millersburg."

"How old was Harley?" Brock asked.

"He was around Margo's and my age, maybe a

little older. But from what I've been told, he spent a lot of time at our house because our *mamm* and his *mamm* were such good friends. He was supposedly an incredibly bright child, and my *mamm* to this day goes on about how pleasant he was." She shook her head. "We didn't see the King family much after that. They began sticking to themselves."

Walking over to the window, Brock looked over the fields of corn spread out as far as the eye could see. "It just seems so odd to me that someone was able to steal into three different houses and snatch up three children who were all about the same age. It's almost like they knew the layouts of each house, as well as where each child's bedroom was, to be so successful with the abductions."

"All the adults thought that very same thing," Sarah said. "I overhead *Dat* talking with Amos Miller a few years ago, and they were wondering if someone we knew arranged everything."

"That is something to wonder about, Sarah, and I can assure you the FBI will be looking into that theory." Brock turned from the window. "But speaking of your father, a horse pulling a plow seems to be moving this way from the fields, so . . ." He smiled at Margo. "We should probably go down and introduce you to your dad."

"I should go out and speak to him first." Sarah

got to her feet and walked across the room. "I'll be right back, and please"—she grinned—"make yourself at home."

With that, Sarah disappeared through the door, leaving Brock all alone with Margo, which was nice, but . . .

"We shouldn't be in this room alone together," he said. "I'm sure your parents would find it . . . What's that old-fashioned word I'm looking for?"

"Untoward," Margo supplied, practically jumping to her feet before they dashed into the hallway.

Moving at a pace that could only be considered fast, they made their way to the first floor, finding a teenage boy watching them from the entrance of the house.

"You're not . . . Sarah." The boy took off his straw hat but his gaze never left Margo's face.

"I'm not." Margo stepped toward the boy. "I'm Margo, or, uh . . . Martha."

The boy blinked. "I'm Isaac, and I suppose you and me must be kin, like I'm your brother and you're my . . . sister." And then, just like a boy, he grinned. "I've been hearing things, not that I should have heard those things, but Sarah's loud. Are you really a movie star?"

Margo grinned back at her brother. "I'm not. I'm just a singer."

"Like a rock singer?"

"More along the lines of pop."

"Huh," Isaac said, as if he wasn't sure he wanted to have a sister who was involved with pop over rock.

Before Brock had an opportunity to ask what type of rock music Isaac might enjoy, or even where he would have heard that music, the sound of a car racing up the dirt drive drifted in through the window.

Running through the door, Brock rushed across the porch just as he saw Robert Hartman grab hold of Sarah, who'd been heading for the fields, then pull her toward his Mercedes.

"No!" Brock yelled as he sprinted forward and then hit the ground when a bullet whizzed by his head. Rolling, he regained his feet and continued forward, dodging behind a large water barrel when more bullets flew his way.

The sound of tires spinning in the dirt warned him Robert was getting away.

Drawing his gun, he took aim at the tires, thought better of it since an innocent woman was in the car, and took off for his Jeep instead.

Yelling at Margo to stay put, he jumped into the Jeep, revved the engine, and took off down the road.

chapter twenty-one

For a moment, Margo's feet refused to move. She was stuck standing on the porch as clouds of dust flew up in the air from the two vehicles racing down the road.

One of those vehicles was manned by her . . . well, Robert, a man who'd just stolen Sarah right from the front yard.

All the air left Margo's lungs in a split second.

He'd mistaken Sarah for her, and there was absolutely no telling what he would do once he realized he'd kidnapped the wrong woman.

Ice filled her veins as unshed tears blinded her. Wiping a hand over her eyes, she saw Isaac run past her and across the front lawn. He didn't stop when he reached the cornfields, and that's when she remembered Sarah had been going to forewarn her dad, or *Dat* as she'd called him, that Margo had come home.

Even though she understood the idea that *Dat* was also her dad, and had probably always loved her, even with her being gone for so long, she had no idea how he would react or how she could possibly explain to him that she was directly responsible for Sarah being taken. She should have shown more caution when dealing with Robert since, clearly, he was a man who wasn't willing to lose whatever game he'd decided to play now.

Squaring her shoulders as she realized she was not being a help to anyone by doing nothing, she moved into the yard, looking around to see if there were any spare horses, bicycles, or anything that else she could use to . . .

The roar of a diesel engine had her turning toward the sound just as a tow truck, the same one she'd seen at Brock's house that morning, burst through a section of corn, decimating stalks of it as it raced her way.

Run!

Having no idea whose voice had just practically screamed in her ear, Margo didn't hesitate, but spun around, setting her sights on fields that were in the opposite direction of where her brother Isaac had run. Just when she reached what she hoped would be the safety of cover within the stalks, she heard what sounded exactly like a howl. She looked up to find a large black dog, a Rottweiler from the looks of it, running toward her.

With her lungs beginning to burn, she pushed herself faster, shoving through the corn stalks, terror causing sobs to burst through her lips every few seconds.

The sound of large paws pounding behind her gave her a split second of warning, but then those paws were on her back and she stumbled, dropping to the ground and then freezing on the spot when she finally rolled to a stop.

Hot breath blew over her face, and not wanting to watch as the beast tore her apart, Margo squeezed her eyes shut and began to pray.

Before she'd gotten much more than a "Help me, God!" out, the dog now holding her in place with his massive paws settled on her chest, let out what sounded like a whine—right before the crunch of someone walking over fallen cornstalks met her ears.

"Good boy, Damien. What a good boy you are. Here's a treat."

As the weight left her chest, Margo opened her eyes and saw Damien loping away, snapping up the treat before he sat on his haunches and took to staring at her with dark eyes that never wavered.

Shuddering ever so slightly, she turned her head and switched her gaze to the man now looming over her.

He was wearing the same baseball cap he'd been wearing when he visited Brock earlier that day, but he didn't look as friendly now. Instead, he looked agitated, a look that was unquestionably *not* going to work in her favor.

What he was doing here, or why he'd set his dog on her, Margo couldn't say. But he obviously had a reason for running her down. All she had to do was figure out what that reason was . . . and figure out why a man would bother to fix her car when he clearly didn't seem all that interested in impressing her, which was why most people went out of their way to do things for her.

"You should have been more careful, little girl," were the first words to come out of his mouth. "You wouldn't be in this mess if you'd just left Millersburg after I gave you that warning."

"What warning?"

"And here I thought you were a bright thing. I forced you off the road and into the lake after I heard talk about people in the diner seeing a woman who looked exactly like Sarah Yoder. I thought for sure that would have you skedaddling out of town, but no, you're like a bad, bad penny. You just keep turning up."

He spat right next to her. "I couldn't believe my eyes today when I drove out to Brock Moore's place to tell him about your car. I was feeling guilty, see, about ruining that car just because I wanted you out of town. So I fixed it, I did, and then how do you repay me? You show up in a window at Brock's house, and that was the last straw. You left me no choice but to act . . . again."

Trying to stall for time, Margo raised a hand to block the sun that was blinding her. "You saw me at Brock's this morning?"

"Sure did. Your hair's like a beacon and drew my eyes right to where you were standing at the window. I parked the truck a ways down the road, waited for you and Brock to leave, and then I followed you here, waiting for the perfect time to make my move. And that perfect time is now."

He pulled her to her feet with arms she distinctly remembered comparing to tree trunks, and the man—Ed, if she remembered correctly—tossed her like a sack of potatoes over his shoulder and began loping through the cornfield, whistling for his dog. Unfortunately, that whistling had Damien charging up to join them.

Drawing in deep breaths to calm a stomach that had definitely turned queasy, Margo's attention centered on the dog sticking to Ed's heels as the strangest feeling swept over her.

She'd been carried through the cornfields before, with a dog running beside her as a man held her in his arms—a very large, yet younger version of Ed, if she wasn't mistaken.

Reaching the tow truck, Ed tossed her inside as if she weighed no more than a rag doll, then climbed in after her to take his place behind the wheel. Damien jumped over Ed and settled down directly beside her.

There'd definitely been a dog the night she was taken—another black dog, with enormous teeth and bad breath. It had nipped at her as she cowered on the seat of some other truck, while a man who'd clearly been Ed roared with laughter every time the dog snarled.

"I didn't expect things to work out this good," Ed said, shifting gears and squealing the tires as he got them back on the main road.

"Why are you doing this?"

"I have to tie up all the pieces."

"What pieces?"

"Things are falling apart. I've watched enough of them TV shows to know that when things go south, someone's always left holding the bag, and it's always the paid help, never the top brass. Well, I'm not going to be the one left holding this bag, no sir. I'm not."

"Are you going to murder me and dump my body in some remote forest beyond Millersburg where poor hikers will discover my picked-over bones in years to come?"

"I'm gonna first try to ransom you for money so I can get out of this town and find me a nice beach somewhere to live out the rest of my days. That right there is why I'm glad I didn't go back and run over your mother, after I missed my opportunity the first time around, back in town and all."

"You tried to run over Caroline Hartman? But . . . why?"

What seemed to be fear clouded Ed's eyes before he shook a thick finger her way. "That's secret information, that is, missy. You don't wanna be asking too many questions because there're bad people involved in this, bad people who would have no trouble killin' you over holding you for ransom."

Margo inched away from Damien as her nerves began to calm and her mind began to work again. "Fair enough. I won't ask why you tried to run over Caroline. But tell me this. Why didn't you use some of that two million dollars I heard Robert Hartman paid to buy me for his wife to get out of town years ago?"

Ed turned his head. "I didn't get no million dollars for you, let alone two. But that's interesting that so much money changed hands. I'm gonna have to do something about that before I leave town. Yes I am, yes I am."

"So it wasn't just you. Others were involved."

"Don't be nosey. It's unbecoming in a woman."

Margo ignored that little bit of absurdity. "Did you take all three of us that night, or did someone help you?"

"I heard tell you've made a lot of money over the years. You think that fancy mom of yours can get me at least a million dollars of that money?" Ed asked instead of answering her question.

"Caroline Hartman is not my mom, and I don't keep a million dollars in an account. My money is tied up in investments."

"Huh. That's gonna be a problem then, darlin'."

Not thinking it would help her stay alive for long if she admitted he might have an excellent point, Margo cleared her throat. "Do you know who shot me?"

"I did. But again, it wasn't to kill you. I didn't even mean to hit you, but that stupid duck you were holding started causing a ruckus and made you, the target I was intending on not hitting, move."

"Did you take a piece of my luggage after you pulled my car from the lake?"

"'Course I did. We emptied everything in my barn since that's where I towed the car to see if I could drain it of lake water and get it working again. But then them policemen—or maybe they was some kind of special agents—started making a log of everything, and that's when I saw the doll." He shook his head. "I couldn't let them have the doll, so I took the whole suitcase, making it appear like a random theft, ya know? I took their camera too."

He drummed his fingers against the steering wheel. "You've got some nice shoes, but I already knew that, seeing as how I've been keeping track of you on and off all these years. It never can hurt to know a few things on people. And your dad, well, he's a good one to have a few notes tucked away about, just in case a person needs a little . . . whadda call that . . . lever . . . ?"

"Leverage?"

"That's the word, *leverage*. And I got me some leverage when it comes to your pop."

"He's not my pop, my dad, or even my father."

"I suppose you have a point, since he bought you and all."

"If you know he bought me, do you also know who bought the other two Amish children?"

"Yep."

"Are they friends of Robert's?"

Ed stopped drumming to whatever invisible song he'd been listening to and turned to level a glare on her. "Stop asking questions. All you need to know is that you and the other two Amish kids were just part of a business deal, a business deal that involved very rich people that wanted children but couldn't get them the normal way. Leave it at that."

"But what about the other two missing children?"

"Do you think Robert Hartman is scary?" Ed asked instead of answering her question.

"I do, but—"

"Then know that the other people involved in this are a million times scarier than him. You need to leave it alone, or you will die. People *have* died over what happened all those years ago."

With that horrific statement, Ed reached over and switched on the CD player, turning it up so loud that further conversation was impossible. To add to the strangeness, the CD he was playing was one of hers, and Ed knew all the words to all the songs.

It took five of her songs before Ed pulled off the road. He pressed on the gas, and the truck bounced along a gravel path for a good five minutes before a large barn came into sight.

The fine hair on the nape of her neck stood up as she stared at the barn.

She'd been here in the past.

Ed had brought her here when she was little, along with Harley and Rebecca.

This barn was where the dogs had been, dogs Ed had set to guard them while he . . . while he what?

The answer to that question eluded her.

"I'm afraid I'm going to have to ask you to wait for me in the barn while I take care of some important business," he said.

Hope that his leaving her there might provide an opportunity for an escape died a rapid death when he whistled and two dogs that looked exactly like Damien raced around the outside of the barn. Their howls of greeting sent the hair on her arms standing up this time.

"That there's Damien's brother and sister. They'll be keeping an eye on you until I return."

Taking a rough hold of her arm, Ed practically dragged her to the barn and straight through the door, letting go of her once they reached some hay bales. Releasing another whistle, he gestured to the entrance, and to Margo's disgust, the dogs moved there and took up what could only be called defensive positions.

"They won't bite, not unless I tell them to." Ed turned and walked outside, sliding the main door shut behind him.

Unwilling to give up that easily, Margo sat down on a hay bale and studied her surroundings. The only possible escape she could see was through the window up in the loft area, but if she climbed out of that window, she'd be she'd be stuck on top of the barn.

Blowing out a breath, she directed her attention to the main floor, squinting when she saw what looked like her suitcase lying open on the floor by a rusted-out old truck. Pushing up from the hay bale, the sounds of her flip-flops—shoes she was suddenly surprised to see still on her feet since they weren't exactly made for running— overly loud in the silence of the barn.

Ignoring the warning growls the dogs imme- diately started making as she made her way across the floor, she sent them a "Shh," then smiled when they quieted.

"Good doggies," she said, regretting that when the growls immediately started up again.

"Best not to get too cocky," she muttered under her breath as she reached the suitcase and bent down to rummage through its contents. She pulled out Martha a moment later.

Straightening, she gave poor Martha a once- over, noticing the doll's coloring had faded and that clumps of dried mud clung to the little apron that made up her outfit. That, unfortunately, was clear proof her suitcases hadn't been nearly as waterproof as promised.

Setting Martha down on the hood of the rusted truck, she walked around to its bed, hoping she'd find some kind of cloth to clean up her doll. Finding an old trunk there, Margo climbed in, flipped up the lid, and found her breath catching in her throat.

Folded ever so carefully in the trunk were pieces of children's clothing—Amish clothing—and tucked against the sides of the trunk were old newspaper articles, along with a camera Margo was fairly certain Ed had mentioned he'd taken from the police.

Unable to stop herself, she pulled out the papers, her eyes skimming over articles that centered around events that had changed her life forever.

Three Amish children missing.

No sign of forced entry.

Law enforcement completely stumped.

Satanic cult suspected.

Margo shivered as that idea settled in her mind. Her parents—her real parents—must have gone through agony hearing that she could have been sacrificed in some twisted ritual, an idea that surely haunted their dreams for years.

Right there and then, any feelings of affection she'd still been holding for Caroline Hartman, however slight, disappeared.

The woman she'd believed to be her mother for over twenty years had chosen to buy a child, knowing, no matter that she claimed differently, that something was wrong about the whole process. She'd carelessly allowed her own selfishness to affect so many people. But even now, after the truth had come to light, Margo knew Caroline would not be thinking about those people. She'd be concerned only with saving her own neck, no matter who she had to throw under the bus.

"I see you found my treasures."

Margo stumbled back from the trunk, the side of the truck bed the only thing that stopped her from falling over. Turning, she found Ed standing a few feet away, his eyes holding what could only be described as rage.

"I don't like people looking at my stuff. That's private, it is, but I guess it doesn't really matter since you already know my secret. Not like it did when that other woman found my trunk."

Time seemed to stand still as tingles spread up her neck and her mouth turned remarkably dry.

"What do you mean, it doesn't matter like it did with that other woman?"

Ed's smile had Margo's blood running cold. "You're a smart girl, Margo Hartman. I'm sure you can figure it out without me helping you along with the answer."

"Stephanie St. James didn't commit suicide, did she?"

"How much is the answer worth to you?"

"How much do you want?"

"A million should do it."

"Done."

"If you're lyin' to me, little girl, I'll kill you."

"Fair enough."

"Dr. Stephanie St. James found that same trunk not even a year back." Ed nodded to his trunk. "She came out to see after one of my dogs that'd come up a little lame. Unfortunately for the good doctor, I forgot I left the trunk open, and she saw what was inside. I don't think she understood what she'd seen, but I couldn't take any chances on having that can of worms opened."

Drawing in a deep breath in the hopes it would help with her lightheadedness, Margo forced herself to ask a question she didn't want to ask. "How did you do it?"

"I just gave her neck a good twist. It broke right away, so she didn't feel no pain. Then I put her in one of my trucks, waited until it was dark like, and took her over to an old barn that gets a lot of stray cats she was always trying to help. I parked clear back from that barn so no one would be seeing any tire tracks. Then I just carried her into the barn, set up a scene that looked like she jumped from the rafters with a rope around her neck, and then I left."

"Why didn't anyone question how she died?"

"Now that's one of them things I just can't answer except to say this town still has its secrets and I ain't gonna be the one to snitch on anyone."

Margo had to sit down in the bed of the truck as tiny black dots obscured her vision, the horror of what she'd just heard making her weak.

Brock's sister had simply been trying to care for an injured dog, and had been killed in return because she'd seen something she couldn't possibly have understood.

"It was almost like an accident."

Raising her head when she was sure she wasn't going to faint, Margo narrowed her eyes. "Breaking someone's neck isn't an accident. It's barbaric and breaks one of those important rules of life. You know, the one that goes something like *thou shall not kill*."

Ed took one step toward the truck. "If there's one thing I can't stand, it's for someone to turn all preachy on me, girl. You think breaking some-one's neck is barbaric? I'll have to see if I have something lying around the house that will give the same results in a more . . . civilized manner." Letting out a chuckle, one that had her feeling less than reassured, he spun around and stalked out of the barn, leaving her in the company of only his dogs again.

He would be back . . . probably soon. There was nothing left to do but try to escape, no matter that his dogs were certain to try to stop her.

Pushing herself up from the floor of the truck bed, Margo looked around and then smiled when she caught sight of something parked in the far corner of the barn.

It was her Mini Cooper, and even though it wasn't looking as good as it had when she left California, it was looking fine for what she needed it for—escape.

Jumping down from the truck, she moved to her car, tried all the doors, and found them all locked. Walking to the front of the car, she bent down and searched with her hand underneath the bumper for the small metal key box Fauna had insisted be welded on there. Fauna had always been an overly competent sort, believing that prevention tactics before a catastrophe occurred were crucial for a stress-free life. That belief occasionally had her reacting a little too neurotically about things. But in this case, welding might just have saved a key box that would otherwise have certainly fallen off when the Mini Cooper took its swim in the lake.

Grinning like a fool when her fingers found what she was looking for, she slid the lid up and the key fell into her hand. Contemplating whether or not the moment was exactly right to burst into a happy dance, Margo shoved that contemplation aside when she heard the distinct growl of dogs that sounded too close for comfort.

Glancing over her shoulder, and seeing the dogs stealing their way closer, she knew it was now or never. Wondering whether or not she'd have time to get a door unlocked before the dogs ripped her to shreds, Margo looked back to the car and blinked.

The sunroof had been left open.

She could fit through that sunroof, not easily of course, but it could be done.

Not giving herself a moment to reconsider, she surged into motion, scrambled over the hood of her car, and dropped her legs through the roof's opening. Howls reverberated all around her as she squeezed her body through the small space, dropped into the driver's seat, shoved the key into the ignition, and prayed that Ed had really fixed her car.

The Mini Cooper sputtered to life and she shoved it into gear and pressed on the gas, causing one of the dogs trying to climb up on her roof to tumble to the ground.

A shot split the air, and then Ed was running through the barn door, a rifle in his hands and murder in his eyes.

Pressing the gas pedal all the way to the floor, she steered directly for him, satisfaction running through her when he jumped out of her way. Aiming the Mini Cooper for the barn door, Margo drove through it, and then she was free.

chapter twenty-two

The longer he drove as he tried to keep the Mercedes in sight, the more Brock was convinced Robert had a destination in mind, one he wanted to get to, but not with Brock on his tail.

Shifting gears when a sharp turn loomed directly in front of him, Brock took the turn and winced when he thought two of his wheels had left the ground, but then punched the gas and shifted again when he felt the Jeep stabilize.

Calling himself all sorts of an idiot as he continued the chase—because he never imagined Robert would return to Millersburg, let alone attempt to kidnap Margo—Brock tried to keep a firm hold on his temper. Losing it wouldn't benefit anyone.

That Robert had mistakenly snatched Sarah instead of Margo added an entirely different level of urgency to the situation. Sarah was certainly someone who could be considered disposable. Or maybe leverage—the type of leverage someone like Robert would have no hesitation in using to his advantage.

Slamming on the brakes when he noticed cows running in a field to his right, Brock blinked when he caught sight of the Mercedes flying through that field. The cows were scrambling to get out of its way, a sight one didn't normally see on a regular kind of day.

Shifting into low gear, Brock steered the Jeep off the road and into the field. He hoped the owners of that field, a couple he wasn't overly familiar with except to know they owned a bed and breakfast that catered to tourists, wouldn't have anyone touring their grounds right then.

Dodging cows still scattering every which way, Brock crested a hill and realized exactly why Robert had chosen such an unusual escape route.

Sitting in the middle of a meadow with what seemed to be daisies was a helicopter. And racing toward that helicopter from the Mercedes, which seemed to have stopped because it had run into a split-rail fence, was Robert, dragging Sarah with him—until she stumbled and fell to the ground.

A large man dressed all in black and with blood covering his face was standing beside the Mercedes, a hired gun if Brock wasn't mistaken, and probably the man who'd shot at him back at the Yoder farm. As Brock stopped the Jeep and opened the door, weapon drawn, the large man jumped back into the Mercedes, revving up a still-running engine. The tires spun for just a few seconds, and then the Mercedes was free of the fence. Then instead of driving it toward Robert, who was trying to pull Sarah up, the man turned the car around and raced it across the field, disappearing over the hill a mere moment later.

"Coward!" Robert screamed before he let go of Sarah, pulled out a gun of his own, and aimed it directly at Sarah's head. "I'll kill her right now if you come any closer."

Brock raised a hand. "I'm not moving, but you need to let her go."

"Do I look like an idiot?"

Swallowing the yes that had been on the tip of his tongue, because that certainly wouldn't aid the situation, Brock shook his head instead. "I'm well aware you're a worthy adversary, Robert. It took a man of remarkable intelligence to be able to keep Margo's abduction hidden all these many years, especially since no one ever really suspected a thing until recently."

"That abduction would have stayed hidden forever if that fool wife of mine hadn't pushed Margo one time too far, making her run." Robert gestured around with his gun. "Of all the places she could have landed, she just had to stop in Millersburg."

"One might call that more than a coincidence."

"Or one might think a person's luck had finally run out," Robert shot back.

Cocking an ear when he thought he heard a car coming his way, Brock glanced past Robert, narrowing his eyes when he saw the pilot of the helicopter running in the opposite direction. The strange thought flashed to mind that, while Robert's luck seemed to be running out, his might be doing the exact opposite, especially since Robert's escape plan had just hit a serious snag.

Suddenly realizing that the pilot might very well have not been a willing participant in the whole flying merrily away plan Robert had apparently concocted, since *Flying Amish Tours* was painted on the side of the helicopter, Brock took a step forward.

"Why didn't you just leave the country when you learned your wife was being interviewed by the FBI?" he called, trying to distract Robert so the pilot could get safely away.

"Do you honestly believe I would have returned if it wasn't absolutely necessary? The FBI has taken my wife into custody, and that means I have no access to the majority of her money. Caroline, bubbleheaded ditz that she certainly is, has been surprisingly savvy with how she's set up the accounts that hold all her lovely funds." Robert shook his head. "I don't like to be controlled, so when she did call me, not that I believed for a second she wasn't being recorded, and asked me to send her help, I laughed right before I hung up on her."

"Probably not your brightest move since, if I were to hazard a guess, Caroline's not going to loosen up your access to her accounts now."

"I won't need her money, not after Margo agrees to my demands, especially when *you* tell her if she doesn't, this woman, apparently a relative of

Margo's, is going to suffer a very, very painful and grisly death."

"What are your demands?"

"I want ten million wired into an off-shore account I've set up. I'll text Margo the account information and codes, and I'll expect that money transferred within the next two hours. Then, if she does exactly that, I'll release this Amish girl, safe and sound with not a hair out of place under that cap she's wearing."

Knowing the situation was going to turn even more dangerous when Robert realized his pilot had taken off, Brock cleared his throat and threw more questions his way. "I'll give Margo your demands, but tell me this. Why did you go through with what sounds like a great deal of bother to buy your wife a child in the first place? You certainly haven't struck me as the paternal type."

"My dear man, do you think I had any choice in that matter? Caroline's parents controlled everything about us. They had all the money, and they were willing to withhold it if we didn't toe the line. Caroline thought she wanted a baby, and Caroline's parents thought a baby might settle their daughter down. Or maybe stabilize might be a better way to describe what they wanted. And I . . . well, I was expected to go along with their wishes if I didn't want the lovely monthly allowance they allotted me cut." He shook his head and smiled a smile that made him look more smug than amused. "It was a *tragedy,* their deaths."

"Why don't you tell me about those deaths."

"While that sounds like a delightful way for me to spend my time—"

Whatever else Robert had been saying got lost as what sounded exactly like a sputtering engine split the air. Black smoke could suddenly be seen crawling over the crest of the hill, and then what Margo had called a *vintage* Mini Cooper rumbled into view, spewing out black exhaust as it puttered toward them.

To Brock's absolute disbelief, Margo drove right past him, heading in Robert's direction as the Mini Cooper began to make a concerning wheezing noise.

Taking off after her, Brock ran as fast as he could as she aimed the car directly at Robert, revving the engine. That had Robert dropping his hold on Sarah, who'd been putting up a fight, and running for his very life toward the helicopter.

When the Mini Cooper let out a screeching whine before it rolled to a stop, Brock passed it just as Margo jumped out.

Pushing even harder, Brock closed the distance between him and Robert, and then he was launching himself through the air, bringing Robert to the ground a second later.

Less than three minutes after that, Robert Hartman could no longer be considered a danger, his gun having skittered through the daisies when Brock punched him. His hands were now securely fastened behind his back, and he was whining in a way that hardly lent him a dangerous air.

Robert, it was plain to see, was not a man who'd ever been physically assaulted, especially since his whining suddenly turned to moaning, as if Brock had mortally injured him instead of simply breaking his nose.

Considering the man deserved much worse than that, he'd gotten off easy.

Leaving Robert blubbering in the middle of flowers that normally provided a more cheerful setting, Brock turned and found Margo helping her sister up from the ground.

After getting Sarah back on her feet, Margo looked up, stilled, and simply stared at him for a long few seconds. She then got a rather determined look on her face right before she was running his way, jumped right into his arms, pulled his head toward her, and kissed him.

chapter twenty-three

For the briefest of seconds, Margo thought she might have made a huge mistake by practically jumping Brock and attaching her lips to his. His arms, she hadn't failed to notice, had dropped to his sides, and his lips seemed to be almost frozen in place.

Calling herself all sorts of a fool as the adrenaline she was certainly going to blame for her impulsive behavior flowed through her, she started to pull away from him. To her absolute delight, though, Brock's arms took that moment to wrap around her, pulling her close as he deepened the kiss.

She wasn't surprised at all that Brock Moore knew his way around a kiss.

His lips softened against hers, and then he was cradling the side of her cheek with his large hand, that delightful move making her sigh just a touch.

A rumble began sounding in her ears, and at first she thought it was just a reaction to the best kiss she'd ever been given. But then she heard Sarah shouting, and then Brock was no longer kissing her but looking at a truck barreling toward them.

"What in the world is Ed doing out here?"

"We need to run," was all she was capable of getting out of her mouth.

With his eyes turning hard, Brock nodded to Sarah. "Get your sister, get to safety, and don't even think about arguing with me."

Not hesitating, Margo ran toward Sarah, grabbing her hand, and they began running toward a grove of trees that might offer them cover.

Unfortunately, before they could reach those trees, the sound of dogs rang out, dogs Margo knew were heading their way.

To Margo's absolute horror, Sarah, for some unknown reason, stopped running, turned, and held up a hand. Damien, along with his two Rottweiler siblings, surprisingly enough, stopped right in front of Sarah, their snarls and growls turning into almost adorable yips as their stubby tails attempted a bit of wagging.

Standing perfectly still, exactly like her twin was doing, Margo drew in a breath and tried to keep her voice even. "Can you keep them from attacking us for long?" she all but whispered.

"Damien, Fluffy, and Kong visit our farm all the time." Sarah's voice didn't have so much as a single tremor in it. "They're not vicious with people they know, but they're not to be trusted with strangers. I'll try to keep them with me, but if—"

The blast of a shotgun cut off whatever else Sarah was about to say, a blast that had Robert letting out what could only be described as a shriek before he scrambled to his feet, his hands still secured behind his back, and started lurching his way toward the helicopter.

Another blast from the shotgun stopped Robert in his tracks, although that shot had been directed Margo's way, not Robert's.

When the dirt the bullet stirred up settled, Margo simply stood in place, her gaze traveling over Ed who was holding a shotgun, pointing it her way.

"Thought you got away from me, girl, didn't you?"

"Put the shotgun down, Ed," Brock said, moving across the meadow with his hands held up even though Margo could see a pistol stuck in the back of his waistband. "No one's been hurt here, so there's still time to do the right thing. Let Margo and Sarah go, and then you and I can talk over whatever it is you've got going on with Robert."

Ed released a laugh that sent chills down Margo's spine. "You'd like that, wouldn't you, Moore? For me to just let the womenfolk go. Well, sorry, but I can't oblige you today, so I'll thank you to keep your hands up where I can see them while I finish me up a bit of business. *Lucrative* business. And just so you know, if you make a move toward that pistol I done know you have on you, I'll shoot Sarah since she's the most . . . dispensable."

With that, and while Brock kept his hands in the

air, Ed nodded toward Robert. "I didn't ever expect to see your rat-face back in Millersburg again, Hartman. I do hope for your sake you can tell me you're flush with cash, because that would improve my rotten mood, and probably save your life."

Temper took Margo by surprise when Robert slowly turned around, blood still oozing out of his nose and the skin under his eyes already turning purple from the punch Brock gave him. The sight of his face was not what had her in a temper, though, but the fact that he was smiling—smiling exactly like he did when he smelled some type of situation he knew could be maneuvered into gaining him an advantage.

"If Margo would happen to . . . die," Robert began in a surprisingly calm voice, especially since he'd just suggested her murder almost as one would discuss the weather, "well, I have an insurance policy on her." He flashed a smile Margo's way.

"It's a tidy sum, and I'll share that sum with you, if *you* take care of the little problem of her still being alive."

Ed seemed to consider that for a moment. "How much is the policy?"

"Five million."

"That seems like a fair price to kill someone for."

"My dear man, I can't give you all that money.

A cool million should be sufficient to compensate you for pulling the trigger. She's standing right there in—"

The shotgun blast left Margo unable to hear for moment, except for a ringing in her ears. Looking down, she expected to find a hole left by the bullet, but Ed had not shot at her. Forcing herself to turn her head, she saw Robert crumpled in a heap on the ground, unmoving as blood seeped into the grass he landed on. The amount of blood left Margo with no other conclusion except to believe he was dead, and she turned her head from the sight as a distinct urge to vomit hit her.

Glancing back to Ed, she found him watching her with his lips twisted into a grin, his shotgun once again pointed her way.

"Civilized enough for you, Ms. Hartman?" he drawled.

"He was going to give you a million dollars."

"But you can get me ten million. I might not be any great shakes at math, but even I know ten is much better than one." He nodded toward the helicopter. "You and me are going to take a little ride."

"You know how to fly a helicopter?"

" 'Bout as well as I know how to fix cars."

Since he'd claimed to have fixed her Mini Cooper, but clearly hadn't done a great job she wasn't exactly reassured by his bragging. Drawing in a breath, she lifted her chin.

"I could just transfer money into your account if you have a cell phone with you."

Ed took a single step toward her. "Why didn't you offer that transfer business before, back at my barn?"

"Would you have let me go if I had?"

"I told you, I don't enjoy killing people."

Margo shot a look to Brock, who still had his hands in the air, although his eyes were now filled with something dangerous. She returned her attention to Ed. "I'm sure that was little relief to Stephanie St. James, that you didn't *enjoy* taking her life."

"I might enjoy killing *you,* though, if you keep trying to cause me so much trouble."

"But then you wouldn't get your ten million, would you?"

"True, this is true. And on that reminder"—Ed gestured with his head toward the helicopter—"we need to get going." He whistled for his dogs, his eyes turning mean when the three Rottweilers stayed by Sarah's side. Their attention never wavered from Sarah, who was saying something to them in what seemed to be the same language Margo had heard the Miller children speak.

"No matter. She can have 'em. Can't take 'em with me where I'm going anyway."

Catching Brock's eye and seeing that he was edging forward, Margo shook her head just a little before Ed grabbed her by the arm and started pulling her toward the helicopter. Keeping her gaze away from where she knew Robert was lying dead on the ground, Margo soon found herself pushed into the helicopter, right before Ed fired it up.

"Is it supposed to smell like gas?" Margo shouted as the distinct smell of gas enveloped her.

Ignoring her, Ed fiddled with the instruments and then the helicopter began to rise. Not allowing herself to reconsider what she knew she needed to do, Margo flung herself out the door and through the air, plummeting the ten feet or so the helicopter had gained, then rolling as she hit the ground.

Not waiting to see what Ed might do next, she was on her feet and running, catching a glimpse of Brock running toward her. But then he passed her—right before the sound of a gun rang out again, followed by the deafening roar of an explosion. The power and heat of that explosion sent her careening to the ground as smoke and debris flew everywhere.

Lying there, stunned, she managed to fling an arm over her face. The helicopter had exploded, which meant . . . Ed was dead.

Before she could fully comprehend that the danger Ed and Robert had presented to her was gone, or dwell on the idea that she, strangely enough, was still alive, even though there had been numerous attempts on her life lately, she suddenly found herself pulled into strong arms.

As Brock whispered in her ear and cradled her against him, even though she had no idea what he was whispering since her ears were still ringing, she allowed herself to simply enjoy the closeness of him.

What felt like only seconds later, but had probably been minutes, he eased away from her and shook his head as he studied her face. "You jumped out of the helicopter."

She smiled. "I know, but since I once had to jump off a burning platform during one of my concerts—on *purpose* for the effects, if you were wondering—I knew there was a good chance I could do it." Her smile faded just a bit. "Although, now that I think about that concert, I did have these really thick, professional cushions to land on. I probably wouldn't have jumped if I'd remembered that."

"I thought you were spectacular."

Swiveling her head, although she didn't move out of Brock's arms, Margo found Sarah standing only a few feet away. The three Rottweilers were sticking by her side, their tongues lolling out as their stubby tails continued to try to wag.

"What did you do to them?" Margo couldn't resist asking.

Sarah shrugged. "While you clearly got the singing voice in the family, I was given a strange ability to get along with animals." She leaned over and gave Damien a pat on the head. "Although I don't know if *Dat* and *Mamm* are going to be receptive to me keeping these little darlings."

"Because they're beasts, not darlings." Margo smiled. "But they do seem to have grown on me, now that they're not trying to rip me to pieces." She sobered when a memory flashed to mind. Catching Brock's eye again, she blew out a breath. "Ed was the one who stole me all those years ago, and he had dogs back then too. He used them to terrify me into silence so I wouldn't draw attention."

Taking a few minutes to explain everything that happened after Brock raced off to rescue Sarah, Margo finished with, "And then, when I found the trunk and saw the proof of the abductions—the clothing I was wearing when I was stolen out of my bed along with the clothing of the other two children, Rebecca and Harley—that's when I thought for sure he was going to kill me."

"And that's when he admitted to killing Stephanie?" Brock asked.

"He did." Margo's eyes filled with tears. "I'm so sorry, Brock. Her death was so wasteful and simply done so Ed could be sure he could continue hiding the sins of the past."

Clearing his throat as he looked off toward where the remains of the helicopter were scattered, Ed's remains mixed in somewhere with that debris, Brock retreated into silence for a long moment before he nodded and lifted his gaze to the sky.

"Stephanie can rest easy now, which is what I hoped to accomplish all along. And Ian will finally be able to have a little closure, and hopefully begin to really heal. My parents will be able to find a small bit of comfort from knowing their most cherished daughter did not take her own life, but had simply been doing what she loved best, taking care of animals. That, unfortunately, had her in the wrong place at the wrong time."

"Will you be able to move on as well?" Margo asked softly.

Brock's gaze returned to hers. "Ever since Stephanie's death, I've been questioning who I am as a man. I've always prided myself on being the protector, if you will. But when she died, my very identity came into question."

"You couldn't have saved her from Ed, because he wasn't a danger to her until she stumbled onto his secrets."

"And you've allowed me to understand that now . . . although I didn't do a very credible job of protecting you, and that's after I knew there was a real threat to your safety."

She nodded to the remains of the helicopter. "Since I'm still alive, I think you need to let that argument go. Ed was definitely unstable, but now he's gone and can never again hurt anyone else."

She shook his head. "I told him I smelled gas when we got into the helicopter, but he just wouldn't listen to me. The fuselage must have been hit when Ed was shooting that shotgun of his at Robert."

"That, or I hit the gas tank when I shot at it, but . . ." Brock brushed her hair back from her forehead, then stood. "Enough about Ed. We need to contact the Millersburg police to come and secure this scene, ask them to let the Yoders know their daughters are safe, and then, after we answer the million and one questions those police are going to ask us, as well as answer some from my associates in the FBI, I'll take you home."

The very thought of that—home—left her smiling, despite the horror of the last few hours.

Taking the hand Sarah was suddenly holding out to her, Margo let her sister pull her to her feet.

Linking one of her arms with Sarah's and the other one with Brock's, and with three enormous Rottweilers trailing after them, Margo didn't look back at the destruction that littered the meadow.

She kept her gaze forward as she walked toward a future that was going to be completely different from anything she'd ever imagined. Then she looked up to the heavens, felt the touch of God's hand running over her, and embraced the sense of peace she felt. She now understood that God, in his own time and in his own way, had shown Margo Hartman how to find her way home.

chapter twenty-four

A few hours later, Margo was back in Brock's Jeep, sitting in the passenger seat while Brock sat behind the wheel. Sarah was in the back, squished in-between her three furry friends.

Brock's associates with the FBI had taken over the case, with the Millersburg local and county law enforcement agencies doing everything they could to help them.

With Robert and Ed both dead, there were still so many mysteries left unsolved. But with Margo having finally found her way home, the case that had been cold for over twenty years had just been given a breath of fresh air. Everyone was hopeful that more answers would be uncovered in the foreseeable future, and that the other two missing Amish children would someday find their way home as well.

After she smoothed down the Nirvana T-shirt Ian had picked up for her, now covered in dirt, grass, and even a bit of dog slobber, Margo turned around and exchanged a smile with Sarah. Sarah had two of the dogs' heads lying in her lap, while the other dog—Fluffy, Margo thought it was named—hung her head out the window, her large jowls flapping in the air that rushed by.

Turning to Brock, Margo shook her head. "For

some reason, I just now realized I'm not exactly dressed to meet . . . the parents." She gestured to her shirt. "I'm wearing Nirvana."

"You look fine, and I'm sure your parents wouldn't care if you came home wearing . . . eh . . . well, I don't know any weird designers, but you get my point. They've been waiting for this day for over twenty years, Margo, and I would imagine they'll love you just the way you are."

"And Isaac, one of your brothers, loves Nirvana," Sarah added.

"I didn't know the Amish listened to grunge music."

"We don't usually, but the younger Amish have been known to get their hands on battery-operated radios, and they might just *happen* on a few rock stations."

Margo quirked a brow Sarah's way. "Did *you* ever do that?"

Pursing her lips for all of a second, Sarah suddenly grinned. "I prefer Taylor Swift over rock, but my favorite artist is Margo Hartman."

"You've heard my songs?"

In answer to that, Sarah started singing one of Margo's songs, proving without a shadow of a doubt that Margo definitely had the better singing abilities over her twin. If she wasn't mistaken, Sarah was tone-deaf.

Joining in with the song, Brock sent Margo a wink as he sang with a surprisingly good voice, and not wanting to miss out on the fun despite the horrifying events of the day, Margo opened her mouth and belted out the words to a song she knew only too well.

By the time Brock pulled into the drive that led to the Yoder farmhouse, the nerves Margo hadn't wanted to address, brought about over the apprehension of meeting her real mom and dad, had disappeared. They were replaced with a warmth that came from sharing a song with her very own sister along with Brock.

"Would you look at that?" Brock suddenly said, his words causing Margo's gaze to turn to where he was staring.

As the Jeep slowed to a stop, Margo's breath caught in her throat because all along the Yoders' drive, were people—hundreds of people.

Tears sprang to her eyes and fell to her cheeks, but she didn't bother to brush them away.

They were happy tears, born of a desire she'd always had—to truly feel as if she belonged to a loving family. And lining up on both sides of the drive was clear proof that she now most certainly belonged to exactly that type of family.

"Are you ready?" Brock asked softly, and when she nodded, that was all it took for him to get out of the Jeep, come around to her side, open the door, and help her out. "Go on," he encouraged as he went to help Sarah from the car.

For a few seconds, Margo found her feet simply wouldn't move as she took in the sight in front of her.

This was her home.

It was what she'd always longed for, and her family, what made a place *home,* was here.

Glancing around, she saw buggy after buggy all the way down the lane as women dressed in their Amish best and men in their suspenders and straw hats looked her way.

A silence had descended over the crowd, and as Margo took it all in, a woman suddenly stepped forward and began moving her way, then broke into a run.

Not hesitating for a single second, because Margo knew the woman was her mother, she ran to meet her, soon finding herself wrapped in what could only be described as a loving embrace.

Holding on as tightly as she could, and wanting to never let go, Margo buried her face into her mom's shoulder. A scent tickling her nose brought a clear memory back, a memory of being held by this very woman long ago, a woman whose scent was exactly the same.

Her mom smelled like apple pie and freshly baked bread and . . . love.

Her mom smelled like *love.*

With tears soaking the front of her mom's dress, Margo continued holding on as her mother whispered words she couldn't understand against her hair. The language was only slightly familiar to her, but the tone of her mom's voice spoke volumes. It spoke of loss and love and hope and of a mother's heart—a heart that had obviously longed for this moment ever since Margo disappeared.

She felt her mom shaking and realized she was shaking in return, but when she tried to speak, to tell her mom it was all right, that everything was going to be fine because she'd found her way home, Margo couldn't get a single word past her lips.

A gentle hand suddenly settled on her shoulder, and her mom's arms dropped away right before she found herself gathered into her father's embrace, an embrace that told her without him saying a thing that he loved her, had missed her, and welcomed her home.

"God has been very *gut* to us today," he whispered before he eased her away from him and looked down into her face, staring at it as if he wanted to memorize her every feature.

"He has been . . . *gut*." Margo smiled when he took out an old-fashioned handkerchief and began wiping away her tears.

It was a very fatherly thing to do, and when he was done, he placed a kiss in the middle of her forehead.

"Thank you . . . *Dat*," she whispered.

Jonas Yoder looked at her for a moment, drew in

a breath that was definitely a little shaky, and returned the smile she was still sending his way. "I've been waiting a very long time to hear that name come from your lips again."

She felt a warm hand take hold of hers and give it a squeeze. Turning, she wasn't surprised to find her mom was touching her again.

Mary Yoder, which Sarah had told her was their mother's name, was a beautiful woman, with kind green eyes and a smile that lit up her entire face. That her eyes were currently drinking in everything about Margo had an ache settling in Margo's heart as she realized the very great loss her abduction had caused the people who had loved her most.

"It's so great to be home, *Mamm*," she whispered, and with that one word—*Mamm*—her mom released a little laugh mixed with a sob, and then Margo was in her arms again.

When they finally let go of each other, and exchanged grins that proved there was a special bond between mothers and daughters that couldn't be broken even when they'd been parted for so long, Margo found herself quickly surrounded by the rest of her family. She was passed from one brother or sister to another, and then what seemed like the entire Amish community stepped forward to welcome their daughter home.

Esta Miller was one of the first to welcome her

home, pulling Margo into her arms as she cried and told her how sorry she was for acting so peculiar the first time they met. She reassured the woman her behavior had been perfectly understandable, but she was thankful when Brock stepped forward, taking hold of Esta's hand as he went about explaining how the case of her daughter and the missing Amish boy was being reopened. That meant there was still hope, and that the search for Rebecca, as well as for Harley, was far from over.

"I must say that Brock Moore is a remarkable man, dear, and I do hope you won't let him slip through your fingers."

Looking from Brock, who was leading Esta away to find her a glass of lemonade, Margo discovered Mrs. Hershberger standing to her right, holding Gabby.

As Gabby let out a quack of obvious greeting, Margo took her duck, and Mrs. Hershberger launched into what sounded exactly like an Amish, or rather Mennonite, version of a matchmaker . . . again.

To Margo's amusement, she soon discovered that Mennonite grandmotherly types were no different from the typical grandmotherly types— not that she'd ever experienced the whole normal grandparent thing. Not yet. But as Mrs. Hershberger kept whispering what seemed to be a long laundry list of Brock's outstanding character traits, Margo found she couldn't disagree with a single one of them.

Knowing now was hardly the time to dwell on matters of romance, though, she handed Gabby back to Mrs. Hershberger, who didn't blink an eye over being handed a duck, told the woman she'd stop by her farmhouse soon so they could have a longer chat, then threw herself back into the midst of the crowd. Before long, she'd met so many relatives and neighbors that her head had begun to swim with names. But she wouldn't have changed anything about her homecoming.

"Here, I brought you some lemonade."

Smiling as Brock stopped by her side, she took the cup he handed her, savoring the taste of freshly squeezed lemonade on her tongue before she swallowed. "Thank you for this. I was parched."

"There's a word you don't hear a pop princess say on a regular basis. But I hope you're hungry as well, because they've put together an enormous spread out in the barn."

Margo lifted her chin. "Parched is a charming word, one that should be used more often, and one that I've noticed my sister uses." She took another sip of lemonade. "Having cleared that business up, I am a little hungry. Breakfast was a long time ago."

"Isn't that the truth?" Brock smiled. "But, before

everyone demands your attention again, I do have something I'd like to discuss with you."

"You're going back to your real home?"

"Well, yes, I will need to go back to Virginia since I'll be returning to the FBI full time, but that's not what I want to discuss with you."

"It's not?"

He reached out and took hold of her free hand. "No, but I'm not sure how to say what I want to say, so I'll start by asking what your plans are for the future."

Shaking her head, she wrinkled her nose. "I hardly know, Brock. When I left California I was determined to take some time for myself after having just finished a national tour. That seems so long ago now, but I think the idea of time off from performing is exactly what I need. And I think I'd like to spend that time here, with my family, getting to know them as well as getting to know more about my Amish roots."

"Do you think you'll ever go back to music?"

"That's like asking if I'll continue breathing. Music is a part of me, like being a protector is a part of you. You'll continue saving the day and I'll, hopefully, continue providing people with entertainment and escapes from the troubles of their everyday lives."

"And . . . what about us?"

Her eyes widened as her knees went incredibly weak. "What about us?"

Raising her hand to his lips, Brock placed a kiss on it. "You kissed me."

She pressed her lips together to keep from smiling. "You kissed me back."

"I did kiss you back, and I *liked* it."

Heat began traveling up her neck to her cheeks. "I might have liked it as well."

"And that's why I would like, in front of all of your relatives"—he gestured to the crowd surrounding them, a crowd Margo just then noticed had gone remarkably quiet—"to ask you a question."

"I think it's too soon to ask *that* question," she whispered as her pulse took to racing through her veins.

Brock grinned. *"Please,* we've known each other for a minuscule amount of time. Give me some credit."

"Sorry."

"Apology accepted." Brock took one step away from her and smiled at everyone watching them. "Since you've only just had Margo returned home, it wouldn't be fair for me to try to convince her to leave with me, so . . ." He turned back to her. "Margo Hartman, I've somehow, and in a remarkably short period time—although I will say it feels as if I've known you forever—fallen somewhat—or perhaps more than somewhat—in love with you. And because I'm not willing to leave

Millersburg without at least asking this question, would you do me the very great honor of allowing me to . . . court you?"

While Margo had been coming to the realization that she'd been falling a little bit in love with Brock as well, his question left no doubt about her being, perhaps, a little *more* in love with him than just a bit.

He'd offered a ritual she knew the Amish embraced to her—the offer of an old-fashioned courtship being one of the sweetest things anyone had ever given her.

Smiling, she tilted her head. "What does that mean exactly, a courting?"

Smiling back at her, he leaned closer and lowered his voice. "I don't know the particulars, which means it's great that we now have people like Mrs. Hershberger around to explain these things, but what I take it to mean is that we'll spend time getting to know each other. And then, after we realize we're perfect for each other, of which I have no doubt, well . . . then . . ."

"Then what?"

"You'll just have to wait and see, but you'll only get to see if you agree to allow me to court you."

"Then I suppose I have no other option but to agree, and—"

His lips touched hers ever so gently before she could get anything else out.

As her family moved closer to offer her their congratulations when Brock stepped back, Margo glanced to the heavens and smiled.

God had certainly not abandoned her even when she'd abandoned her faith, and because of that, and because of God's obvious love for her, she was finally home.

epilogue

Six months later

Whipping the chocolate mousse with a hand mixer until it turned frothy, Raven Vanderlyn turned off the mixer, set it aside, and then scooped what she knew would be a delicious dessert into bowls she'd found in an antique mall. After placing the bowls on a tray, she struggled with the tray over to the professional-grade refrigerator she'd had installed in her downtown loft and slid the tray inside.

"I do wish you weren't so obsessed with your little hobby," Elizabeth Vanderlyn said from the high stool she was sitting on by the kitchen island. "It's embarrassing to have to admit to our friends that our daughter, our darling Raven, wants nothing more in life than to be a . . . baker."

"Since I just signed a lease for my own bakery, it's a good thing my main goal is to be a baker," Raven said lightly, having had this particular conversation with her mother so many times in the past that it hardly even annoyed her these days.

"Why don't you come to the club with me later, darling?" Elizabeth continued, abruptly changing the subject since she evidently wasn't getting the response from Raven she wanted. "I heard

Jonathon's family is supposed to be there. We could have your father meet us after he's done at the office, and"—she smiled—"you could have Jonathon meet us there as well. We can all enjoy a nice dinner together."

"Jonathon already told me he's meeting clients tonight for a business dinner—" Raven suddenly stopped talking as a news story popped up on the small TV that was installed underneath one of her kitchen cabinets. Nodding to the show, she looked back to her mother.

"Did you see where Margo Hartman got engaged?"

"Who?" Elizabeth asked.

"Margo Hartman. She's been in the news for months now. She's the singer who discovered she was abducted from the Amish as a child and just found her way back home." Raven nodded toward the TV again. "She's marrying the FBI agent who helped her uncover the truth, and they're hopeful the authorities will find some new clues that might lead them to the other children who went missing from the Amish."

"Other . . . children?" Elizabeth repeated.

Opening a cabinet, Raven began pulling out the ingredients to make some red-velvet cupcakes she'd been itching to try all week. "Yes, two of them. A boy and a girl, if I'm remembering correctly." Setting baking powder on the counter, she shook her head. "I can't imagine finding out you'd been stolen, growing up believing you're one person, but then finding out you're completely someone else."

Elizabeth picked up the remote and aimed it for the TV, then muted the sound even though the volume had been on one of the lowest settings. "That would be distressing, but not something you need to worry about, darling." She picked up her Chanel bag that had been lying on the kitchen island, and got off the stool. "Now, how about if we treat ourselves to facials and then make our way to the club? It'll be my treat."

Knowing she wasn't going to be able to get out of accompanying her mom for facials and then a meal at the club, Raven began returning all of her ingredients back to their proper places. Closing the cupboard door, she turned and found her mom staring at the TV, her face looking incredibly white.

"Mom, are you okay?"

Shaking herself ever so slightly, Elizabeth smiled. "Of course, darling. I'm fine, and I'll be even better after our facials."

Linking arms, mother and daughter walked out of the kitchen as the story of Margo Hartman continued to play out on a TV that had been merely muted. It was a story that Raven completely forgot about as she left her loft with her mother, out to enjoy a day with facials and then dinner.

Forgot until . . .

meet the author online!

Website: jenturano.com
Twitter: @Jenturano
Facebook: www.facebook.com/jenturanoauthor

Center Point Large Print
600 Brooks Road / PO Box 1
Thorndike, ME 04986-0001 USA

(207) 568-3717

US & Canada:
1 800 929-9108
www.centerpointlargeprint.com